"Captain Hawke, I presume." The Gaian Chancellor extended his hand.

Aurora clasped it. "Thank you for meeting with us Chancellor."

He shook his head. "I'm the one who's grateful for your assistance. This way." The Chancellor gestured to the corridor to their left. "I'll introduce you to the Corps Director first. She controls all operations here and at the station for the other community that was affected. She can put you in touch with Corps members who can assist you in your investigation."

"So your own people won't be working with us?" Cardiff asked.

He glanced back at her. "No. While we're well known for our agricultural skills, most of that knowledge is from practical, hands-on experience, not scientific study." His expression looked strained. "What we're seeing now is unlike anything we've ever encountered. We're at a wall. That's why we contacted the Council, and why they sent you. This is beyond our ability to analyze or investigate."

"Do you think it's a natural occurrence, a mutation or infection that's native to the planet?" Aurora asked.

The Chancellor stopped and faced her. "Captain, I'm not certain what's happening here could be labeled a natural occurrence *anywhere*."

THE DARK OF LIGHT

LIGHT

Starhawke Rising Book One

Audrey Sharpe

Ocean Dance Press

THE DARK OF LIGHT
© 2015 Audrey Sharpe

ISBN: 978-1-946759-01-6

Ocean Dance Press, LLC
PO Box 69901
Oro Valley AZ 85737

This is a work of fiction. Any resemblance to actual persons, living or dead, business establishments, events, or locales is entirely coincidental.

Cover art by B&J

Visit the author's website at:
AudreySharpe.com

This book is dedicated to my mom.
My champion, my mentor, my friend.
I could not have done this without you.
I love you.

Prologue

"Where do you think *you're* going, little green man?"

The harsh voice echoed in the early morning air, a discordant note amid the cheerful chattering of birds and the whispering of the wind in the pines overhead.

On the trail below, Aurora Hawke paused in mid-stride. The sound had come from up ahead, where the path curved around a rock outcropping. The boulders prevented her from seeing the owner of the taunting voice, or the intended recipient. The speaker's attitude, however, came through loud and clear.

"Is the alien trying to contact the mother ship?" a second male jeered.

The comment was followed by harsh laughter, and then a third male joined in. "Nah, they probably left him behind 'cause he's a runt."

Great. Bullies before breakfast. What the hell were they doing on the hiking trail before sunrise? She'd been on this same path every day before dawn for weeks now and had never run into a soul. Even her new roommate, Reanne, had flatly refused to join her when she'd realized how early Aurora left each day. So what had lured these three Neanderthals out of their beds?

Shifting her weight to the balls of her feet and tightening the straps of the small pack on her back so that it fit snugly against her, she crept as soundlessly as possible up the path toward the rocks.

A breeze ruffled the branches of the pines and aspens that rose in graceful columns along both sides of the trail, the air unseasonably warm for mid-September in northern Colorado. The rustling of the leaves helped to conceal her approach. When she reached the rock edge, she flattened her back against the stone and peered around the corner.

Her first look confirmed what she'd suspected— these were not Academy cadets. The three large teenage boys stood in a rough semicircle across the trail, their haphazard clothing and long, unkempt hair a sharp contrast to the crisp uniforms and short hairstyles favored by most cadets. The ruffians were using the steep drop-off on the left to cage in their victim, making it difficult to see him. However, judging from the size of the boy's shoes, he wasn't more than eight years old, far too young for even a junior cadet.

He could be the child of one of the professors or staff, but why would they allow him to hike alone in the early morning? The area around the Academy was relatively safe, but as this situation proved, it wasn't harmless. With the cliff behind him and the three boys in front of him, he was trapped.

The teenagers had tossed assorted rubbish near the base of the rocks. All three looked as though they had slept in their clothes. When the breeze shifted, she discovered they smelled like it, too. They'd probably fallen asleep on the rock after a night of drinking, and been roused by the child's approach down the trail. She hadn't encountered the boy on the main trail, so he must have been hiking the Pine Loop that branched off near the trailhead.

One of the boys moved slightly, giving her a glimpse of the victim's profile. His hair was wavy, with a blend of colors from light tan to milk chocolate, like a dappled fawn. But it was his skin that made her catch her breath. It was tinged a pale green, with thin ribbons of brown swirling in non-linear patterns, giving the boy's golden eyes the appearance of gazing out from behind fern fronds. *Kraed.*

That changed things considerably.

The Academy administration had trumpeted the arrival of Professor Signal Clarek as a member of the staff this year, the first Kraed to ever accept a long-term position. His lectures were notable for the incredible wealth of information provided and the warm tropical setting in which they were taught, which mimicked the more humid environment of his homeworld.

Professor Clarek was her physics instructor and faculty advisor, and the boy with his heels backed up to the cliff was his son, Jonarel. Apparently the boy didn't share his father's aversion to the dry Colorado air.

She still didn't like the odds, but she felt better knowing the boy's identity. The bullies had chosen their victim poorly. For one thing, Kraed entered puberty at a much later age than humans. Jonarel wasn't the child he appeared to be. He was at least as old as the boys he was facing, possibly older.

He'd also grown up on a planet that was populated with very large, very lethal predators. Even though the Kraed had long since learned how to safely co-exist with the creatures of their world, Kraed children were still taught to defend themselves from infancy. Jonarel could probably handle these three without her assistance, but she wasn't prepared to bet his life on it, especially given his precarious position.

One of the teenagers snatched the tablet Jonarel was carrying from his hands and dangled it above the Kraed's head. "What you doing with this, little green man?" He waved the device in the air. "You studyin' humans so you can grow up to be a *real* man?"

Despite his small size, Jonarel managed to look haughty as he stared at the giants in front of him. "If I wanted to learn anything valuable about humans, I certainly would not begin with you three."

Aurora slapped a hand over her mouth to stifle a bark of laughter. The boy had guts. And no sense of self-preservation.

The bullies looked ready to tear him to pieces. "Is that so?" sneered the largest of the boys, the apparent ringleader. "Well maybe it's time to find out if little green men can fly." He grabbed the front of Jonarel's jacket in both hands.

Aurora didn't wait to see what he planned to do next. "Let him go." She stepped around the rock and pinned the ringleader with the authoritative look she'd perfected in her Academy leadership prep classes.

The boys looked startled by her presence, but Jonarel didn't show any surprise at all. In fact, he looked like he'd been expecting her. That was disconcerting. Then again, Kraed were known for their acute senses. He'd probably heard her approach.

The ringleader's attention switched to her. "Not gonna happen, girlie." He leered as his gaze lingered on her ample chest. "But if you want to wait until we finish here, I'd be happy to take care of *you.*"

Ugh. She fought down the bile that rose in her throat as the other boys snickered. Keeping her expression carefully neutral, she stared hard into the leader's eyes, refusing to respond to his taunt.

He dropped his gaze. "Just keep walkin'," he muttered.

"I'm afraid I can't do that." She took a step closer. The two boys standing on either side of the ringleader glanced nervously between her and the large bully, clearly unsure what to do next. Good. She wanted them to be uncertain.

"And why is that?" The leader faced her, dragging Jonarel with him. That was an improvement at least. Now the larger boy's body was between Jonarel and the cliff.

"Because that's my friend you're threatening. He was supposed to meet me here." She couldn't see Jonarel's face, but she hoped his expression wouldn't give lie to her words. "I'd appreciate it if the three of you would head home so we can work."

The ruffian snorted. "Work? You're jokin'. This kid is just outta diapers. What're you gonna do with him, play house?" That comment brought on a roar of laughter from the other boys.

Aurora spoke over the racket. "What you don't seem to understand is that this *kid* is a Kraed. They don't reach their adult size until they're in their twenties. He's probably older than you are."

"Eighteen." Jonarel said.

So he was two years older than she was. Good to know.

He turned his head so his gaze met hers. Intelligence and awareness shone in those otherworldly eyes. Maybe his age wasn't the only thing about him that wasn't what it appeared.

"*Eighteen?*" The bully jerked Jonarel onto his tiptoes and brought their faces centimeters apart. The larger boy's lip curled as he snarled, but Jonarel remained completely relaxed, his arms hanging loosely at his sides.

The Kraed had courage to spare.

The bully glared at Aurora. "*If* you're telling the truth." His tone indicated she was lying. He was right. "What's your *friend's* name?"

"Jonarel Clarek."

"What kinda name is that?"

"A Kraed name."

Jonarel pointed to the device one of the boys still held. "My name is on my tablet."

"I didn't ask you." The bully gave Jonarel a hard shake that made his teeth click together.

"Knock it off!" Aurora took a step toward the leader. She spoke slowly, giving weight to each syllable. "I said, let...him...go."

The bully's pupils widened, showing the first flicker of uncertainty. He had about five inches and at least fifty pounds on her, but her forceful attitude seemed to be unsettling him. He was probably used to picking on the weak. She certainly was not weak.

But instead of releasing his hold on Jonarel, he gave her a lecherous smile that bared his crooked teeth. "I don't think so." A predatory gleam appeared in his eyes. "I think we'll make this into a party, instead."

Jonarel's hands flexed as the bully stepped forward, dragging him along. Her heart rate picked up. She didn't know what the Kraed planned to do, but she wanted to avoid a physical confrontation if at all possible.

Instead of reacting to the implied threat, she sighed dramatically. "That's a shame." She gave the leader a look of pity. "I was hoping to save you boys from a trip to the hospital."

"Oh yeah? *You* gonna put us there, girlie?"

"No. But the boy's father will."

That brought him up short. "Whadda you mean?"

She used the patient tones of a teacher explaining a particularly difficult problem to a student. "Did any of you happen to notice his last name?" She looked each boy in the eye before returning her focus to the ringleader. "Clarek. As in *Professor* Clarek, the new head of the Astrophysics department at the Academy, who happens to be built like a grizzly bear."

All three boys paled, so she pressed her advantage. "It's clear you three don't know anything about Kraed, so let me share another fun fact with you. Kraed males are incredibly protective, especially when it comes to their families. You're threatening a Kraed male's only son. A very *large* Kraed male. Do you have any idea what is likely to happen to you if he finds out you hurt his child?"

The boys stared at her with rapt attention. So did Jonarel, though his expression was one of fascination, not fear.

"I don't know about you, but I wouldn't relish infuriating a man who could knock my head from my shoulders with one swipe of his hand. But, it's your call." The silence stretched out as she gave them time to ponder her words.

Finally, one of the boys shuffled his feet and looked up the trail with an expression of longing. "Uh, maybe we should head back to town." He glanced nervously at Jonarel.

"Yeah." The other boy kicked a rock with his shoe. "This is boring."

The ringleader seemed torn between his need to maintain his macho image and his desire to keep his body in one piece. Physical preservation won out.

"Whatever." He gave Jonarel a little shove and brushed his hands together like he'd touched something dirty. "You space geeks aren't worth my time, anyway." His gaze flicked insolently over Aurora before he gestured to the other boys. "Let's go."

They gathered their few belongings from the rocks and started up the path. Jonarel stepped to the edge of the trail to give them room. The ringleader plucked Jonarel's tablet from the hands of his friend as they passed and shoved the device hard into Jonarel's chest, knocking him off balance.

As Jonarel's arms pin-wheeled, time contracted to a single point, bringing every detail into sharp relief. The rustle of Jonarel's jacket sleeves against his torso. The look of surprise that flashed across his face. The crunch of a pebble under Aurora's foot. The rush of air into her lungs as she inhaled.

Then he pitched backward over the cliff.

"No!" She lunged forward, her left hand making contact with his ankle as his torso disappeared from view. She held on, but her momentum pulled her over the edge, face first.

The decline was sharp, but not the vertical drop she had anticipated. They were sliding, not falling. As they tumbled past a large tree, she reached out with her right hand and grabbed for an exposed root. Her fingers tightened on the rough wood and her left arm jerked as she and Jonarel came to an abrupt halt.

She stifled a groan, grateful that Jonarel was a featherweight and the sudden stop hadn't dislocated her shoulder. She looked up at the trail. They'd fallen about ten meters down the side of the cliff. A moment later, three heads appeared over the edge, like prairie dogs from a burrow, their expressions a matched set of shock.

"Help us!" she called, her voice weakened by the strain of holding onto Jonarel with one hand and the tree root with the other.

The boys exchanged a quick glance, and then their heads disappeared. The sound of fading footsteps trickled down as the miscreants ran up the trail, away from the Academy.

"Perfect." So much for outside assistance. She glanced down. Jonarel was dangling by his right leg, his hands planted firmly on the ground on either side of his torso. Below him the ground sloped at roughly forty degrees for about a hundred meters. She could just make out the shattered remnants of his tablet where it had slammed into the ground at the bottom of the ravine.

"Jonarel? Are you okay?"

He curled up slightly so he could meet her gaze. "I am filthy and bruised, but unharmed."

"Good." She took a deep breath to oxygenate her straining muscles. "Let's keep it that way."

"Agreed. How?"

The area around them consisted of mounds of fallen leaves and a few sharp rocks. Nothing of substance. He'd have to hold onto her instead. "How strong are you? Can you climb onto my back?"

A strange expression ghosted across his face, but he nodded. "Yes."

"Let's start there. I'll keep us steady while you pull yourself up."

The pressure on her left arm intensified as he moved. Thank the universe for daily yoga and calisthenics intensives. She needed that upper body strength right now.

He grabbed onto the denim of her jeans and pulled, allowing her to release her grip on his leg. Small pricks pierced her skin through the material, like a thorn or a claw. Kraed didn't have claws, did they? Although Jonarel certainly was agile as a cat. In no time his small arms wrapped around her shoulders and his legs clamped onto her waist. She rolled to the left so she could grab the tree root with both hands, bringing instant relief to her burning shoulder.

His mouth was right next to her ear. "What now?"

"There's a coil of rope in the small compartment of my backpack. Tie one end around your waist."

The zipper rasped and his weight shifted as he pulled out the rope. He pressed into her as he followed her instructions. "Done."

"Now tie the other end around my waist so I won't lose you."

A brief silence greeted her request. "You are more concerned with my safety than your own?"

"At the moment, yes."

He didn't reply, but he moved the rope around her waist. She arched her back so he could maneuver it under her. When it tightened, she let out the breath she'd been holding.

"Now what?" he asked.

"Give me a minute." She examined the tree root, running her left hand along the edge to check the thickness. "Do you see the small ledge off to the left?"

He twisted around her. "Yes."

"We may be able to pull ourselves up onto it and climb the tree trunk that's connected to this root."

"Understood. What should I do?"

"Grab the root and crab walk to the ledge."

"Crab walk?"

She smiled in spite of herself. "A crab is a small Earth crustacean that walks sideways. Can you get a grip on the root?"

"Of course."

His legs locked onto her torso as he reached up. A moment later he was next to her, moving with ease toward the ledge. Maybe he *was* using more than his fingers for traction.

She followed behind, the rope a gentle arc between them. She tried to get a toehold with her boots to take some of the stress off her shoulders, but she only succeeded in loosening a pocket of gravel that rattled down the steep slope.

The rock ledge was only about twenty centimeters deep, but as tiny as Jonarel was, he'd be able to stand on it. Using a smaller rock just below the ledge as a foothold, he pulled his torso up until he was partially balanced on the ledge. Then he lifted his foot and pushed with his legs until he was standing, his body pressed against the side of the hill.

Unfortunately, when he stretched his arms toward the tree trunk, he was still half a meter away.

She sighed in frustration. "I'll have to climb up." She hoped her voice didn't betray her concern. She'd been holding onto the root for five minutes and her arms were shaking. She might not have the strength to pull herself up. But at this point, they didn't have any other options. She didn't share her other observation, either—that the ledge didn't look wide enough to support them both.

She grasped the ledge with her left hand and placed her foot on the same rock Jonarel had used to boost himself. He moved to the far side of the narrow ledge, giving her as much room as he could. She focused on her balance, pushing with her foot while hauling her upper body with her arms.

She yelped as the rock under her foot gave way. With only her arms to support her, she swayed. Jonarel grabbed the material of her jacket to steady her, but the rock ledge shifted beneath them.

"Hang on!" The ledge pulled away from the cliff face, taking them with it. She released her hold on the stone and yanked Jonarel into her arms, wrapping his small body in a bear hug. The motion carried her onto her back as they plummeted down the cliff face.

They slid rapidly toward the rocky ravine. Aurora shifted her focus to the molecules surrounding them, generating an energy field that increased the friction with the ground underneath them and significantly slowed their momentum. It also provided a buffer between their bodies and the leaves, rocks and sticks that were tumbling down the cliff face with them.

Even with the increase in friction, the ground rushed up to meet them. She concentrated on the molecules at their feet, generating as deep a field as she could to act as a shock absorber when they hit the gulley. Even so, the impact jarred Jonarel out of her arms and knocked the air from her lungs.

She lay on her stomach, drawing labored breaths as debris rained down over her head and arms, coating her jacket and hair. Pins stabbed her chest with each inhale, but she didn't sense any internal damage. She wasn't so sure the same would be true for Jonarel.

As soon as she could move, she flipped over on her side. Jonarel was sprawled on the ground about a meter away, the rope still around his waist and his face hidden by his thick hair. Ignoring the vise that continued to squeeze her rib cage, she pushed onto all fours and touched his arm. "Jonarel?" she croaked. "Are you hurt?"

Slowly, he rolled onto his back and met her gaze. But the expression on his face took her completely by surprise. Rather than shock, or pain, or even concern, he looked like he was trying to solve a riddle or puzzle.

Panic flared in her chest at his scrutiny. "Are you hurt?" she asked again, breaking eye contact and looking him over for signs of trauma. He remained silent, and her initial panic morphed into terror that he'd sustained a head injury.

But finally he responded. "I am uninjured. That is surprising, however, given our unexpected descent. By all calculations, I should have one or more broken bones, and possible internal injuries. And yet, I am unharmed."

"That's a good thing, right?" She forced cheerfulness into her voice.

He sat up. "Certainly. The question is, how? I have studied the laws of planetary physics since I was a child, and nothing I have learned would explain what occurred."

"What do you mean?" Her heart thumped erratically as she searched for a logical explanation for their situation. "We fell down a cliff and landed in a ravine. That's gravity at work."

"Yes, but the rate of our descent decreased steadily, and we landed with less force than we should have. How did you achieve that?"

Don't panic. "I don't know what you're talking about." She fought to keep her voice even. "Maybe you hit your head and aren't thinking straight, because we landed hard."

He opened his mouth to reply, but his gaze suddenly shifted over her shoulder and his eyes widened. A split second later she heard a terrifying sound–the crack and rumble of falling boulders. Judging from Jonarel's ashen expression, the rockslide was almost upon them.

Acting on instinct, she tackled him, knocking him to the ground and covering his body with hers as her energy field snapped into place around them.

The first boulders struck the shield a hand's breadth from her head. A flare of light and a loud bang followed as the stone smashed into thousands of harmless pieces and dribbled down around them. More boulders hit, each causing a jarring of the energy field as the rocks broke apart.

The deluge continued for seconds that felt like hours, but eventually slowed, replaced by the gentle rustle of shifting pebbles and dirt. She remained motionless, staring sightlessly at the collection of debris around them. This was it. The moment she'd dreaded for years, ever since the heartbreaking day she'd learned she was different from other children, that she had to keep a part of herself hidden forever. She'd given her mother her solemn oath that she would never reveal her ability to anyone. Ever.

Well, that plan was shot to hell. She couldn't hide now. She might have been able to bluff before, but she was huddled in a crater of evidence that couldn't be denied. For better or worse, the truth was about to be revealed.

Taking a deep breath, she pushed onto her heels and looked into Jonarel's upturned face, bracing for whatever she would find there.

"You saved my life."

That wasn't what she'd been expecting. Should she deny it? But what was the point? He was right. She didn't have to confirm anything, though.

Unsure of how to respond, she wiped her hands on her jeans and glanced away. "We should get moving."

"Wait." He placed his small hand on her arm.

She froze. Now the questions would come. The accusations. Her worst fears brought to vivid reality.

He sat up, facing her, and grasped her hands in his. "Do not fear me." His grip was strong, but there was no aggression in it. "I can see the worry in your eyes, the uncertainty."

She'd never felt so vulnerable in her life. It terrified her.

"It is all right." He gazed at her. "You have an ability that I have never encountered in my travels or studies. An ability you want to keep hidden."

Her heart provided a staccato beat for his words.

Warmth steadily lit his golden eyes. "You understand much of my race, but we too have our secrets." Releasing her hand, he raised his and made a subtle movement with his fingers. Wickedly sharp, nearly translucent claws unsheathed from the pads of his fingers.

Her breath caught. He *did* have claws!

"In earlier times, they were necessary to help us escape predators." He moved his fingers again and the claws disappeared seamlessly into his flesh. He held his hand out, palm up, offering it for inspection.

Fascinated, she placed her hand underneath his and ran the pad of her thumb over his fingertips. She couldn't detect any trace of the sheath openings or the claws that lay just below the surface.

"This is something we have chosen to keep secret, as it might inspire fear." He grasped her hand again, raising their hands together so they were palm to palm. His expression grew solemn. "My race is an honorable one, Aurora Hawke. When we make a pledge, we keep it." His golden gaze held hers, revealing a glimpse of the man

Jonarel would become after his body caught up with his mind. The concept was both intriguing and intimidating.

His voice deepened. "On the honor of my forebears, the future of my descendants, and the forfeit of my own life, I pledge that I will honor the sanctity of your secret for as long as I draw breath."

Her heart stuttered to a halt. The forfeit of his life?

And the expression in his eyes indicated he meant it. That he would make this pledge to her, a virtual stranger, left her speechless.

It also triggered a new emotion—hope.

She had to clear her throat before she could reply. "Thank you." What else could she say? But she had a question for him, too. "How do you know my name?"

"I know who you are."

"You do?"

"Yes. My father has spoken of you often. He considers you his most promising student."

"Oh." What was she supposed to make of that statement? She'd remained near the top of her class during her three years as a junior cadet, and was on track to be an officer when she graduated. But she'd never considered the possibility that her professors might talk about her to their families.

However, now was not the time to think about it. Untying the rope from around her waist, she stood and assessed their situation. The V-shaped gulley ran downhill in the direction of the Academy and the terrain looked fairly clear of obstacles. With luck, they'd find an easy slope that would allow them to get back up near the trailhead.

Turning to Jonarel, she gestured toward the winding dirt path.

"Let's see where this leads us."

One

As the sun set on the horizon, dusk tiptoed toward the fields of grain that encircled the farmhouse at their center. The fading light burnished the tips of the stalks golden and umber, while a gentle breeze tickled their leaves, making them bend and sway with silent laughter.

Light spilled from the windows of the house, the sounds of clattering plates and boisterous conversation announcing the end of the long workday. Rich aromas from the evening meal wafted on the breeze and scattered toward the hills beyond.

As the light waned, burrowing creatures poked their heads out of the open doorways of their underground homes beneath the stalks. It was dinnertime for them as well, and one by one they scampered through the never-ending maze of greenery, foraging for their evening delights.

Small invertebrates added their voices to the growing symphony, while the winged creatures of the day called out their goodnights before flying home to their roosts. Above them, the deep purples and reds of sunset gave way to the sparkle of a million stars, each one a glittering jewel dropped into a sea of midnight blue.

The night slowly laid a blanket of darkness over the field, except for the small halo that encircled the farmhouse and those within. The cheerful hum of activity filtered out in a gentle background murmur as the hours passed, until the lights were extinguished and the soft veil of sleep descended. The creatures of the valley settled into their cozy dens as the nighttime sounds provided a soft lullaby.

But as the midnight hour approached, a subtle tension cut into the peaceful tranquility. From out of the darkness, figures appeared like shadows, crafted from blackness so absolute that it seemed to swallow light wherever it dared touch. An eerie silence followed in their wake. The very ground beneath them seemed to hold its breath. Even the wind hesitated, as if reluctant to touch them with its gentle caress.

The figures raised their grotesque and misshapen limbs and placed them against the silky surface of the plants. For a moment, all was still. Then the stalks began to tremble. One by one, the plants recoiled, withering as their leaves turned brown and then black. Their silent screams went unheard.

The figures pressed forward, their limbs sweeping out to encompass more and more of the proud stalks, leaving a barren, wasted battlefield in their wake. The devastation moved with them, and animals fled in all directions. Those who ran away from the inky blackness survived. Those who cowered among the tall stalks were not so lucky. When the darkness reached them, their shrieks of terror quickly staggered and died on the breeze.

In the distance, the rising crescent moon struggled to cast a sheltering light on the farmhouse, the sleeping occupants unaware of the nightmare that waited just outside their small sanctuary. But their childlike innocence would hold sway this night, keeping them safe until the rising sun revealed the truth.

In the valley beyond, nothing moved. No sounds drifted in the air. All was still as a crypt as the black shadows melted into the darkness from whence they came, and were gone.

Two

"Will he agree to leave the Fleet?"

Aurora glanced at the man lounging in the chair to her right. His features were clearly defined in the otherwise dim room by the shimmering blue and green light cast by a neon bar sign on the wall beside him. His large hands rested comfortably on the polished wood tabletop, and his long legs stretched out on either side of the table's pedestal base. But she didn't buy his relaxed posture for a moment. It belied the seriousness of his question.

Anyone who looked at Jonarel now would not recognize the boy Aurora had met thirteen years ago. She still marveled at how much he had changed since that fateful day on the hiking trail. At eighteen, he'd been just a little more than a meter tall. Now, even seated, his muscular frame towered over her.

And his physique wasn't the only difference. His skin tone had shifted to a rich forest green when he hit adolescence shortly after his nineteenth birthday, and his thick hair now brushed his shoulders in shades of dark chocolate and caramel. It created a stunningly beautiful visual for anyone lucky enough to come into contact with him. More than one female had turned to stare as Jonarel had made his way through the crowded bar to their table.

Music rippled from the sound system, enveloping the packed space in a rhythmic heartbeat that vibrated through the table. Aurora tapped her index finger against the smooth surface, keeping time with the music as she considered his question. "Kire loves being a member of the Fleet. If I asked him to serve on an ordinary starship, he'd probably turn me down." Picking up her drink, she tilted the glass in Jonarel's direction. "However, you and the ship are my ace in the hole."

His eyebrows lifted. "Indeed."

Jonarel had been best friends with Kire Emoto since the Academy, and parting ways after graduation had been tough on both of them. She was counting on their friendship and Kire's strong intellectual curiosity to make the challenge she and Jonarel were about to present to him irresistible.

She'd met Kire in a linguistics class during her fourth year at the Academy. They'd bonded over a shared love of language, and the following semester they'd made a pact to sign up for Teelian, the newest and most challenging Galactic language. Kire had taken to it like a duck to water. She had not. But he'd willingly spent countless hours in the Academy library with her, studying and practicing.

During one of their sessions, he'd mentioned that he was struggling with his engineering courses, so she'd asked Jonarel to tutor him. The two had quickly formed a close friendship. However, after they were assigned to different posts, it had become nearly impossible to get together. The opportunity to work on the same ship should be a powerful enticement, even if it meant leaving the Fleet.

Jonarel's gaze shifted to the front door. Judging by the change in his posture, he'd spotted Kire.

Kire's slim form appeared a moment later, clothed in his gray Fleet uniform. Aurora raised her hand in a short wave. A smile lit up his face as he worked his way through the crowd.

She stepped around the table so she could give him a hug. "It's good to see you, Kire."

He squeezed back. "It's good to see you too, Roe. How long has it been? Two years?"

"About that. Since shortly before I left the *Excelsior.*"

He looked her up and down like a proud papa. "And became the youngest Commander on a Fleet ship. The *Argo*'s damn lucky to have you." He gave her a nod of approval. "I think being a Commander agrees with you."

You have no idea. Kire liked to stay informed, especially when it came to his friends. The only reason he didn't know she'd left the *Argo* was because she hadn't officially resigned until a week ago, and her former captain was holding off making an announcement until he decided who would replace her.

Kire turned toward Jonarel. He extended his hand, his expression solemn. "Clarek."

Jonarel dwarfed him as he stood, his expression equally devoid of emotion as they shook hands. "Emoto."

Kire cracked first. His smile broke through as he pulled Jonarel into a quick hug and slapped him on the back. "How have you been you big lug?"

"I have been well." Jonarel gestured to the empty chair on his right as he and Aurora reclaimed their seats.

"I still can't believe you left the Fleet to return to Drakar." Kire glanced at Aurora as he sat. "What did you have to do to get him back on Earth?"

"Oh, the usual things. Bribery. Blackmail." She laughed when Jonarel scowled. "Can I get you anything?" she asked Kire as she picked up her drink.

"Sure. It's been a while since I've had a good pale ale."

"Coming right up." She caught the attention of the server and ordered the drink. "So, how are things on the *Odyssey?*"

"Stellar." Kire settled back in his chair. "We've had a few run-ins with Setarips lately, but nothing we couldn't handle. I was promoted to Lieutenant-Commander and took over as the communications chief about six months ago. It's more work and longer hours, but I love the challenge."

Damn. A promising promotion in the Fleet would make her offer less appealing. "That's great!" She refused to let her anxiety show. "I'm glad your commanding officers appreciate you."

The server set Kire's drink on a coaster in front of him. He nodded his thanks. "Yes, they do." He took a long pull of the amber liquid as he studied Aurora. "But I get the feeling you're not asking out of idle curiosity." He lowered the glass and rested his forearms on the table. "What's up?"

He'd always been able to read her like a book. Time to lay her cards on the table and let the chips fall where they may. "I've recently become the captain of a ship."

She'd stunned him into silence. But he recovered quickly and grinned. "Wow! I had no idea. Congratulations." He raised his glass and clinked it with hers, but a crease appeared between his narrow brows. "I would have expected that announcement to be all over the Fleet newsfeed. When did this happen?"

If she had been offered the captain's position on a Fleet ship, he might have known before she did. He was that good at his job. She glanced at Jonarel, drawing strength from his steady gaze. "It's not a Fleet ship. It's privately owned."

"Really?" Kire sat up straighter. "You mean you've left the Fleet?"

She nodded.

He frowned, his expression puzzled. "Huh. First Jon here, and now you. I never would have imagined that." He traced the rim of his glass with his finger. "So what's the story? If it's not a Fleet ship, who owns it?"

Here's where things got tricky. "I do."

He blinked. And stared. And blinked some more. "What?" As her words slowly registered, his expression upshifted from puzzled to confused. "I don't understand. Even if you've been saving everything you've earned since you left the Academy, there's no way you could afford to buy a ship at this point."

"That's true." Fleet salaries were a matter of public record, so he knew what she made. He also knew she didn't come from a wealthy family. The next bit of information was only going to generate more questions. "The ship is Kraed. Jonarel designed and commissioned it."

Kire's gaze shifted to Jonarel. "Is that what you've been up to these past two years? Building a ship?"

Jonarel nodded.

Understanding slowly dawned. "You used your succession money to finance it, didn't you?"

Another nod.

Kire glanced at her, his brow furrowing again. "But you said that *you* own it." He paused, clearly trying to make the pieces of the puzzle fit together. "Did you buy it from him?"

"Certainly not!" Jonarel roared, his face darkening with anger.

Several of the customers at nearby tables jumped and glanced nervously in their direction.

"Okay, okay." Kire held his hands up, palms out. "Take it easy big guy. I didn't mean to upset you. But I'm trying to figure this out and it's not making any sense."

He had no way of knowing he'd unintentionally insulted Jonarel's honor. Aurora worked to cut through the sudden tension. "Kraed never sell their ships. To do so would dishonor the family for all generations."

"Uh-*huh*." Kire kept his focus on Jonarel, whose face still resembled a thundercloud. "So, if Jon designed it, and now you own it, but you didn't buy it, then how..." He trailed off and his eyes widened. He opened his mouth, but nothing came out. He tried again, his voice barely a whisper. "Did you two pair bond?"

"No," she and Jonarel said simultaneously.

Thank the universe Jonarel had answered as quickly as she had. It was the one question she'd dreaded more than any other, especially with Jonarel sitting right next to her. "The ship was a gift from Jonarel and his family."

Kire looked like he was waiting for the punch line.

"The only way a non-Kraed can own a Kraed ship is if it's gifted to them." She paused. How much more could she say without prompting questions she wasn't prepared to answer?

Jonarel jumped into the breach, his deep voice filled with warmth. "Aurora is an honored friend. She was my father's favorite student and is considered a part of my family. My parents supported my decision to use the money from my succession to design and construct a starship for her."

"And you just gave it to her?"

"Yes."

Kire's face showed his disbelief. She could relate. She'd been battling her own doubts ever since Jonarel had taken her to see the ship. *Her* ship. She'd been overwhelmed, and more than a little concerned about the motivations behind his decision and what it signified.

However, she'd had no choice. She'd accepted that the ship was hers. To refuse such a gift would have destroyed their relationship forever. She'd deal with the repercussions later.

The flicker of emotion in Kire's eyes told her they would be revisiting this topic. But he apparently had picked up on her unease and had decided to forego any more probing questions, at least for now. Sitting back in his chair, he lifted his glass and took a healthy swallow, his gaze never leaving hers. "So, you're the captain of this ship?"

She nodded.

"And I'm guessing Jon is the engineer?"

"Yes."

The corners of Kire's mouth started to twitch. "And I'm here because...?"

"The ship needs a communications officer. I want the best in the Fleet."

He laughed, relaxing against the back of his chair. "And you're not above using flattery to get him." He sipped his drink. "What's this ship of yours going to be doing?"

"We're designated for scientific investigation and exploration related to planetary and interstellar disturbances. We're still putting the crew together, but the Galactic Council wants us to be ready for service in two weeks."

"Why would the Council hire an independent? Why not just use Fleet ships?"

Jonarel fielded that one. "Scientific study is time-consuming. Given the option, the Council would prefer to pay a small team of trained specialists rather than pull one of their Fleet ships from active service. It is more efficient."

Kire considered the answer. "Makes sense." He looked back at her. "And you need to be ready in two weeks?"

"Yes. But I'm hoping to recruit my communications officer today." She stared pointedly at him.

He stared right back. It was a big decision. She understood that. But one way or another, she had to know his answer now.

A twinkle appeared in his hazel eyes. "You can check that one off your list, Captain."

Hallelujah! Aurora resisted the urge to punch her fist in the air as the tension in her neck and shoulders eased. She hadn't realized how much she had been counting on his presence on the ship until he'd said yes. "Thank you, Commander."

"Commander?"

She grinned. "Oh, didn't I tell you? You'll also be the ship's first officer."

He set his glass down with a thunk. "*Damn.* You sure know how to bury the lead."

She chuckled. "Let's just say I wanted to make sure you took the job for the right reasons." She folded her hands in front of her. "And now that we have that settled, there's one more key position to fill on the bridge."

"Which is?"

"Navigator. I'm having trouble locating someone who has the skill and talent to handle a Kraed ship confidently. Any suggestions?"

Kire glanced at Jonarel. "Wouldn't a Kraed be the best choice?"

Jonarel shook his head. "Unfortunately, that is not possible. Those members of my clan who have sufficient experience all have bonded mates and young. They will not leave Drakar. And those in training are not yet ready to handle the position."

"Then how about someone from another clan?"

Jonarel looked at Kire as though he had suggested they put an elephant in charge of navigation. "I would never ask nor would anyone accept a position onboard a ship belonging to another Kraed clan. It indicates one does not have strong family connections."

And the Kraed were the most family-oriented species Aurora had ever met.

"But the ship belongs to Roe, doesn't it?" Kire asked. "And she isn't a Kraed."

"No, but she is part of my clan."

And there it was. Jonarel hadn't said she was *like* a part of his clan, or that he *considered* her part of his clan. No, he'd said *she* is *part of my clan*. She'd always felt like the Clarek clan had adopted her, but Jonarel's comment confirmed her official standing in the eyes of his people. What exactly that meant to Jonarel, she didn't know. And she was in no rush to find out.

Kire was giving off equal parts of bewilderment and frustration, which made for a really fascinating expression on his face as he gazed at her. He was probably realizing how much he didn't understand about her relationship with Jonarel. That made two of them. However, he wisely chose to drop that line of questioning. "I'm guessing the navigator on the *Argo* isn't a candidate?"

"No. His style is very structured and by the book, which works fine on a Fleet ship. But he doesn't have the creativity and sensitivity required to work with a Kraed vessel."

"Okay. So we need someone who's intuitive, who can think outside the box." Kire's expression grew thoughtful.

"In that case. I do know someone who's perfect, if she's available. Her name is Bronwyn Kelly. She's young, and she didn't attend the Academy, but she's the best navigator I've ever seen."

"So she doesn't work on a Fleet ship? How did you meet her?"

"About six months ago a Setarip destroyer attacked the ship she was piloting. I saw the vid logs of the maneuvers she did to keep that ship out of target range until we arrived to deal with the destroyer. What she accomplished was amazing. No casualties. either. She's a cool character. Nothing seems to bother her."

"Can you contact her?"

"Consider it done."

Her comband vibrated against her forearm. She glanced at the display. "It's Admiral Schreiber." She selected the incoming message. Her heart rate accelerated as she scanned the contents. "Our timetable just changed. The Admiral wants us to report to his office for immediate assignment."

Kire frowned. "Why the sudden urgency?"

"He doesn't say." The tone of the message indicated time was of the essence. She panned her comband over the payment portal as she stood. "But I think you'd better contact Bronwyn Kelly on the way."

Three

Kire walked briskly toward Admiral Schreiber's office on the tenth floor of the Council headquarters building. He was still wrapping his head around the idea that he had resigned his post on the *Odyssey*, accepted a new position as the communications officer on Roe's ship, *and* was now a first officer, all in the past thirty minutes. He was either incredibly blessed or certifiably nuts. The jury was still out on that one.

Good thing he could work on very little sleep, because it looked like he wouldn't be getting much in the next few days. Roe had often commented on his ability to power nap, and he'd need that talent if her suspicions about their meeting with the Admiral were correct.

He'd also contacted Bronwyn Kelly. The young navigator had been intrigued by the possibility of piloting a Kraed vessel. She was arranging transport to Earth. The decision to hire her would ultimately be up to Roe, but he had a feeling she'd approve of Kelly.

As he stepped into the Admiral's office, he spotted Roe standing by the doorway to the small conference room, talking with two women. The woman on her left was about Roe's height, with an athletic build that showed even in her Fleet grays. The woman to her right was taller, with short dark hair that didn't reach the collar of her light blue medical tunic. Her face seemed vaguely familiar, although he couldn't place her.

Roe turned as he walked toward them. "Kire." She nodded in greeting and then gestured to the woman in blue. "You remember Mya, don't you?"

Recognition clicked into place. "Of course." He clasped the hand of Roe's childhood friend. He hadn't seen Mya Forrest since he'd left the Academy seven years ago, and her brown hair had been much longer then, almost to her waist. The shorter pixie cut she wore now suited her and was much more practical in her line of work. Roe had mentioned she'd already hired a medical officer. Now he understood why that job had been so easy to fill.

"I see she managed to talk you out of the Fleet." Mya glanced at Roe with sisterly affection.

"It wasn't tough to do." He grinned. "She knows my weaknesses."

"Mine, too." Mya made a face.

Roe's green eyes sparkled with mischief, but she refrained from commenting. Instead she turned to the woman on her left.

Despite the woman's modest, tailored uniform, she was stunning, with shoulder-length hair the color of milk chocolate and a face that Helen of Troy would have envied. Her toned physique spoke of strength and agility, and her dark brown eyes were almost hypnotic as they analyzed, categorized and detailed every millimeter of the space and the people in it. He'd bet good money he was about to meet the ship's security officer.

"Kire Emoto, may I introduce Celia Cardiff." Roe said. "We served on the *Argo* together. She's the head of security and weapons systems on the ship. She's also a walking encyclopedia of pharmacology." Laughter tinged her voice as she looked at Cardiff. "I'd introduce Kire to you, but since you ran his security background checks, you probably know more about him than I do."

If they were talking about raw facts, Roe might be right. However, they'd been close friends since they were teenagers. She'd been his confidant on many occasions. Those types of things didn't show up on official transcripts.

"I don't know, Sahzade," Mya said, echoing his thoughts. "You have a way of learning everyone's secrets, too."

He glanced at Mya. "What did you call her?"

"Sahzade."

"Which is...?"

"Her nickname when she was a child."

He frowned. "But I've never heard you call her that before."

Mya chuckled. "That's because I was told on pain of death that no one was to hear that name while we were at the Academy."

Roe grimaced. "A rule that she conveniently forgot as soon as we started serving together on the *Argo*."

Mya shrugged nonchalantly, clearly amused at Roe's discomfort.

"What does Sahzade mean?"

"Nothing." Roe looked like she wanted to leave it at that, but he wasn't about to let her off the hook so easily. He stared at her expectantly until she relented. "It's just something she made up when I was a child. From the way she tells it, I tended to ignore anyone who called me Aurora."

Kire grinned. "I can believe that. You were probably one of those kids who tried to change your name every month, weren't you?"

"Yes," Mya said.

"No," Roe replied, giving her friend a stern look. "But I liked running around outside and getting dirty. Aurora sounded like someone in a white dress with bows in her hair. Sahzade fit me better, at least as a child."

"Hmm." Mya covered her mouth with her hand to hide her smile.

Roe ignored her. "As I got older, I realized I really liked my name. But by then, the nickname had stuck."

And he'd given her another one when they met. "What about you?" he asked Mya. "Did she ever give you a nickname?"

"Actually, Mya *is* my nickname. My real name is Lelindia."

"You're kidding."

She shook her head. "Nope. Aurora couldn't pronounce my name when she was a toddler, just the *ah* sound at the end. However, like most two-year-olds, she was pretty good at saying *my* and *mine* so anytime she wanted me, she'd say *my-ah*. Over time, it became Mya, and she's never called me anything else."

Roe's pale skin had always shown a blush easily. A telltale flush of red was creeping up her cheeks now.

He grinned. "I should have known you were a precocious kid."

Before she could respond, Jon appeared at her side. "We're ready to begin, Captain."

"Thank you." Roe looked delighted by the interruption. "Shall we?"

The conference room contained a small round table and eight chairs. Admiral Schreiber was already seated at the far side. Kire settled in on the Admiral's left, next to Cardiff and Mya, while Jon and Roe sat to the Admiral's right.

"Thank you for getting here on such short notice." The Admiral clasped his hands in front of him. "I know your ship was not supposed to be put into service for another two weeks, but an hour ago we received a distress call from Gaia that requires an immediate response."

"Gaia?" The concern in Mya's voice was reflected on the faces of the rest of the crew.

Gaia was the first Earth colony, established in the mid twenty-second century. Kire knew the history by heart, as did every Academy graduate. Aggressive corporate monoculture crop production and rampant destruction of natural resources triggered the onset of a cascade failure in Earth's ecosystem that had nearly made the planet uninhabitable. However, the dire situation accomplished what years of war and diplomacy had not, galvanizing the world's governments and scientists into working together toward a common goal. It was the roots of what would eventually become the Galactic Council.

A three-pronged approach was launched. First, seeking solutions to correct the dramatic imbalances that had triggered the collapse, and the institution of eco-based agricultural production of edible plant life. Second, the development of a method for interstellar travel so that, if the worst happened, there would be somewhere for the human race to go. And third, the creation of a global communications network that broadcast a continuous call for assistance out into the void of space.

Without the crisis, it might have been centuries before humans would have developed the ability to travel through space. Their cooperation resulted in the successful completion of the first interstellar vessel, the *Odyssey*. It also caught the attention of the Kraed, who made contact with Earth's leaders and offered their help. They located a suitable planet for human colonization, and the *Odyssey* transported the first settlers to what would become Gaia.

Thanks in large part to the scientific assistance provided by the Kraed, Gaia never had to become the human race's new homeworld. Changes in ecological and agricultural management combined with the support and participation of the global community brought Earth back from the tipping point. The colony that had remained on Gaia was considered by most as part of Earth, a sister planet that had been a beacon of hope in a dark period.

"Gaia's in trouble," the Admiral said. "We need you to be ready to depart in twenty-four hours."

Roe snapped to attention. "*Twenty-four hours?*"

"I know that's asking a lot, Captain, but your crew's expertise is exactly what we need in this situation."

Roe loved a challenge. Her eyes revealed the steely determination Kire knew so well. "Then we'll be ready."

The Admiral's lined cheeks crinkled in a brief smile. He tapped the table's control console and an image of Gaia appeared above them, its lush green and blue surface so similar to Earth's it could be mistaken for its twin. "The last census put the resident population at just under one million." Yellow circles appeared on the image indicating the ten populated areas. "And ships traveling in the sector have always depended on Gaia as a safe food and water source. However, that may be about to change."

His gaze settled on Roe for a moment before he continued. "About two weeks ago, one of the communities suffered massive, unexplainable plant destruction. They thought it was a blight, though the pattern of loss was unlike anything they had seen and their science teams were unable to find a cause. It was isolated to one community until yesterday, when the same destruction occurred in an area more than a thousand kilometers away. They've lost at least fifty percent of the food resources and native vegetation for the affected communities. If it continues to spread to the other inhabited areas, all of the planet's agricultural resources could be wiped out in a matter of months."

The image shifted, and Kire sucked in a breath.

"It looks burned." The horror in Roe's voice matched the look on her face.

The pictures showed a barren wasteland of blackened hills and valleys, with houses and other structures sticking up at odd intervals like some giant child's grotesque sandbox creation. Only the roads and scattered groves of trees provided any break to the devastation.

Kire turned to the Admiral. "You said the plants died mysteriously. What about incendiary devices? It certainly looks like heat-induced destruction."

The Admiral shook his head. "In all cases, the devastation occurred at night and there was no indication of smoke, light, or heat. No one even realized what had happened until they went out in the morning."

"A foreign biological infestation?" Mya suggested.

"So far they have been unable to detect any life forms that are not indigenous to the planet, and there are no known creatures or entities capable of this type of rampant damage."

"How about an outside pathogen?" Cardiff leaned forward, her dark eyes intent. "Perhaps brought in accidentally by a visiting ship?"

"Possibly, although the problem began in a region that is rarely visited by outsiders, three hundred kilometers from the nearest relay station. To reach that community, a visitor would have to pass through one of the larger towns and the relay first, yet neither have reported any destruction."

Cardiff frowned, her gaze returning to the images.

The Admiral continued. "At this point, we don't have a working hypothesis. The damage has affected all vegetation with the exception of wooded areas, but we can't rule out the possibility that it could spread. Right now it's hurting their agricultural viability, but if a solution isn't found, it's conceivable that the planet's entire ecosystem could be wiped out."

Which essentially meant the death of the planet. The room grew quiet as the significance of that statement soaked in.

The Admiral ran his hand over his head, a gesture that probably dated back to a time when he had hair. "We've already sent a Rescue Corps team to begin setting up temporary quarantine and housing areas for the two affected communities. We'll be delivering supplies and non-perishable goods via freighter over the next few days, which should cut down on the general sense of panic."

He touched the console and the images disappeared. Confidence shone in his eyes. "You are some of the best scientific minds in the known galaxy. It's your job to find a solution before the destruction ripples out any further." He turned to Roe. "Any questions?"

Her lips pressed into a thin line. She glanced at Jon before replying. "The ship can be ready in time, but we have a problem. We don't have a pilot."

"Do you have any prospects?"

She nodded. "We've contacted someone, but right now she's closer to Gaia than Earth."

The Admiral steepled his fingers. "I have someone who could fill in, at least to get you to Gaia. He's a talented navigator who works for the Rescue Corps. He's scheduled to pilot one of the freighters to Gaia tomorrow, but I can assign someone to fill in for him. Would that be acceptable?"

Roe looked uneasy. "Has he ever been onboard a Kraed vessel?"

The Admiral seemed amused by her concern. "No. But he's flown just about everything there is to fly. I'm sure he can handle it."

She glanced at Kire, and he shrugged. What choice did they have?

"Then we'd be happy to have him onboard, Admiral."

"Good. I'll contact him with instructions. What time can you leave?"

Roe looked at Jon.

"The ship can be ready by nine hundred hours tomorrow," he said.

Admiral Schreiber clapped his hands together. "Very good. Unless you have any other questions, we'll adjourn so you can get moving." Everyone rose as the Admiral pushed back his chair and stood. "I'll expect to hear from you when you reach Gaia."

Four

A steady flow of Fleet crewmembers and civilian passengers crowded the platform for the high-speed tramway that connected the Council building to the transport hanger. Aurora stepped quickly through the open tram doorway and chose a spot near the front window, even though at this late hour, there wouldn't be much to see.

The doors to the small cabin closed and the tram surged forward. The walls of the tunnel flashed by until they gave way to the inky black of a moonless night. By day, the bright sunshine of southern California would have bathed the area in its warm glow, reflecting off the surface of the ocean to her left. Right now the only lights shone from the nearby buildings and the track markers up ahead.

Tapping her comband, she reread the most recent message from Admiral Schreiber.

I've spoken to the pilot and he's agreed to fill in. It was an easy sell. Once I mentioned it was a Kraed vessel, he jumped at the chance. My assistant has sent his credentials to your security chief.

She should be thrilled, but she couldn't shake a nagging feeling of apprehension. It wasn't that she doubted the Admiral's judgment—the pilot he'd recommended would certainly be capable. It just seemed wrong to have someone she'd never met piloting her ship. Especially on their first mission.

However, given the time constraints and the necessity of reaching Gaia as soon as possible, she didn't

have any other options. At least Celia would have a chance
to familiarize herself with their temporary crewmember
before departure. If there was anything Aurora needed to be
aware of, Celia would alert her. Most people, especially men,
tended to tell Celia anything she wanted to know.

After working together on the *Argo* for the past
two years, Aurora had grown accustomed to the attention
Celia drew when she walked into a room. Few people
realized the sharp mind and lethal grace that hid behind the
lovely exterior.

Not that Celia cared. Being underestimated was an
advantage in her position. Only one thing mattered to her—
protecting those around her. It was a point they'd bonded
over. She'd originally sought Celia out shortly after joining
the crew of the *Argo*. The ship's captain, Admiral Schreiber's
son Knox, had mentioned that Celia was a master at hand-to-
hand combat. Aurora hadn't received much instruction on
advanced fighting techniques at the Academy, since she'd
focused her attention on leadership and cultural studies.

However, as commander of the *Argo*, she'd realized
situations could arise on a mission where she needed to be
able to defend herself without using her shielding abilities.
So, she'd asked Celia to become her sparring partner.

Over the past two years Celia had taken great
pleasure in knocking her flat on her butt every time they
faced off. To date, she'd never bested her teacher, but she
didn't know anyone else, man or woman, who had either.
That was another reason she'd been determined to convince
Celia to leave the *Argo*. Since their future missions would
involve the bizarre and unknown, she wanted someone by
her side who could handle anything the galaxy might throw
at them.

The tram slowed as the bulk of the transport hangar rose out of the darkness. The vehicle slid to a stop at the arrival platform and she joined the mass exodus, heading for the stairs that led to the main departure wing. Kire stood at the top landing, waiting for her.

He smiled as she approached. "Captain."

She smiled back. "Commander."

He fell into step beside her as they made their way through the crowd. "Mya and Jon are already onboard the shuttle, and Cardiff will be on the next tram. Unfortunately, the pilot was unable to join us in time for our shuttle, so he'll take the next crew transport in a couple hours and report in at the station."

So she'd have to wait a while longer to meet their mysterious crewmember. "What time will our supplies be ready for loading?"

He checked his comband. "The Admiral put a rush on our requests, so the ground crews estimate all items will be prepped by four hundred hours. That should give us a few hours after everything's onboard to get settled in and familiarize ourselves with our stations before we depart."

As they continued through the busy port, she thanked her lucky stars that Kire had been willing to make this leap of faith with her. She couldn't imagine anyone else stepping into the role of commander with such ease and efficiency, especially with only a few hours' notice.

They reached the shuttle launch platform and crossed the elevated walkway to number four. Kire followed her up the ramp and into the main cabin. Mya and Jonarel were already seated in the second passenger row.

She and Kire took the two seats in front of them and reached for their safety harnesses. Snapping the broad straps into place. she turned to Mya. "Did you have time to gather all your medical supplies?"

"The supplies. yes. although I had to give up on my plan to bring a few potted medicinal plants. I had hoped to make a quick trip home next week to take some cuttings. but that will have to wait until later."

"You should be able to make do with what we already have onboard. at least for now." She caught Jonarel's gaze and suppressed a smile. Mya would discover soon enough that more awaited her on the ship than she ever imagined. *A lot* more.

Celia appeared in the shuttle doorway. her gray Fleet uniform replaced by a dark brown tunic and legging combination that emphasized her athletic physique. She claimed a seat behind Mya near the window and clicked her harness into place. "All set."

The shuttle pilot glanced over her shoulder into the main cabin. "Are we still waiting for one more?"

Aurora shook her head. "He's catching the crew transport instead."

"Then I'll notify the tower we're ready."

As the pilot spoke to the ground personnel. the loading ramp retracted. sealing the outer door in place. Vibrations rumbled up through the floor as the launch sequence engaged and the thrusters built up a head of steam. The braces retracted and the shuttle shot along the channel and out the open hangar door. continuing along the inclined track for a few more seconds before breaking free of the runway.

Aurora's breath caught as the engines engaged and the craft rocketed upwards. She'd made this type of shuttle jump dozens of times over the years. but this felt completely different. And no wonder. She wasn't on her way to a Fleet ship—she was on her way to *her* ship.

As they escaped the grip of Earth's atmosphere, emerging into the vast expanse of space, she glanced over her shoulder at the beautiful vista of green and blue. No matter how many times she saw this view, she never tired of it. From this perspective, it was hard to imagine that a hundred years ago, Earth had been on the brink of ecological collapse. And now they were tasked with preventing that same fate from befalling the planet that had been Earth's beacon of hope.

She shifted her attention to the window on her left as they approached the busy space station. She'd specifically requested a shuttle with wide view panels along both sides. In a moment, her crew would know why.

The shuttle fell in line behind a patrol yacht and a freighter. The pilot's voice drifted back from the cockpit. "We'll be arriving at the L5 hanger in about five minutes. You should get a good view of the ship out the port windows as we pass."

Aurora spotted the ship a moment later. "There. Just to the left of the freighter."

Mya inhaled sharply and Kire whipped his head around to stare at Aurora. "*That's* our ship?"

She smiled, enjoying the look of incredulity on his face. She knew the feeling. "Yep."

The foundation of Kraed design was flowing beauty, so all Kraed ships were graceful. But what Jonarel had accomplished was beyond words. While Fleet ships were crafted in neutral metallic tones that stood out in sharp contrast to the blackness around them, Kraed vessels used a compound in the outer hull that allowed the ship to take on the look of whatever surrounded it, much like a chameleon.

When the ship's defenses were fully activated, the vessel became nearly invisible, even to scanners. At the moment, the ship was mimicking the star field, giving the hull the appearance of black velvet embedded with tiny diamonds.

The other enchanting quality was the complete lack of straight lines. Kraed favored curves, so every part of the ship flowed seamlessly together, like a cascade of water frozen in an instant. The only break in the fluidity was the windowed airlock on the cargo level that attached the ship to the space station.

"It's beautiful." Mya's voice was reverent, a combination of awe and delight.

Just the reaction she'd hoped for.

As they drew alongside, Mya pointed to the elegant script underneath the ship's bridge. "*Starhawke?*" She glanced at Aurora in surprise. "You named the ship after yourself?"

Jonarel replied before Aurora could. "I named her."

"Why *Starhawke?*" Kire asked.

Jonarel held Aurora's gaze as he answered. "All Kraed ships are named after the family that created them. Clarek would have been part of the ship's designation, however, because this ship was a gift to Aurora, her family name was chosen instead. The second name identifies the essence of the ship. This would normally be a word in the Kraed language, but a word in Aurora's native language seemed more appropriate."

Everything he'd said was one hundred percent true, but as the crew would soon learn, there was a lot more to the name of the ship than he'd revealed. It was one reason she had carefully avoided telling anyone the ship's name, even though she loved the imagery of Jonarel's choice—a hawk in flight among the stars.

They left the ship behind as the shuttle glided through the hangar doorway and touched down on the landing platform. The airlock doors closed and the bay's interior pressurized.

Aurora unsnapped her safety harness. "Thank you," she called out to their pilot.

"Safe travels," the pilot replied as Aurora and her crew headed down the loading ramp.

Mya walked beside Aurora as they made their way through the throng in the main corridor. "Are there any other secrets I should know about?"

Mya was gazing at her with the same expression she used to have when Aurora was a child and had talked Mya into joining one of her many adventures, which often included bending a few of their parents' rules. But there was a deeper meaning to the question. After all, Mya had experience keeping secrets, too.

For one thing, neither of her parents were human. They belonged to the same virtually extinct race as Aurora's mother, having barely escaped the destruction of their homeworld fifty years ago. It was a topic that had only been brought up in the household once, the day her mother had sworn her to secrecy about her abilities. Neither she nor Mya had been given any details.

However, Mya's parents hadn't placed the same restrictions on Mya regarding keeping her ancestry secret. Instead, they'd used logic to obtain obedience. Because Mya could pass for a human, revealing she wasn't one would invite questions she wouldn't be able to answer. And since her special abilities didn't draw attention the way Aurora's did, they weren't a burden.

In this instance, however, the secrets were all positive. Aurora smiled. "A couple more."

Mya studied her. "Any heart-stoppers?"

Aurora chuckled. Mya knew her well. "Nothing you can't handle."

She led the way through the station's main hub and into the corridor for the *Starhawke*'s docking berth. At the entrance to the airlock she stepped in front of the security scanner. The doors parted, the windowed upper half of the spacious cylinder providing them with a stunning view of the ship rising above. From this perspective, it looked enormous, though in reality it was less than a tenth the size of a standard Fleet ship. It didn't take nearly as many crewmembers to manage it, either—just a very special one who never left the ship.

They reached the end of the airlock and Aurora placed her hand gently on the ship's hull. Her fingertips tingled as the cargo bay doors materialized out of the smooth surface and slid open to reveal the spacious interior.

"Nice." Kire followed her onto the ship.

"Coded touch sensors?" Celia asked as she, Mya and Jonarel joined them. Her gaze swept over the doors and interior walls, which were smooth as glass with no visible controls.

"Not exactly." Aurora stopped a few meters into the cargo bay. "The entire ship registers biological signatures, so almost any surface can function as an interface." She glanced at Jonarel. His golden gaze was focused intently on her. This was the big reveal. "But the Nirunoc directs the ship's response."

Celia frowned. "Nirunoc? What's that?"

"Not what. Who."

"*Who?*"

Aurora focused her attention on her security-minded friend. The next bit of information might increase her unease. "The Nirunoc are a race of non-biological beings that were created on Drakar just as artificial intelligence entities were developed on Earth. However, unlike the power struggle that developed between humans and the AI race, the Nirunoc and Kraed have a familial relationship. The Nirunoc are raised like children, the clan providing for their needs and encouraging them to choose their own path. As a result, the two species are intertwined as an extended family. They work together for the betterment of all."

She swept her arms out. "One of the factors that makes Kraed ships more advanced than anything humans have achieved is the presence of a Nirunoc onboard. Essentially, they bring the ship to life."

Celia looked stunned. "Are you saying the ship is *alive*?"

Aurora nodded. "The Nirunoc is a living, sentient entity, and she has integrated with the ship's systems. Whatever happens to the ship will impact her."

"Then why haven't we heard of them before?" Kire asked.

Jonarel spoke up. "Human history with sentient non-biological entities shows a decided lack of understanding for their individuality. My people have seen no advantage to sharing the existence of the Nirunoc, at least until human attitudes toward AI move toward a desire for partnership rather than dominance."

His tone indicated that might take a while. She agreed. Even the most recent attempts at communication with the AI homeworld had failed to open a dialogue, largely because the Council still believed they had a right to dictate how the relationship would develop. The AI had been firm in their assertion of self-governance.

"Meaning this knowledge stays here?" Kire asked.

Jonarel nodded. "Yes."

"You keep saying she." Mya's gaze swept around the room. "Do they have gender?"

Aurora smiled. "They can. Since the Kraed have gender, and the Nirunoc are part of their families, they have the option of choosing a gender to help identify themselves. In this case, she wanted to be viewed as female. She's also chosen a vocalization and visual that matches her choice." She glanced to her left, where a very realistic holographic image of a Kraed female with long dark hair and deep green skin had appeared. "Haven't you, Star?"

The image's lips moved, but the melodious voice came from everywhere and nowhere, the ship acting as a speaker. "Yes."

Celia tensed, her hand dropping instinctively to the weapons belt concealed beneath her tunic.

Aurora placed a reassuring hand on her arm.

Kire, however, looked like a kid in a candy store. "So your name is Star?" He stepped closer to the three-dimensional image.

"Yes and no," she replied. "My given name is Tehar, but when I made the decision to bond with this ship, I chose to accept a new name that echoes my own. Star, rather than Tehar."

Kire glanced at Jonarel. "So when you said the second name of the ship was its essence, you didn't mean its function. You literally meant her." He indicated Star.

Jonarel inclined his head.

Kire grinned. "That is so cool!"

Aurora hadn't known how her crew would feel about working on a ship that had a mind of its own, but Kire's reaction delighted her. She suspected he and Star would have a lot to talk about. And now that the shock had worn off. Celia seemed more relaxed as well. It wouldn't take long for her to realize the security benefits that such an arrangement presented.

As for Mya, she was shaking her head in amusement. Jonarel stood next to her with his arms folded loosely over his broad chest, enjoying the moment. And this was only the beginning.

Aurora stepped toward the far wall, the doors parting to reveal the corridor beyond. "So, who's ready for a tour?"

Five

Three hours later, Aurora was ensconced in the captain's chair on the bridge, reading over the information Admiral Schreiber had provided about Gaia. Kire sat at the communication console, monitoring all messages from the crew, station command, and Council headquarters. Jonarel was in engineering working with Star on priming the engines. Celia was in the cargo bay overseeing the delivery of their supplies, and Mya was settling into her office in the med bay.

"Roe?"

She looked up as Kire pivoted to face her. "Yes?"

"Our pilot's here. Cardiff's escorting him to the bridge."

Finally. She'd been trying, rather unsuccessfully, to ignore the vacant chair on the lower level of the bridge ever since she'd sat down to work. But as the minutes had ticked by, anxiety had crept in. Uncertainty always made her twitchy.

She'd considered going down to the cargo bay to ask Celia for a quick rundown regarding their new pilot, but she'd held off. Celia had plenty to do without handholding her. Still, it would be nice to know the pilot's name before he showed up on the bridge. "Did she upload his bio into the system?"

"Let me check." Kire turned back to his console.

She glanced at the readout on her comband. They still had a couple of hours before departure, so the pilot would have time to look over the navigation controls before he had to take the helm.

"Looks like it's here," Kire said.

But as she rose to join him, Kire abruptly hit the console and it went blank. She froze. "What's wrong?"

His expression was carefully composed. "You're not going to like this."

Judging from his reaction, he was probably right. "Tell me."

"The pilot is—"

He halted, his attention shifting to the open lift doors as Celia stepped onto the bridge. A broad shouldered man in a Rescue Corps uniform followed her, his gaze sweeping the bridge, stopping when he spotted her.

Aurora's heart stopped at the same time. "*No.*" The word was barely a whisper, more exhalation than speech as all the air evacuated her lungs. But that one word echoed in her head over and over as she stared at a man she had hoped never to see again.

He was taller than she remembered, or maybe he just looked taller because he'd filled out in the intervening years. Youthful softness had been replaced by the hard muscle and lean physique of adulthood. He still wore his blond hair short on the sides but longer in front, which gave him a roguish look.

He was watching her, and that realization broke through her paralysis. She slammed the door on the wave of emotions his arrival had triggered and took a calming breath. Adopting the neutral expression she had perfected in her years as a Fleet officer, she stepped forward to greet her new pilot.

Celia started the introductions. "Captain, may I present Cade Ellis from the Galactic Council Rescue Corps.

Mr. Ellis, may I present Captain Aurora Hawke." Celia's words flowed smoothly, but she had a speculative look in her eyes. She had definitely registered Aurora's initial reaction.

Cade, however, didn't look the least bit surprised to see her, which made sense. The Admiral would have informed him that she was the captain of the ship he'd be piloting. He'd had time to prepare for this meeting. She had not. The fact that he'd still agreed to take the assignment, knowing she would be his commander, posed some interesting questions. Maybe she'd ask them later. Right now, she was at a disadvantage.

She forced herself to meet the sea-green gaze she knew so well. She extended her hand. "Welcome to the *Starhawke*, Mr. Ellis."

A flicker of surprise crossed his face, but after a slight hesitation, he reached out and enveloped her hand in his. "Thank you, Captain."

The brush of his palm against hers caused an instinctive reaction that sent rivulets of warmth up her arm. She fought the urge to jerk her hand away, determined not to show any weakness in front of this man. Not now, not ever.

"I appreciate your willingness to fill in on such short notice." She managed to keep her voice steady as she extricated her hand from his grip.

The corners of his mouth lifted slightly, although no humor showed in his eyes. "It was an impossible offer to refuse, especially from the Admiral. I've studied Kraed technology for years, but I never expected to have the opportunity to pilot a Kraed ship myself."

"The Admiral mentioned that was a selling point."

His gaze shifted to her right. Kire stood next to her, his posture relaxed but his eyes as hard as flint as he stared at Cade.

"You may remember Commander Kire Emoto from the Academy. He's the ship's communications chief and my first officer."

The two men locked gazes for a few heartbeats, neither making a move as tension snapped between them. Finally Cade nodded in acknowledgement. "Commander."

Kire returned the gesture. "Mr. Ellis."

For a man who usually had a hint of laughter in every syllable he spoke, Kire's voice was pure ice. He wasn't any happier to have Cade onboard than she was. That was comforting.

She glanced at Celia. "Have Mr. Ellis's personal belongings been delivered?"

Celia nodded. "I have them in a transport crate in the cargo bay."

"Good. Then please show Mr. Ellis to cabin G4 and deliver his belongings there." Guest quarters, including G4, were located on a mid-ship deck, while the crew cabins were on the upper decks. Aurora had originally planned to put their interim pilot in the navigator's cabin on the crew deck. Not anymore.

Celia didn't seem surprised by her choice of accommodations. "Of course."

Aurora turned to Cade. "We depart at nine hundred hours, so you have a little time to get settled in your quarters before you report back here."

If he realized he'd been downgraded, he didn't show it. "Thank you, Captain. I'll do that." He headed back to the lift, with Celia right behind him.

As soon as the doors slid shut. Aurora closed her eyes and willed the muscles in her neck and jaw to unclench.

Kire placed his hand on her shoulder. "I'm so sorry. Roe."

Opening her eyes. she gave him a mirthless smile. "The universe has a wicked sense of humor."

Six

Aurora stood in front of the wide viewport in her office, her hands clasped behind her back, watching the ships that moved across her field of vision. But she wasn't seeing them. Not really.

Cade Ellis onboard her ship. She still couldn't believe it. If anyone from her crew could fill in as the navigator for this mission, she would have ordered him off the moment he set foot on her bridge. With a little help, Star could get them away from the station, but she didn't have the skill required to navigate through their interstellar jump. Neither did anyone else onboard, except Cade. Like it or not, she needed him. That was a bitter pill to swallow.

The door chimed. "Come in."

Mya stepped into the room, the doors sliding closed behind her as she joined Aurora in front of the viewport.

"Kire contacted you."

Mya nodded. "Yes."

She waited to see if Mya would elaborate, but her friend just gazed out the window at the passing ships, her demeanor completely unruffled.

Finally, the silence became unbearable. "And?" She crossed her arms over her chest. It was a defensive gesture, but dammit, she *was* defensive.

Compassion warmed Mya's brown eyes. "This is your battle, Sahzade. How can I help you?"

A million thoughts raced through her mind while emotions played tug of war in her chest. Mya would understand, as she always did, but now was not the time to dredge up the past. She went for irony instead. "How would you feel about shooting a member of the Rescue Corps out of the airlock?"

Mya laughed. "Tempting as that might be, I don't think that's in anyone's best interests at the moment."

A smile tugged on her lips. "No," she admitted. "I suppose you're right." She gazed at the buzz of activity beyond the window. "But thinking about it sure makes me feel better."

Mya nodded, her eyes sparkling with amusement. But her voice held a note of concern. "Will you be all right working with him for the next twenty-two hours?"

It was a fair question, given the history she and Cade shared. But she wasn't a starry-eyed Academy cadet anymore. "This is my ship. I may need him at the navigator's console, but he's still under my command. Either he will respect that, or..."

"He'll have an unfortunate run-in with an airlock?"

"Something like that."

Mya studied her for a moment. "You'll be fine."

She hoped Mya was right.

As they stepped onto the bridge she motioned Mya to the console to the left of the captain's chair. Celia was already seated at tactical on the lower level, with Cade to her right at the navigator's console. They both looked up as Aurora approached.

"All supplies have been delivered and stored, Captain," Celia said. "The exterior doors have been closed and secured for departure."

"Thank you." She turned her attention to Cade. "Any issues to report, Mr. Ellis?"

He was the picture of efficiency, without a hint of emotion shadowing his expression. "None, Captain. The course and heading are laid in and navigation systems are online."

"Very good." Whatever she might think of Cade personally, he'd been an exceptionally skilled pilot even before they'd parted ways. She had every reason to believe he'd spent the past ten years adding to his knowledge and experience. For the next few hours at least, she needed to trust him to do his job.

She moved over to Kire's console. "What's our status?"

He checked the panel. "All diagnostics have been completed." He scanned the incoming messages. "Station command has given us clearance to depart."

Excitement strummed along her nerve endings. She settled into the captain's chair and opened a comm channel. "Hawke to engineering."

Jonarel's deep voice rumbled over the connection. "Clarek, here."

Did Cade just flinch? Or was that her imagination? "We've received clearance for departure."

"Engines are primed and all systems are fully functional, Captain. The ship is ready on your command."

Her pulse shifted into high gear. She'd been thinking of this moment since the day Jonarel had brought her onboard. Now that it was here, she had so many things she wanted to tell him, so many thoughts and emotions she wanted to share. She settled for the one thing she could say.

"Thank you." She put emphasis on her words, hoping that Jonarel would understand. He wanted to be in engineering just in case something went wrong, but it felt strange that he wasn't on the bridge for this moment.

A ping sounded from the arm console. and she glanced down.

You are welcome.

Her heart squeezed. None of this would have been possible without him. And that made this moment precious.

Cade glanced back, his gaze locked on her. "Captain?"

"Mr. Ellis, you have the helm."

"Roger, that." He swiveled back around. "Disengaging mooring clamps and engaging thrusters."

A nearly imperceptible vibration slipped up through the floor as the engines came to life. Aurora kept her gaze on the main screen, memorizing every detail as they maneuvered away from the station.

A freighter and a couple shuttles passed in the distance, headed for destinations unknown, but Aurora's focus stayed fixed on the star field up ahead as the ship picked up speed.

"We've cleared the perimeter. Course is laid in to Gaia," Cade said. "Approaching our jump window. Interstellar engines are online."

"Then let's see what she can do."

She sensed a subtle shift in the energy field as the ship switched from the main drive to the interstellar engines, almost as if Star had taken a breath. Then they launched into the glittering void of space.

Seven

"Sahzade, this is incredible!" Mya stepped to the center of the spacious room and pivoted slowly, her face lit with child-like excitement.

Aurora knew exactly how she felt.

Nearly every available surface was draped, twined, or stacked with edible plants—vegetables ripe on the vine, leafy tubers, salad greens, herbs, melons and succulent berries. Stone pathways meandered through the dense foliage, ducking under trellised archways and climbing over several small bridges that crossed a babbling brook. The stream originated from a fountain near the doorway and ended at a reclamation pond on the opposite side of the room. Strategically placed lighting created the illusion of dappled sunlight, but could also simulate the night sky, or even clouds and storm conditions.

Mya glanced at Jonarel, who stood watching her. "I suppose this was your idea?"

He inclined his head.

Mya's voice was reverent as she stroked the glossy leaves of an orange tree. "It's beautiful. Just...beautiful." She trailed her fingers over the dark green orbs hanging from the tree, promising future delights. Her expression grew thoughtful. "Don't take this the wrong way, but why on earth did you go to so much trouble?"

Jonarel looked bemused. "The ship is designed to be self-sufficient for extended periods of time. Creating a space to grow a replenishing food source was a necessity."

Necessary, yes, but Jonarel had gone above and beyond. Aurora had been amazed by the design of this room when he'd first shown it to her a month ago, and together they'd made quite a few additions. It was a plant-lover's wonderland, and Mya's reaction was everything she had hoped it would be.

Jonarel gestured to a wooden rack covered with rows of ceramic pots to Mya's right. "Aurora also thought you'd enjoy having a dedicated space for medicinal herbs, given your interest in the subject."

Like everyone from their race, Mya had been born with the innate ability to grow plants. It was as much a part of her genetic code as her dark hair and brown eyes. Unlike her parents, who specialized in herbal therapy, Mya's passion lay in studying extraterrestrial vegetation, especially those with potential medicinal applications. One of the perks Aurora had promised when she'd offered Mya the job of ship's medical officer was the opportunity to study plants that few Earth physicians had ever seen.

"And you conveniently located it right off the med bay." Mya faced Jonarel. "That seems like quite a coincidence."

"Not at all. I believed Aurora would succeed in recruiting you as the ship's doctor. I planned the layout accordingly."

Mya nodded. "Good guess." She strolled down one of the winding pathways, her fingertips dancing across the tops of the plants as she passed. She gestured to the doorway on the far side of the room. "What's in there?"

"The storage pantry, which connects to the kitchen. You will find equipment and supplies for drying and storing your herbs there."

Mya shook her head. "You've thought of everything." Retracing her steps, she stopped in front of Jonarel and rested her hip against one of the raised planters. "So Mr. Clarek, are there any impossible feats for the functioning of this ship that you *haven't* been able to make a reality?"

Jonarel's dark brows lifted, and his gaze swept across the room. He shook his head, his thick hair brushing across his shoulders. "Not yet."

Aurora snorted with laughter.

"Good to know you're still humble," Mya said under her breath.

That comment earned her a rare Kraed smile. "Of course."

Aurora met Mya's gaze and grinned. It was wonderful to be together again. She'd enjoyed being a Fleet officer, and certainly had no regrets, but she'd missed moments like this, moments that highlighted the easy camaraderie created by years of friendship and shared experiences. Thanks to Jonarel, she had that again.

However, as captain, she couldn't play hooky from her duties for long. And she had a task she still needed to accomplish here. "I'm sorry to break things up, but I should get back to the bridge." She paused and fixed her gaze on Jonarel. "But before I go, there's something I need to tell you."

Jonarel's stance shifted, as though he was bracing for impact.

Good thing. There was zero chance he'd like what she had to say. "I want to alert you that the temporary navigator the Admiral sent is someone you know." She gazed into his golden eyes. "Cade Ellis."

As soon as the words left her mouth, the emotional temperature of the room dropped.

Jonarel stood ramrod straight, his hands curling into fists. He took a step toward her, seeming to grow in the process. "*Cade Ellis?*" His voice was barely a whisper, but it cut like glass. His eyes flashed with a wild intensity that signaled barely contained rage.

She resisted the urge to flinch. Forget the airlock. Judging from the look on Jonarel's face, if Cade wasn't careful, the Kraed might serve him a punishment far worse than being blown out into space.

As she'd feared, she'd poked a sleeping tiger with a very sharp stick. But she couldn't allow the situation to get out of hand. Not that she was in danger. Jonarel would sooner chew off his own arm than allow anyone, including himself, to harm her. But Cade might as well have a target on his chest.

"Yes." She met his anger head on. "Is that a problem?"

Of course it was a problem. She was the one who'd spouted off about the dangers of overprotective Kraed males on the day she and Jonarel had met. He certainly looked the part of an enraged grizzly right now.

But when his only response was a low growl as his lips pulled back from his teeth, her temper flared to life. "This situation is not what either of us would have chosen." Her voice took on a hard edge.

He opened his mouth to respond but she cut him off.

"*However,* I am the captain of this ship and he is a crewmember under my command, at least until we reach Gaia. As such, I expect you to treat him with respect."

The look Jonarel gave her raised the hairs on the back of her neck. She took a step closer, her words rumbling out of her throat as she worked to control her temper and her fear. "If I see or hear *anything* that is unprofessional in your behavior toward him during that time, you and I *will* have words. *Is that clear?*"

Waves of raw emotion rolled off of him, so thick she had trouble drawing breath. She'd only seen this type of behavior from him once before, and she'd been frightened then, too. She had to get through to him. Otherwise, things were going to get ugly.

The silence stretched out as tight as a drum. She waited, giving him time to regain control. She could sense Mya's fear too, skittering around the edges of the black cloud of anger coming from Jonarel, but Aurora didn't dare break eye contact to check on her.

Finally, his expression shifted, the burning hostility leaving his eyes, replaced with a wary tension. He stepped away from her, his taut muscles flexing beneath his tunic. But the lethal edge had disappeared. He gazed at her for several long moments before he responded. "Yes, Captain."

She searched for any sign that the storm would return, but he appeared to have locked it down. Satisfied, she nodded in acknowledgment. "I'll be on the bridge." She exchanged a quick look with Mya before pivoting on her heel and walking out of the room.

The minute the doors closed behind her, she sank onto the nearest med platform and took a few deep breaths. Her pulse pounded in her ears as she struggled to calm her chaotic emotions.

She'd known her revelation wouldn't be welcome, but she'd seriously underestimated how Jonarel would react. She'd hoped the calm of the greenhouse and Mya's presence would soften the blow. It hadn't. Jonarel had been ready to attack Cade. Correction. He'd been ready to *kill* Cade. She knew it as surely as she knew her own name. And yet somehow the two men would have to exist on the same ship without doing bodily harm to each other.

What had been going through Jonarel's mind? Even knowing him as well as she did, and understanding why he hated Cade, his reaction seemed far more intense than she would have expected. Did he know something she didn't?

She'd like to ask him, but not right now. Considering how he'd looked—eyes flashing fire, large hands curled with claws unsheathed, neck and shoulder muscles flexed—that discussion could wait until Cade was safely off the ship.

Star's gentle voice interrupted her thoughts. "Are you all right, Captain?" The Nirunoc materialized next to her on the med platform.

Even after a month spent working with Star and Jonarel to get the ship ready, Aurora was still adjusting to the reality of a crewmember who could appear and disappear at will.

Part of Star's job was monitoring the wellbeing of the crew, so she'd probably heard most of the confrontation in the garden. Without any background information as to why Aurora and Jonarel would suddenly be arguing, Star's appearance in the med bay made sense, especially with Aurora sitting like a stone.

She met Star's gaze. "Yes, I'm fine. Just working some things out."

Concern showed in Star's honey-colored eyes. "Is there anything I can do?"

Aurora shook her head. If only this situation were that simple. "No. But thanks for offering."

Star smiled gently and placed a hand on Aurora's arm. Then the image dissipated.

Standing, Aurora walked through the med bay doors and continued onto the lift. "Bridge."

The doors slid closed and the lift glided up, but her thoughts continued to churn. Jonarel was a study in contradictions, much like the classic Jekyll and Hyde. He had created a ship of incredible grace and beauty, one that was a perfect blend of science and art, yet he possessed a feral side that was capable of violent destruction. She was one of the few who had seen both extremes. Which one represented the real Jonarel?

When the lift stopped and the doors opened, her gaze locked with the man who had triggered Jonarel's Mr. Hyde impersonation. She wasn't in the mood to deal with him, either, but she needed to get an update.

"Status, Mr. Ellis."

His fingers danced over the console. "On course and on time, Captain. We should arrive at our destination in nineteen hours, thirty-five minutes."

"Thank you." She started to turn away, but stopped herself. She'd just ordered Jonarel to treat Cade like a member of the crew. She needed to do the same. "I know you're scheduled to be on duty for another three hours, but the ship has an excellent auto-pilot system. It can maintain our heading now that you've entered all the coordinates. If you'd like to get something to eat, I can have food sent to your quarters." She gestured to Kire. "We can watch over things while you're gone."

The first crack appeared in Cade's professional veneer. "Trying to get rid of me, Captain?" His eyes sparkled with amusement and his voice lost some of its Fleet efficiency, sliding toward easy familiarity.

The question startled her, as did the way he was looking at her. Teasing her had been one of Cade's favorite activities once upon a time, but she certainly hadn't expected him to do it now.

She kept her response neutral. "Not at all. You're welcome to stay on the bridge until your scheduled off hours if you prefer. But you were rushed getting here and might not have had time for a decent meal before we departed."

His mouth softened into a smile, and the look in his eyes grew warmer. "Thank you for thinking of me."

Was he *flirting* with her? Surely not. And yet something in his manner had definitely changed. For a reason she could not possibly fathom, Cade Ellis was trying to charm her.

For all the good it would do. She kept her voice cool as a Colorado autumn. "If you change your mind, inform the Commander before leaving the bridge." She headed toward the door to her office.

"Yes, *Captain.*"

Damn him. Only Cade could make that word sound like an endearment.

"Nineteen hours and thirty-four minutes to go," she muttered as she entered her sanctuary.

Her comband vibrated a moment later.

"Yes?"

"Captain, you have a message waiting for you from the Admiral," Kire said.

She paused. Why hadn't he told her while she was on the bridge? *Because you didn't even look at him.* Cade had rattled her so badly she'd completely ignored her first officer. Not good.

"Thank you. I'll review it now."

She sat down at her desk and tapped the screen to bring up the message.

We've received an update from Gaia. They suffered more losses last night. The Rescue Corps teams will have a base camp set up by the time you arrive. Report there. The Chancellor said they're starting to see the first signs of panic, so you'll need to do whatever you can to keep everyone calm. We don't want to add fear-induced pandemonium to the list of problems.

Report back as soon as you've conducted your preliminary evaluation.

Of course the Gaians were terrified. Their planet was dying.

Her concerns about Cade and Jonarel faded into the background as her focus returned to her mission. Clearing the vid screen, she called up the files the Admiral had provided. One way or another, they would find out what was causing the destruction and stop it. They had to. The alternative was simply not an option.

Eight

Celia Cardiff leaned over the pot of simmering tomatoes and took an appreciative sniff before adding a pinch of basil to the mixture. "So what's the deal with Aurora and Ellis?"

Mya stood like a statue beside the counter in the *Starhawke's* galley kitchen, her body language telegraphing tension and anxiety. She glanced at the doorway to the greenhouse and sighed. "It's a long story."

"Uh-huh. I figured as much." Celia lifted a strand of pasta and popped it into her mouth. Perfect. She snagged a colander and dumped the contents of the pot into the basin. "I'm guessing they dated once upon a time."

"Yes. Back at the Academy."

"Did he end it, or did she?"

"He did."

Oh boy. After studying his personnel file and talking to him during the trip to the bridge, he'd seemed like an intelligent man. But if he'd dumped Aurora, he'd just been reclassified as an idiot.

"Emoto doesn't think much of him, does he?" The first officer's glacial attitude toward Ellis was a stark contrast to his behavior on all previous occasions.

"No, he doesn't."

She divided the pasta into two bowls and ladled the pomodoro sauce over it. Heaven. She'd never imagined such a feast would be possible onboard a starship, or that she'd have the freedom to prepare it. Prior to her trip to the med bay to find Mya, she'd spent the previous hour with their ghostly crewmember going over the ins and outs of the ship's abilities.

She'd been unnerved when Aurora first introduced Star, but the Nirunoc was a security officer's dream come true—the ultimate watchdog. That was an unexpected bonus, and freed Celia up for other things. Like cooking. And getting answers to the questions that had been swirling in her head ever since Aurora had blanched at the sight of Cade Ellis.

She'd planned to serve the meal in the observation lounge that opened off the kitchen to the stern of the ship, but this conversation seemed to call for privacy. She carried the bowls to the small wooden table in the alcove near the pantry, settling onto the bench facing the kitchen while Mya sat across from her.

"What about Clarek?" she asked, placing her napkin in her lap and picking up her fork. "He must have known Ellis at the Academy, too."

Mya didn't answer, and not because she was eating. The tension radiating from her increased, giving Celia some idea what, or rather who, had triggered her friend's unease in the first place.

"He doesn't care for Ellis, either, does he?"

Mya swirled her fork in the long strands of capellini. "No, he doesn't."

Hmm. Judging by Mya's tone, their engineer *hated* Ellis. And from the way Clarek looked at Aurora, it was easy to imagine why.

Aurora had never talked about Clarek as though they were romantically involved, but there was something there, a vibe that spoke of more than just friendship. Aurora might not be certain whether she wanted to pursue it, but

Clarek's behavior indicated he'd be open to the idea. If Ellis had dated and dumped Aurora at the Academy, that would have given Clarek cause for his anger. A Kraed's protective streak ran deep. "Is there anything I should be aware of?"

Mya's lips thinned. "Let's just say those two should not be allowed in the same room together."

"Is Ellis a security threat?"

Mya shook her head. "No, nothing like that. He's always had a strong sense of duty to his work."

Strange. There was a touch of admiration in the way she said it. "What do *you* think of him?"

Mya's eyes took on a far-away look, like she was watching scenes from the past playing in her head. "Honestly, I don't know. For a while, he was good for Aurora. She became so intense at the Academy, so focused, almost to a fault. Cade helped her loosen up, not take herself so seriously." She put down her fork and rested her chin on her hands. "But in the end, he couldn't accept her for who she was. And that hurt her worse than any physical blow could have."

That confirmed it. Ellis was an idiot. Physical wounds, even those that seemed unbearable at the time, could heal. Emotional scars were a lot harder to overcome. She'd learned that the hard way. If Ellis had inflicted that kind of pain on Aurora, he would have to tread very carefully during his short stay on the *Starhawke* if he wanted to arrive at Gaia in one piece.

Nine

Nineteen hours later, Cade Ellis couldn't decide which he hated more—having to spend another moment tethered to the navigation console of the *Starhawke*, or having to leave and never setting foot on the ship again.

When the Admiral had informed him that he'd been assigned to a temporary post that would get him to Gaia sooner than originally planned, he'd been thrilled. Learning that the trip included the opportunity to work on a Kraed vessel that just happened to be under the command of Aurora Hawke had piqued his interest even more.

But as soon as he'd heard Jonarel Clarek's voice over the comm, his attitude about this assignment had changed. It didn't take a genius to figure out the oversized Kraed was the engineer on Aurora's ship. In fact, given Clarek's course of study at the Academy, there was a good chance he'd helped design and construct the damn thing.

Cade had wanted to dismiss the ship as a piece of space junk. But after a day at the helm, he couldn't. Much to his dismay, the ship fascinated him. The design was nothing like the many Fleet ships he'd served on, with their sharp corners and utilitarian systems. Everything about the *Starhawke* flowed with a grace that delighted the eye without detracting one bit from the ship's efficiency. In fact, he'd come across several modifications to traditional design concepts that could shoot the next generation of Fleet ships into a new class.

His interest in the ship had prompted him to remain at his post for eighteen of the twenty-two hours of the journey. He'd spent an hour of his off-duty time in his cabin going over the encrypted data the Admiral had given him to analyze in preparation for joining the rest of his team when he arrived at the Rescue Corps headquarters. He'd also taken a quick nap and eaten some of the emergency rations he always carried.

He'd been touched by Aurora's offer of food, but it was unwise to interact with the rest of the crew any more than he had to. He might come face to face with the one person onboard he didn't want to see. Getting into a brawl while on temporary assignment would earn him a sharp reprimand from the Admiral, but that would be a cakewalk compared to the reaction from the *Starhawke*'s captain.

And that was the real thorn in his side. Seeing Aurora again was a challenge. He'd anticipated a chilly reception, but true to her nature, she'd been a consummate professional, treating him with respect and even kindness. She could have pulled rank and made this trip a nightmare. She hadn't.

However, hearing her words of gratitude over the intercom to the Kraed skulking down in engineering had been a different kind of challenge. Something about the way she'd said *thank you* when they'd left the space station had made Cade's blood boil. He'd unwisely attempted to get a reaction from her when she'd returned to the bridge after her break. It hadn't worked. In fact, he was pretty sure he'd only succeeded in irritating her.

What was going on between Aurora and Clarek? It seemed likely there was more to it than friendship. She was the captain on a Kraed vessel that bore her name. Jonarel Clarek was a Kraed and her engineer. They'd known each other since Aurora was sixteen. All signs pointed to a *close* relationship. And if he stayed onboard much longer, that hypothesis might be confirmed. He didn't want it confirmed. For the sake of his mission and his sanity, he wanted off the ship.

"Time to destination, Mr. Ellis?"

An eternity. He tapped the console to check their progress before facing the object of his musings, who sat calmly in the captain's chair. "Ten minutes until we enter the system. Another five to reach Gaia."

Aurora's eyes had taken on a focused gleam he knew well. She loved a challenge, especially when it involved helping those in need. This current crisis would have her itching to take action and make things right. And when Aurora Hawke set her mind to something, the universe tended to respond.

She turned her attention to Emoto. "Any communications from Gaia?"

"Bronwyn Kelly has arrived. The transport is in orbit and they'll shuttle her over when we get there."

Aurora glanced at Cade, the corners of her mouth tipping up. "Looks like your job is nearly finished, Mr. Ellis."

Actually, it's just beginning. But he couldn't tell her that. In fact, there was an entire mountain of things he couldn't tell her, so he kept his reply noncommittal. "So it would seem."

Her focus sharpened and he instantly regretted his choice of words. As she continued to hold his gaze, he got the distinct impression she was trying to read his mind. That was one skill she didn't possess, but he'd learned long ago not to underestimate her empathic ability to pick up on subtle clues that most people missed.

Keeping his emotions in check and his expression blank, he turned back to the console. Only fifteen minutes to go.

Ten

Cade was hiding something.

Aurora couldn't put her finger on it, but it was more than unresolved issues from their shared past. He seemed concerned that she might see through his façade and uncover his secret. She wasn't sure whether she should be flattered or alarmed.

Wasn't it odd that the one person the Admiral had recommended to fill in as the navigator on her ship wasn't even a member of the Fleet? Cade was with the Rescue Corps—working as a freighter pilot, of all things. But the man she knew didn't fit the job description of an RC pilot. He took charge and made things happen. Picturing him at the controls of a ponderous transport hauling supplies, even for the Rescue Corps, was like picturing a Tyrannosaurus Rex attending a tea party. It just didn't work.

By the Admiral's admission, Cade could pilot almost any craft, so why was he working for the Rescue Corps instead of navigating one of the newer Fleet vessels? And if she was right, what the hell *was* his purpose in coming to Gaia? The Admiral obviously trusted him, so Aurora had to believe Cade's intentions were good. But why hadn't the Admiral trusted her with the truth?

The star field appeared on the bridgescreen as the main engines took over from the interstellar drive.

"We've reached the system," Cade said.

Kire pivoted to face her. "I've alerted the Chancellor to our arrival."

"Do we have visual on the planet yet?"

"Bringing it up now."

The image of Gaia filled the bridgescreen and she sucked in a breath. The planet was beautiful, a vision of how Earth might have looked five hundred years ago before technology lit up the night side. She'd read about the Gaian colony in her history classes, and she admired the brave women and men who had agreed to risk their lives on a largely unknown world to save those they had left behind.

Cade's hands moved confidently over the controls as he guided the ship into orbit. The task was simplified by a complete lack of cross-traffic. With the quarantine in place for the past forty-eight hours, no ships were allowed on or off the planet without Council approval. The only other vessel in orbit was the small passenger transport that awaited them. Cade maneuvered the *Starhawke* into position, nose to tail with the much smaller craft.

"Standard orbit established."

Kire glanced over at her. "All crewmembers have been cleared by Gaian security for access to the planet. A shuttle has been dispatched by the Rescue Corps to pick up Mr. Ellis."

She stood. "Thank you. Tell Celia to report to bay one and direct Mr. Ellis's shuttle to meet her there. Ms. Kelly's transport can be routed to shuttle bay two. Escort her to the conference room as soon as she arrives. I'll join you in a moment."

"Yes, Captain." Kire headed for the lift.

Cade rose and she moved to intercept him. "May I speak with you?"

He paused. "Of course."

She tipped her head up so she could hold his gaze. He really was taller than she remembered. "I wanted to thank you for your assistance in getting us here so quickly. The Admiral's faith in your abilities is well deserved."

His eyebrows rose at the compliment, and the corners of his mouth softened. "It was my pleasure." A spark of emotion flashed briefly in his eyes. "You have a beautiful ship."

"Thank you." There was something funny about the way he said it though, as if the comment cost him. Being under her command might have been harder for him than he'd indicated. But he seemed sincere.

Maybe if she pushed a little, she could extract information regarding his plans after leaving the ship. "Will you be staying at the Rescue Corps headquarters until the freighter you were scheduled to pilot arrives?"

Her question seemed to amuse him. "Were you hoping to see me again?"

His non-answer caught her off guard. She hadn't stopped to think how he might interpret her interest in his whereabouts. She shook her head firmly. "No, that's not why I asked."

"Then why did you?"

Why indeed? Not only was he not answering her question, he was cornering her. She couldn't provide the real answer—that she was fishing for information—so she came up with a plausible alternative. "Curiosity. I don't know much about how the Rescue Corps operates, but I have trouble picturing the pilots sitting around when they aren't transporting the freighters."

"They don't. Most pilots shuttle Corps members and supplies to the various staging points after the freighters are secured."

That made sense. But he still hadn't specified what *he* would be doing after he left the ship. Interesting. Her instincts told her he was up to something. However, she couldn't pursue the matter without tipping her hand. Maybe the Admiral could provide some insight. For now, she'd just have to live with the mystery.

"I see. Well, then I won't keep you any longer." She held out her hand. "Safe travels."

He stared at her, his expression growing serious as he clasped her hand. When their palms touched, the strangest thought popped into her head. *Cade was worried about leaving her.* Not sad. Not glad. *Worried.* As though he feared for her safety.

"Take care." He gave her hand a gentle squeeze before releasing his grip and heading toward the lift. As he stepped inside, he glanced back with a cocky grin. "Try not to miss me." He winked as the doors closed.

She rolled her eyes. He always liked to have the last word.

She could live with that. It was the uncertainty regarding his reasons for being here, and his inexplicable concern for her safety that puzzled her. She crossed her arms and she stared at the closed lift doors. "What are you up to, Cade?"

Eleven

The sleek shuttle glided past the wide valleys and steep mountains of Gaia's equatorial zone, skimming over swaths of lush vegetation that spread out to the horizon.

From his seat behind the cockpit, Kire watched Bronwyn Kelly at the controls. She was as cool as a cat, even with Roe sitting next to her, observing her every move. She'd shown the same composure during her interview. They'd discussed her navigation experience, beginning with her first job as a space station shuttle pilot, but Roe hadn't been interested in a list of facts. Instead, she'd delved into what had driven Kelly to become a pilot in the first place. Kire had been curious as well.

Her mother had been a navigator in the Fleet, a very talented one by all accounts, who had met Kelly's father, a pub owner, while she was visiting her parents in Dublin. Even though he wasn't fond of space travel, he'd agreed to join the crew of the Fleet ship she was assigned to, where he'd worked as a bartender in the crew lounge. Kelly had been born a few years later, and had spent her early childhood onboard the ship.

She'd inherited her mother's talent and passion for flying, and by the time she was eleven years old, she'd been able to detail every aspect of the starship's navigation system and plot a course better than some of the officers. However, not long after her twelfth birthday, her mother and six other crewmembers were killed while transporting supplies to a colony that had suffered a Setarip attack.

Three Setarip destroyers had returned and attempted to capture the shuttle. During the ensuing conflict, the smaller craft was destroyed.

Kelly's father had been devastated. He'd insisted that they return to Earth. He'd also made her promise that she would never join the Fleet, and that she would remain in Ireland as long as he lived.

He'd died before she reached adulthood. Officially, he'd drowned in the lake behind their house after falling out of a rowboat. But his blood alcohol level had been off the charts, a condition that had become common in the last years of his life.

Her promise had kept her from applying to the Academy, so she'd sought work where she could make use of the navigation skills she already possessed. Her abilities, combined with her willingness to go anywhere, had earned her steady promotions and job offers.

It was a tragic story, but Kelly delivered it with unflappable stoicism. Roe had listened quietly, and then she'd taken Kelly to the bridge so the young pilot could check out the navigation system. She'd also offered her the opportunity to pilot the shuttle for their visit to the Rescue Corps headquarters. So far, Kelly seemed to be handling the ship effortlessly.

Kire and Cardiff were in charge of directing the shuttle's cameras, gathering images of the countryside for Jon and Star to analyze back on the ship. Mya had also stayed behind to run baseline tests on the healthy crop samples the Rescue Corps had sent when they'd picked up Ellis.

The shuttle crested a mountain, revealing a sea of black that stretched fifteen kilometers to the southeast.

Kire's breath caught. It looked like the remains of a giant's funeral pyre.

To the west the landscape shifted back to lush green, a jarring juxtaposition to the desolation. What could possibly cause this kind of rampant destruction without leaving any trace?

Kelly took them on several passes over the affected areas while Kire and Cardiff recorded the images and sent them to the *Starhawke*. When they finished, the shuttle banked, leaving the barren wasteland behind. A few minutes later, the large collection of beige tents and scattered permanent structures that comprised the temporary Rescue Corps headquarters appeared in the distance.

The majority of the Gaian residents made their living from farming or the distribution of crops to supply ships, so very few other industries had developed. As a result, they didn't have large metropolitan areas. The Rescue Corps had converted a site that normally functioned as a warehousing center for the crops that were exported to other locales or off-planet.

Kelly opened the communication channel. "*Starhawke* shuttle to Rescue Corps command. We're approaching RC headquarters. Requesting permission to land." Her lilting Irish voice seemed fitting for their surroundings, her accent softening her vowels so that *to* sounded more like *tuh*.

"*Starhawke* shuttle, you are cleared for landing."

"Beginning our approach."

The landing pad came into view as the shuttle descended. Within moments Kelly had settled the shuttle onto the platform with nary a bump. Impressive.

Kire glanced at Roe. She met his gaze, the corner of her mouth tilting up as she gave a subtle nod. They had found their navigator.

The shuttle door slid open. He followed Cardiff as they headed down the ramp, with Roe and Kelly joining them a moment later. A man approached from the main building and Roe stepped forward to greet him.

"Captain Hawke, I presume." He extended his hand.

Roe shook it. "Thank you for meeting with us Chancellor."

The Chancellor shook his head. "I'm the one who's grateful for your assistance."

Introductions continued all around, then the Chancellor led them to a security station just inside the building where a Corps guard scanned each member of their party.

"This way." The Chancellor gestured to the corridor to their left. "I'll introduce you to the Corps Director first. She controls all operations here and at the station for the other community that was affected. She can put you in touch with Corps members who can assist you in your investigation."

"So your own people won't be working with us?" Cardiff asked.

He glanced back at her. "No. While we're well known for our agricultural skills, most of that knowledge is from practical, hands-on experience, not scientific study." His expression looked strained. "What we're seeing now is unlike anything we've ever encountered. We're at a wall. That's why we contacted the Council, and why they sent you. This is beyond our ability to analyze or investigate."

"Do you think it's a natural occurrence, a mutation or infection that's native to the planet?" Roe asked.

The Chancellor stopped and faced her. "Captain, I'm not certain what's happening here could be labeled a natural occurrence *anywhere*."

Roe's eyebrows lifted and Cardiff stiffened, but neither said anything more as the Chancellor continued down the hallway. They passed through another security checkpoint that opened onto the temporary command center.

"The Director is meeting us in tent twelve. We've gathered a few families who are willing to talk to you about their experiences." The Chancellor nodded to several Corps members as their group crossed to a doorway on the far side that took them out of the building. A collection of tents had been set up in long rows in the clearing.

"How well are the residents coping with the losses?" Roe asked as they walked down the packed dirt path that led between two rows of tents.

The Chancellor sighed. "As well as can be expected. The hardest part is not knowing what's causing the destruction. We have no way to prepare for it or prevent it from spreading."

The refugees stared at them as they passed, but no one smiled or acknowledged them in any way. Every face had a nearly identical look of bleak sadness. It was like walking through a warzone, although it wasn't only the people who were struggling for survival—it was their planet, too.

The Chancellor ducked under the flap of a larger tent near the end of the row and ushered them inside. The space contained a collection of chairs and tables set at intervals, with about twenty adults and small children seated around one of the larger tables. The soft murmur of conversation cut off as the refugees turned to face them, their expressions filled with a mixture of apprehension and curiosity.

The Chancellor's gaze swept through the crowd. "Apparently the Director has not arrived yet." He turned to Roe. "Would you like to wait for her?"

Roe shook her head. "If it's all right with you, we'd like to get started."

"Very well." He cleared his throat. "I would like to introduce you all to Captain Hawke and her crew. They have been sent by the Galactic Council to investigate the destruction and help us find a solution." He nodded at Roe. "Captain."

She stepped forward, taking time to make eye contact with each person, her body language radiating quiet confidence. Several of the refugees sat up straighter, their expressions showing the first glimmers of hope Kire had seen. Roe had that effect on people.

"Thank you for agreeing to meet with us today," she said, her voice calm and measured. "This is Commander Emoto, my first officer." She gestured to him. "Lieutenant Cardiff, my head of security, and Ensign Kelly, our navigator."

Kelly's head turned as she met Roe's gaze, but that was the only indication of surprise she gave at being acknowledged as an official member of the crew.

"They are all highly trained officers, so please give them your complete cooperation. I know that discussing your losses will likely be difficult for you, but it's imperative that we gather as much detail as possible regarding the events that have occurred. We will—"

"I'm so sorry I'm late!"

Kire turned as a woman in a Rescue Corps uniform stepped through the tent opening and walked briskly toward them. The light from the doorway cast her features into shadow, but when she stopped in front of Roe, Kire's jaw dropped open.

"Reanne?" Roe's voice indicated the same bewilderment he felt, but she'd confirmed the identity of the new arrival. The lock of white hair above her forehead that blended with the straight brown of the rest was a dead giveaway.

"Yes, I'm..." Reanne Beck's blue eyes widened. "Aurora!"

Roe looked like she'd been hit with a stun gun as Reanne gave her a quick hug. As far as he knew, the former roommates hadn't seen each other since Roe had graduated from the Academy, and their friendship had been rocky even before then.

"You two know each other?" The Chancellor looked back and forth between them.

"Oh, yes!" Reanne clasped Roe's hands. "Aurora was my mentor and roommate for my first three years at the Academy. We were like sisters." A hint of sadness crept into her voice. "It's been too long."

Roe's smile looked forced. "It has been a long time."

"And I had no idea you were part of the investigation team."

Roe extracted her hands from Reanne's grip. "Actually, I'm the head of the team. The *Starhawke* is my ship."

Reanne blinked. "You're the captain?"

"Yes." Roe's gaze shifted to the insignia on Reanne's uniform. "And I'm guessing you're the Rescue Corps Director."

Reanne smiled. "Guilty as charged."

Roe turned to Kire. "You remember Commander Kire Emoto."

A world of meaning passed between them as she held his gaze. He resisted the urge to grin. Roe was not entirely happy to see her old friend.

Reanne crossed her arms over her chest and regarded him with a badly concealed smirk. "Of course. Commander now, is it? I see you're still following where Aurora leads."

During their Academy days, Reanne had always enjoyed belittling him whenever she got the chance. Apparently the impulse was still alive and kicking.

"Hello, Reanne." He used his most banal expression as he gazed back at her. Sure enough, her attention moved quickly past him.

Roe introduced Cardiff and Kelly before glancing over her shoulder at the refugees, who were watching them all intently. She gave Reanne a pointed look. "I was just beginning to explain what we needed to—"

"Oh, of course, of course." Reanne cut her off and stepped back. "I know you have a job to do." She made a rolling motion with her hand. "Please continue with your investigation. We can catch up later. I have a few matters to discuss with the Chancellor, anyway, but we'll be nearby if you need anything." She led the Chancellor into the far corner of the tent.

Roe's gaze followed her.

At that moment, Kire would have given his first month's pay to know what was going through her mind.

Twelve

An hour later, Aurora had a plethora of notes, but no answers. All of the families had described the same scenario, yet no one had seen or heard anything that might indicate the cause of the destruction. No light, heat, smells, noise, nothing. In each case, they went to bed with the vegetation healthy and thriving, and woke up to total devastation.

"Reports?" She glanced around the table at Kire, Celia and Kelly.

"No one appears to have noticed anything unusual," Kire said. "Even with the heightened awareness of the problem, they haven't been able to detect anything when it's happening."

Celia frowned. "It's hard to believe such destruction could occur without some evidence, unless it's a naturally occurring contamination."

"Is there any reason to think it could be a natural phenomenon, despite the Chancellor's comments?" Aurora asked.

Celia shrugged. "We won't know for sure until we examine the affected areas. However, I find it difficult to believe it's a biological infection, based on the pattern of destruction and the lack of anything similar in their history."

"But that doesn't rule out a contaminant that could've been brought in from another planet," Kelly pointed out.

"True, although most of Gaia's off-world visitors are on their way to or from Earth," Celia replied. "It wouldn't take long to track down who's been here recently. I'll look into it once we're back on the ship."

Aurora nodded. "Then we'll—"

"Excuse me, Captain?"

One of the refugee women Aurora had interviewed stood just behind her chair, with her young daughter clasping her skirt in her pudgy fingers. The child looked to be about five years old, and was tucked most of the way behind her mother's legs, peering shyly at Aurora.

"Yes?"

"I don't mean to interrupt, but you said anything might be important. I wanted you to see the drawing my daughter just did."

The woman held out a piece of paper. Aurora took it and glanced down at the crude image. It depicted a dark creature, bipedal, with a hunched, misshapen back, thick, twisted limbs, and an almost skull-like head. "What is this?"

"She said she saw this the night the crops around our farm were destroyed."

Aurora's head snapped up and her heart thumped. The woman looked uncomfortable, clenching her arm by her side and glancing down at her daughter. Kire, Celia and Kelly were all staring at the paper, their expressions intent, so Aurora spun the drawing around so they could see it.

After studying the image, Kire looked at the girl. "Did you see this thing *before* the plants died?"

The girl shoved her face against her mother's skirt, refusing to look at him. Her mother spoke. "The moon was nearly full that night. She told me that she got up to go to the bathroom, but when she passed by her bedroom window and looked down, this is what she saw killing the plants."

"You *saw* it kill the plants?" This from Celia, whose body was now tight as a bow.

The girl peeked out at them, then nodded.

"How did it kill them?" Kelly asked.

The child hunched her body and turned away. Her mother knelt down and placed her hands gently on her shoulders. "It's okay, sweetie. Can you tell me?" The girl whispered something and her mother frowned. "She doesn't know how. It just reached out to touch them and they died."

Aurora felt Kire's gaze on her. The same questions were reflected in his eyes that were racing through her mind.

"Have you ever seen this creature before the night the plants died?" he asked.

The girl shook her head.

"How many did you see?"

The girl whispered to her mother, who swallowed nervously. "Lots."

Aurora gazed at the hideous figure on the paper in front of her. *Lots.* What the hell were they dealing with here? Was this thing even real, or had the child's imagination conjured up an image to explain her fear after seeing her family's farm destroyed?

"Is it all right if I keep this?" she asked the girl, gesturing to the drawing.

The little girl nodded.

Aurora could feel their anxiety and fear, which bordered on panic. No one would want to believe such creatures existed, let alone that they were massing in large numbers, steadily reducing everything to ash. Placing hand lightly on the woman's arm, she allowed a gentle wave of energy to wash over mother and daughter that eased some of their tension. "Thank you for sharing this with us. It's a big help. If we have any more questions, we'll be in touch."

The woman smiled weakly before leading her daughter back to the other side of the tent.

Aurora faced her crew. "I think it's time for an onsite investigation. I'll be right back."

As she approached the table where Reanne and the Chancellor sat talking, she considered the best way to obtain what she needed without giving Reanne any more information than was absolutely necessary. She was usually good at reading people, but for some reason she'd always struggled with Reanne. She just couldn't seem to get a bead on what the other woman was thinking or feeling. It unnerved her.

Reanne had been unpredictable as a teenager, prone to fits of anger. Aurora doubted she'd changed, although her promotion to RC Director indicated she'd achieved a certain level of maturity. Reanne's presence could make the situation more challenging. They'd been close once, but the last few years at the Academy had been filled with tension that had fractured their friendship beyond repair.

Reanne looked up as she approached. "Any luck?"

She'd left the drawing with Kire. She didn't plan to mention it, at least until they knew whether it represented a real threat or an imaginary one. "We need to visit the area that was hit last night. Can you arrange ground transportation for us?"

"Absolutely." Reanne touched her comband. "Mr. Byrnes, the *Starhawke* crew needs a ground transport outside the main hanger in five minutes."

"Acknowledged," came the reply.

"Thank you." Aurora turned away.

"Let me know what you learn out there," Reanne called after her.

She gave a non-committal wave and motioned to her crew to join her at the front of the tent.

"She's arranged for transport. The driver will meet us outside the security checkpoint."

"Do you think the little girl made up these monsters to explain what happened to her family's farm?" Celia asked as they retraced their path through the hangar.

"I'm not sure. Children use monsters to explain anything that frightens them, so that's certainly possible. However, as no one else has been able to provide any concrete information, I'm prepared to assume she saw something." They exited the building, where a small transport waited. "She may be imaginative, but she might also be observant."

Thirteen

She wasn't prepared for this.

As Aurora gazed out the windows of the transport at the apocalyptic panorama around them, her brain stalled. From the absolute silence in the vehicle, she suspected the others were in a similar state.

It took about thirty minutes to reach the destination that their driver, Mr. Byrnes, had recommended. The cream colored two-story farmhouse with the deep green accents would have been picturesque, except for the total annihilation of all life in the surrounding fields and hills. It reminded her of images of atomic bomb sites she'd seen in her history classes. Everything was just...gone. No plants of any description remained. Not a blade of grass or a stalk of grain. Just kilometers of blackened dirt.

Her stomach clenched. The family who owned this farm had lost everything in a single night.

The house looked completely untouched, as though at any moment rowdy children would push through the screen door and spill out onto the spacious porch, intent on an afternoon adventure. The paint was unblemished in any way—no sign of ash or soot, heat damage, or mold and fungus on the wood boards. But fifteen meters away, blackness stretched like an ashen blanket.

To their right, a dirt road led away from the clearing to what looked like a property border that curled like a ribbon into the distance. She shaded her eyes from the sun's bright glare as she looked up at Mr. Byrnes. "Do you know if that road follows the border of the farm?"

He nodded. "I believe so."

"I want Cardiff to examine the property line. Can you drive her out there?"

"Absolutely." He looked pleased to be paired with Celia. No surprise there. Most men were.

"Is there anything in particular you want me to look for?" Celia asked.

She shook her head. "Anything could be significant. See if there's any surviving plant life and take samples of the remains of the crops and the soil. Also check the road and any pathways for tracks or marks that seem out of place. We're looking for anything unusual, such as variations in the pattern of decay or other physical evidence."

As Celia and Mr. Byrnes returned to the transport, Aurora turned to Kire. "I want you and Kelly to begin collecting samples from the areas closest to the house. Keep an eye out for anything out of the ordinary."

"Like something that might indicate a bipedal creature of some kind?"

She pictured the monster the child had drawn. "Perhaps. Or anything that would disprove that possibility. If you see something, let me know. I'm going to examine the house exterior. I'll join you in a few moments."

Kire and Kelly each shouldered a collection pack and headed toward the nearby field as Aurora walked to the farmhouse. Silence followed them. No bird calls, no rustling of small animals, no insects. No one had mentioned anything about the local wildlife being affected by the destructive force, but if they'd survived, they'd obviously abandoned the area.

The wooden boards creaked as she climbed the steps to the wraparound porch. From the front of the house, she could see the clearing and the dirt track they had driven in on, which curved to the right back toward the main road. She continued around to the side of the house. Only the day before gently sloping fields would have stretched down to the wooden border fence that ran along the front side of the property, parallel with the main road nearly half a kilometer in the distance. But instead of green fields, dark ash covered the ground.

Her body gathered tension like a spring. Whatever had happened here, it had left a darkness behind that clung like tar. Her empathic senses were going haywire.

She touched her comband. "Hawke to Clarek."

"Clarek here."

"We've reached one of the farms. I'm sending you images of the fields from the farmhouse porch. Stand by."

She raised her arm to eye level and slowly panned from right to left, including the space just in front of the farmhouse where the flower border continued to bloom cheerfully, a spot of color that mocked the destruction beyond.

She stepped into the shadows on the porch. "Have you had any success with the images from the shuttle trip this morning?"

"Not yet, but we're still analyzing them. We'll have a report ready before you return."

"Very good. Hawke out."

She retraced her steps and continued around to the other side of the house. Standing near the railing, she could see Kelly crouched at the field edge, placing sample vials into the storage kit at her feet. Kire had moved farther from the house and was scanning the ashen ground.

She took a deep breath and focused on relaxing her muscles. No luck. Apparently the tension had set up permanent residence.

Her comband vibrated. "Yes?"

Kire's voice sounded strained. "I think you should see this."

"On my way."

She left the porch and headed in his direction, but as she drew closer to the field, the tension in her body increased. Her stomach pitched in response and bile rose in her throat, followed by a dull ache that spread through her limbs like a fever. She paused, fighting down the sensations. Her gaze swept over the ground, searching. Whatever had happened here, it was wrong. Very, very wrong. Swallowing hard, she kept moving.

When she finally reached Kire, a frown line showed between his thin brows. "Are you okay?"

The pain in her muscles was damned unpleasant, but she kept her voice even. "I'm fine. What did you find?"

He studied her for a moment before turning toward the field and gesturing to a spot about ten meters in. "What do you make of that?"

She looked where he'd indicated, but it took her a few beats to process what she was seeing. When she did, her lips parted in surprise.

A space about twenty-five centimeters long by ten centimeters wide was mostly free of the debris, but that wasn't what had caught Kire's attention. The shape of the outline showed five distinct marks at the top, pointing toward the rest of the field, with a curved wedge below. It was a footprint. A *bare* footprint, but one that was misshapen to the point of being almost unrecognizable.

Kire's expression was grim. "Looks like we may be dealing with something real, after all."

She nodded. "Although that generates more questions, not answers. Have you seen any other tracks?"

He shook his head.

Her comband vibrated.

"Captain?" It was Celia.

"Go ahead."

"I'm at the border road. There's no sign of living vegetation, but I've spotted something you should see."

An image came through and she switched it to projection mode so Kire could view it, too.

"I'll be damned," he whispered.

The image matched the print they were looking at, only this one was coming out of the field onto the border road. A second image appeared, showing more prints leading across the road and then disappearing into the ash on the other side.

"We've found something similar. Get exact measurements on the prints, and take samples of the surrounding soil, then report back here." She turned to Kire. "We need to get samples from this one, too."

"Walking out there will disturb the surrounding area."

"I know, but I think obtaining the data's more important than keeping the area untouched."

Kire fetched a few sample vials from the collection pack before heading back toward the field. As she followed him, her stomach churned. She placed a hand over her mouth and closed her eyes, focusing on her breathing.

Kire's placed a hand on her arm. "Roe, what's wrong?"

She opened her eyes and gave him a weak smile. "Just a little stomach upset. I can handle it."

He frowned. "I've never known you to have stomach issues. How bad is it?"

She lied. "Not bad."

His eyes narrowed. "Why don't you go sit on the porch while I finish up here? It should only take a few minutes."

Her stomach thought that was a fine idea, but she shook her head, determined to get a closer look at the footprint. Her body was revolting, and she wanted to know why. "I'm okay. Let's go."

Years of friendship had apparently taught him the futility of arguing when she'd made up her mind. He relented, turning to the field.

She forced herself to do the same, but each step increased the feeling that she was sinking into a noxious sludge that threatened to overwhelm her.

He glanced back. "Do you want to go first?"

She shook her head. "You should lead. Your feet are larger than mine, so I'll follow in your footsteps to minimize the disturbance to the area."

"Okay." He slipped the sample vials into the pockets of his jacket. Then he stepped carefully onto the blackened soil, trying not to disrupt the surrounding ash.

As his foot lifted and he moved forward, she set her foot down into the center of his first footprint. Instantly her muscles tensed to the point of immobility as every cell in her body promptly forgot how to function.

She tried to call out to Kire, but her mouth refused to obey her command to form words. She must have made some sound though, because he turned.

A look of alarm spread over his face. "Roe!"

His voice grew faint, and he began to tilt away from her. No, wait. She was the one tilting as the ground rushed up to catch her. She slumped onto the blackened remains of the crops, and the horrifying sensations intensified, blotting out everything around her. As her vision and hearing cut out, leaving her with only scattered thoughts, she tried desperately to summon her energy shield. But as she fell into the darkness that surrounded her she sensed...nothing.

Fourteen

Kire had taken a few steps toward the footprint when a small sound, like a whimper, made him turn his head.

Roe was a couple meters behind him, but her skin had drained of color and her eyes were wide and vacant. She staggered, crumpling to the ground.

He slapped his comband and dropped to his knees by her side. "Emoto to Clarek!"

Jon replied immediately. "What's wrong?"

"Roe collapsed. Tell Mya we're on our way and to be prepared for—" *What?* He didn't know. "Anything."

"What happened?"

"I don't know. But we'll get to you as quickly as we can."

Jon's voice vibrated with tension. "Understood."

Kire slipped his arms under Roe's head and upper body and cradled her while she twitched and moaned. Kelly appeared on her other side a moment later. "I contacted Cardiff. She'll be here soon."

Thank the universe for the unflappable navigator. "Thank you. Let's move her into the shade over by the house."

Working together, they lifted Roe and carried her to the dirt path in front of the flowerbeds. They lowered her to the ground and Kelly placed one of the sample packs under Roe's legs to elevate them.

Kire crouched, circling Roe's wrist with his fingers to check her pulse. He'd expected it to be weak. Instead, it pounded through her veins in a frenzy. Her tremors had subsided but her gaze jumped all over the place, her expression indicating disorientation and terror.

Panic clawed at him as he placed a hand on her shoulder. She flinched. "Roe?" No response. "Captain?" Still no response.

The transport arrived and footsteps raced across the ground. A moment later Cardiff knelt beside him.

"What happened?" She clasped Roe's hands in hers, checking her pulse as he had.

"We were walking into the field and she suddenly collapsed."

Cardiff frowned, but didn't comment.

"Should we move her into the transport?" he asked.

She gazed at Roe's face, assessing, then shook her head. "No. She's in shock, but I can help her."

He stepped back as Cardiff placed her body directly in Roe's field of vision. Her thumbs drew small circles on the backs of Roe's hands, her gaze never leaving Roe's face. She murmured something, but he couldn't make out the words.

Whatever she was saying or doing appeared to be working. Roe blinked once...twice. Then she suddenly sucked in a huge lungful of air, like a diver breaking the surface of the water.

Her breath stuttered out in a staccato beat, but with each inhale the color steadily returned to her face.

Cardiff didn't move, just held her gaze and talked to her. After several long minutes that felt like years, Roe gave Cardiff's hands a squeeze, and Cardiff's lips turned up in a soft smile. She released Roe's hands and sat back on her heels, removing the collection bag from under Roe's legs.

"Can you sit up?" she asked.

"I think so." Roe's voice sounded like she'd been gargling gravel, but she braced her hands on either side of her body and pushed herself upright. She took one more deep breath, straightened her shoulders, and pulled her tunic into place. "Thank you."

Cardiff nodded.

Roe's gaze flickered to Mr. Byrnes. He was staring at them from his position near the transport, his expression a mixture of curiosity and concern. Clearly he didn't know what to make of this turn of events, either.

There was zero chance Roe would say anything as long as they had an audience, so Kire tapped his comband. "Belay that order."

Mya replied. "Is she okay?" She sounded frantic.

He knew the feeling.

Roe tapped her own comband. "I'm fine. We'll be heading back to the shuttle as soon as we finish up here."

There was a pause. Mya's tone changed to the no nonsense briskness of a physician preparing to deal with a difficult patient. "I'll be waiting for you."

She'd put a wealth of meaning into those words. Roe's expression indicated she knew it, too.

Fifteen

Cade was exhausted. In the three years since he'd accepted the command of Admiral Schreiber's Elite Unit, he'd faced many hardships, including hiking to the top of Mt. Killanis in eight hours and wrestling a fanged sheetak who'd decided he'd make a nice dinner. But nothing he'd endured had been half as challenging as keeping an eye on Aurora Hawke and reporting his team's activities to Reanne Beck. He was in his own private Hell.

After he'd left the *Starhawke*, he'd immediately sent a message to the Admiral to apprise him of the situation. When the Admiral had first informed him that his number one priority on Gaia was to insure the safety of the *Starhawke* crew, especially Aurora Hawke, Cade had been stunned. He'd assumed that the Admiral wanted his unit to determine if the destruction was the result of a planned attack. However, while that job was part of his assignment, his primary responsibility was to provide surveillance and security for the *Starhawke* crew, without letting them know they were being watched and guarded.

Cade rubbed a hand over his eyes and leaned back in his chair. As commander of the team, and someone Aurora would recognize, he had been unable to take an active role in the surveillance. Instead, he was ensconced in a tiny room in the Rescue Corps headquarters, trying to figure out how he was going to avoid reporting what he'd witnessed to Reanne.

She was not an official part of his team, but as the director of the Rescue Corps, she had been instructed by Admiral Schreiber to comply with any requests Cade's team made. In return, Cade was expected to keep her in the loop regarding their activities so she could accommodate them while carefully cloaking all their movements as official Rescue Corps business.

He could work with that arrangement, but he'd learned long ago that volunteering non-essential information to Reanne Beck was a bad idea. Aurora's collapse fit into that category.

He'd stationed his tech specialist, Bella Drew, on tactical so that she could monitor and track the movements of the *Starhawke* crew. When she'd reported that a shuttle was headed down to the surface, Cade had contacted Reanne. She'd confirmed that a contingent from the ship was due to arrive at the RC headquarters. However, she'd given no indication that she knew the identities of the crewmembers, even though she would recognize most of them. He had a suspicion the Admiral may have withheld that information on purpose.

Reanne had also informed him that the crew wanted to investigate the site of the most recent attack. That fit his plans perfectly. Cade had arranged for his number one, Justin Byrnes, to act as the transport driver. While Aurora and her crew met with the refugees, his team had equipped the transport vehicle with concealed interior and exterior cameras and audio surveillance so Cade could hear and see everything that occurred. The exterior cameras allowed for a nearly three-hundred-sixty-degree view around the vehicle.

Justin had also managed to attach similar devices to the exterior of the field specimen packs when he loaded them into the storage area. That turned out to be fortuitous. Thanks to the devices attached to the pack Emoto had chosen, when Aurora suddenly slumped to the ground, Cade had a front row seat.

He'd been out of his chair and shouting orders to his team before Emoto had even turned around, but he'd still heard the fear in the other man's voice when he'd contacted Clarek on the *Starhawke*. That fear had matched the emotion coursing through Cade's veins as he'd watched the scene unfold. Thankfully, Kelly had notified Cardiff of the situation immediately, which had given Justin an excuse to head back to the house. He'd followed Cardiff as she'd sprinted for the transport.

Cade's view of Aurora had been partially blocked by Kelly as they carried her off the field and laid her down, but he was pretty sure he'd left a nose print on his monitor as he'd strained to see if she was responding in any way. He wasn't aware of drawing a breath until after Cardiff arrived and he'd seen Aurora sit up without assistance.

That had been an hour ago. Her crew had returned to the RC headquarters and boarded their shuttle, heading back to the *Starhawke*. Justin had already been to his office and given his report, but it hadn't helped with the growing number of unanswered questions. What the hell had happened to Aurora out there? Why had she collapsed? Why had walking into the field affected her, when no one else had any reaction at all?

He didn't know for certain that the decimated plants were the cause, but the unexplained nature of the destruction, combined with the fact that Aurora had fallen the moment she stepped on the decayed vegetation, seemed like too much of a coincidence to ignore. Add in the

Admiral's cryptic warnings to keep her safe, and it was hard not to speculate.

Aurora Hawke was the strongest woman he knew, in many ways. For her to suddenly break down like that was unimaginable. He wanted answers. Now.

"Reanne to Cade."

He tapped his comband. "Ellis here."

"I'd like to see you in my office."

Great. Talking to Reanne was not at the top of his list at the moment, but her cooperation was critical to his team's success. He needed to maintain a positive working relationship, no matter how challenging the upcoming discussion might be.

"On my way."

Justin had mentioned that Aurora had recovered quickly after they'd left the farm. She'd seemed a little stiff and weak but otherwise okay. Her crew hadn't talked about the incident during the drive back, respecting Aurora's silence. Cade admired that. It showed how protective they were of their captain, and of their investigation. Unfortunately, that stance was preventing him from doing his job, and his frustration level was rising.

He knocked on the door to Reanne's office.

"Come in."

Reanne was seated behind her desk. She glanced up as he entered.

"Cade. Good. Have a seat."

The only two chairs in the room sat in front of the desk with their backs to the door. He'd made it a habit to never place himself in a vulnerable position, even in the most innocuous situations. Rather than sitting in one of the chairs, he moved off to one side and lounged against a side table stacked with supply crates.

She crossed her arms and scrutinized him. "After today's events, I have a new appreciation for your gifts of secrecy. But I'm curious. Is there a reason you didn't tell me that Aurora was the captain of the *Starhawke*?"

So that's what she wanted to talk about. He should have guessed. He shrugged. "Was it a problem for you to see her again?"

She seemed surprised by the question, but she shook her head and smiled. "Of course not. I always regretted that we lost touch over the years." Her gaze sharpened. "I'm more concerned about you. Was it hard to see her? I know you didn't part on the best terms."

He didn't need to be reminded. "It was fine."

"So it won't be a problem having your team working in secret alongside hers?"

"Why do you ask?"

Her lips pressed together as she stood and walked around the desk, stopping in front of him. "I'm worried about you."

That was interesting. "Why?"

She sighed. "Where Aurora's concerned, you've always been a bit, well...*intense*. Reactionary, even. And I just want to make sure her presence won't negatively impact you. Or in some way interfere with the job we're here to do."

She was questioning his professionalism? His temper flared, but he tamped it down. "It won't."

"You're sure about that?"

"Yes."

"Okay." Her tone indicated she didn't believe him. She rested her hand on his arm. "But just so you know, if you need to talk about anything, I'm here."

An image flashed through his mind of a similar conversation many years earlier, shortly before he'd left the Academy. Reanne had offered her assistance then, too. And he'd learned that her compassion came with a price. It wasn't a mistake he intended to repeat. "I'll keep that in mind."

He took a small step backward and her hand fell from his arm. She looked startled by his subtle rejection, but she recovered quickly. She rested her hip against her desk, her posture relaxed.

He didn't buy it. She wanted something from him. He just wasn't sure what.

"So, tell me what happened during the investigation."

Out of the frying pan and into the fire. "Not much. They surveyed one of the recent locations and took samples for analysis."

"They weren't out there very long. I was under the impression they were going to stop at several sites. Did they find something that prompted them to return early?"

She was fishing for information, but he wasn't about to tell her that Aurora had collapsed, or that her crew had seen footprints. However, if he didn't say anything, that wouldn't sit well with her. She had to obey the Admiral's orders to cooperate with him, but if she wanted to, she could make his job a whole lot harder.

"Byrnes indicated that the crew found enough to work with at the first site. They wanted to get back to the ship to begin their analysis."

The corners of Reanne's eyes tightened slightly, a sign so subtle most people wouldn't have noticed. But it was his job to notice. She was not happy with his response. Then she snapped her fingers as if something had just occurred to her. "The ship! That's right. I almost forgot you've been onboard. What's it like?"

Yet another question he didn't want to answer. His gaze flicked to the doorway, willing someone to interrupt them so he could make his escape. He forced his lips to relax into a smile. "It's nice."

"Nice?" She smirked. "You're one of the first humans to ever pilot a Kraed vessel and the only word you can find to describe it is *nice?*"

He shrugged. "What else can I say? I didn't have time to wander around, and my job was to navigate, not inspect. It seemed...nice."

Reanne rolled her eyes skyward. "Heaven help us from the single-minded male of the species." She crossed her arms. "But then again, you've always been single-minded, especially with anything involving Aurora."

She smiled and said it like a joke, but he suspected she was trying to get a reaction out of him. Refusing to rise to the bait, he waited until she finally pushed away from the desk and reclaimed her chair. "Do you have anything else you need?" she asked, her attention already shifting to the data pad in front of her.

"Not right now."

She waved a hand toward the door. "Then I won't keep you any longer. You know where to find me."

Yes, he did.

As he walked out of the office, he resolved to take an active part in the next surveillance operation, which would accomplish two goals—creating distance from Reanne Beck, and placing him in a better position to protect Aurora Hawke.

Sixteen

As soon as Aurora stepped off the shuttle, Mya was waiting for her, medical scanner at the ready and a very determined look on her face.

Aurora held up her hand, indicating she needed a minute. She pulled Kire aside as Kelly and Celia unloaded the specimen bags from the shuttle. "Take the samples to the medical lab and have Celia begin a chemical analysis. Then I want you and Kelly to take a look at the images of the prints we found and see if you can come up with a hypothesis for what we're dealing with. We'll all convene in the conference room in an hour."

He hesitated, looking as tense as she felt. "Are you going to tell me what happened down there?"

I wish I knew. She understood his concern, and appreciated the stress he was under after what he'd witnessed, but she wasn't ready to talk about it. She was still too raw. "Not right now. But I promise not to pass out unexpectedly anytime soon." She pushed the corners of her lips up into an approximation of a smile.

He relented, although concern remained etched on his features. "Okay. See you in an hour." He and Kelly picked up two of the specimen bags and headed toward the door.

Celia grabbed a bag as well, but she paused briefly to slip an arm around Aurora's shoulders and give her a reassuring hug before following Kire and Kelly.

Mya approached, nodding to Celia as they passed each other. Aurora almost expected them to slap palms like a tag team in a wrestling match. Apparently Mya was her official handler now.

Her friend began assessing her condition before she'd even reached her, although she'd slipped the medical scanner into her pocket the moment the doors closed behind Celia. The device was only for show. Everything Mya needed to know she could see without the aid of electronics.

"I'm fine."

Mya didn't pause in her assessment. "So you say."

Mya wouldn't find any sign of weakness, trauma, or abnormalities in her energy pathways, but she waited patiently for her to reach that conclusion on her own.

When she finally seemed satisfied that Aurora wasn't about to keel over, she fixed her with a pointed stare. "What the hell happened down there, Sahzade?"

The trillion-dollar question. She needed Mya's help to frame her reaction in a way that made sense. Her current state of mental and emotional free fall wouldn't last forever, and she had no idea when she'd slam into the ground. She wanted to be prepared. "It's complicated."

Mya's brow furrowed. "With you it often is. Was it tied to what's happening on Gaia?"

She swallowed. "Let's just say there's more going on than meets the eye."

Mya's gaze was steady. "Tell me."

"Let's go to my office."

They were both quiet as they entered the lift and ascended to the bridge. As they exited, Jonarel rose from the captain's chair and covered the distance between them in a few long strides.

"Are you all right?" He gripped her shoulders as he scrutinized her from head to toe, confirming she was still in one piece.

"I'm fine."

He exchanged a glance with Mya. Clearly neither of them believed her, and why should they? She'd collapsed while investigating a farm. That wasn't exactly normal behavior, especially for her.

However, as much as she understood everyone's concern, right now she needed to talk to Mya. Alone. She redirected the conversation. "Kire and Kelly are analyzing the images we took at the farm site. I need you to share your findings with them. Star can monitor the bridge for now."

Jonarel's eyebrows lifted. "Does Kelly know about Star?"

She shook her head. "Not yet. But now that she's our navigator, we need to inform her. I'm leaving it to you to introduce them. I've called for a crew meeting in an hour so we can discuss our strategy. I'll be in my office if you need me."

He didn't relax his grip. His eyes looked like liquid gold as he stared at her, tension accentuating the patterns of deep green and brown on his face. "Are you sure you're all right?"

She smiled, though it took some effort. She placed her hand over his and squeezed. "I'm fine. I promise. I just need some time."

The brackets around his mouth eased somewhat, and he nodded as he released her, though he still looked reluctant to let her out of his sight.

She continued to her office with Mya right behind her. As they stepped into the soothing confines of the small space, she glanced out the viewport, where Gaia hung just off the port side. An involuntary shudder made her tremble.

Mya's hand settled on her shoulder. "Sahzade, talk to me."

She drew strength from Mya's reassuring presence and the understanding in her eyes. She gestured to the two plush chairs by the viewport before sinking into the nearest one and closing her eyes. Residual tension radiated through her body like a live wire, and she silently commanded her muscles to relax.

When she opened her eyes, she found Mya perched on the edge of the chair to her left, watching her. Worry flowed off of her in waves.

"I really am okay." Aurora shifted into a more upright position. "I'm just having trouble processing the experience."

Mya nodded, her warm brown eyes filled with empathy. "What happened?"

Aurora blew out a breath. "It started when we reached the outskirts of the affected area on our way to one of the farms. I felt tension creeping in, but I brushed it off as a reaction to the devastation we were seeing. But when we reached the farm, I felt...weird."

"Weird, how?"

"Like someone had dunked me in a vat of toxic goo."

Mya's nose wrinkled. "Is that when you collapsed?"

She shook her head. "No, I was still managing okay until I approached the decayed plants." She paused as she tried to put into words the feelings that had descended on her. "It was like a virus had been mainlined into my bloodstream."

Mya's eyebrows lifted.

"Kire had spotted a footprint about ten meters in, so I told him to lead and I followed." Her chest tightened and she inhaled slowly, battling her mind's reluctance to return to that moment. "But something happened when my foot touched the ash. It concentrated the sensations somehow, swamping me." She shuddered as an echo of the feelings reverberated through her.

Mya slipped her right hand into Aurora's left, holding it gently but firmly as a soft current of soothing energy flowed between them.

The energy halted the growing tension in her neck, and her constricted throat relaxed. Swallowing and breathing both became easier. "I locked up. My muscles...hell, my *entire body* stopped responding in any way. I toppled over because gravity works well on an inanimate object in motion." She flinched at the memory.

Mya frowned. "What about your shield? Why didn't you engage it?"

Aurora shifted her gaze to the viewport, focusing on the beauty of the star field so that she could keep her emotions reined in. "Just before I blacked out, I tried. Nothing happened." And that terrified her more than anything else. Shielding was as natural to her as breathing, especially when she felt threatened. And it had never failed her...until now.

Mya stared at her, her lips parting in disbelief. "But...but you've always shielded whenever you're scared or hurting." She shook her head in denial and her voice grew louder. "Hell, when you were two years old and I got mad at you for breaking the microscope my parents had given me for my eighth birthday, your shield engaged, and that was before you even understood what you were doing." She gestured in the direction of Gaia, her voice roughening with fear. "What could possibly be down there that paralyzed you *and* prevented you from protecting yourself?"

It was a very good question, and one she couldn't answer. "I don't know."

A flash of pure terror appeared in Mya's eyes, and that shocked Aurora more than her own collapse. She was used to seeing concern and even anxiety in Mya's expression from time to time, but fear was not an emotion Mya allowed herself to show. Ever. It went against her personal and professional pride.

Aurora didn't believe in showing fear either, yet she'd experienced a planet-sized dose today. The immobility had been scary, but if she was honest with herself, that wasn't the worst part. No, the bone-deep horror lived in the discovery of her own vulnerability. She'd never understood the mental and emotional sensations that came from feeling helpless in the face of danger. Now she did.

The first glimmer of hope had been a vague awareness of Kire's voice, and she'd grabbed hold of that tether with the panic of a drowning victim. But that hadn't been enough to pull her out of the void.

No, it was Celia who had managed that. She'd given her something to focus on, something other than the terror that had snarled and snapped all around her, driving her out of her mind and body. She couldn't remember anything Celia had said, but she'd never forget the look in her eyes. She'd known. She'd known the darkness that Aurora had fallen into, the desperation. Because she'd been there herself. And she'd survived.

That realization had galvanized Aurora back into reality.

She took a calming breath, resting her forearms on her knees. "Whatever affected me is tied to the plant destruction. I'm certain of it. So in a way, my reaction is good. I'm like a divining rod for whatever's happening down there. We might be able to use that to our advantage."

Mya looked wary. "How?"

"If I reacted this strongly to the remains of the plants, I have to believe I'll also react to the root cause of the destruction. We might be able to use that to track them down."

Mya's eyes widened. "Them?"

She nodded. "The evidence indicates a humanoid attack. How or why, I don't know. Yet." She reached into the pocket of her jacket and pulled out the drawing of the black figure. She opened the folded paper and handed it to Mya. "But one of the local children saw something."

Mya stared at the image for several moments. When she looked up, the worry had returned to her eyes. "You want to act as a divining rod to track this?" Her tone clearly indicated what she thought of that idea.

Aurora ignored the sudden pounding in her chest. "That's right. But first, I need to take a look at those plant samples." She hauled herself to her feet.

Mya stood and put a restraining hand on her arm. "Are you sure that's a good idea, considering what just happened to you? Speaking as your doctor and your friend, I don't think you should be anywhere near those samples until we ascertain what's triggering your reaction."

The frown on Mya's face had carved a deep line above the bridge of her nose. But Aurora couldn't accept her friend's advice. Too much was at stake.

"That's exactly why I *need* to work with the samples." Conviction gave her voice strength. "I have to know why whatever is out there is affecting me, *and only me*, this way." She thought about the decimated landscape, the footprints, and the little girl's drawing. "Because whatever it is, it's our job to stop it."

Seventeen

Celia stared at the data on her screen and sighed. Nothing. She'd been testing the plant and soil samples for everything she could think of and still had zip to show for her efforts. How could something cause this much destruction without leaving a trace of evidence that would explain how it was done?

Still, she was enjoying the hunt. She'd discovered her passion for pharmacology at the Academy, initially because so many plants could be used as poisons, and as a security officer in training, she needed to be able to identify them. But she'd also learned all the ways plants could help people, and that had motivated her even more.

She and Mya had spent many of their free hours together while they'd served on the *Argo*, working with new plants they'd encountered and sharing tips and tricks they'd learned. The rest of the time, she'd had fun challenging Aurora on the sparring mat. Aurora had spirit, but her fighting skills had been pathetic when they'd first started. Now she could hold her own, and their workouts took a lot more concentration and effort.

When Aurora had offered her the job on the *Starhawke*, saying yes had been the easiest decision she'd ever made, even though it meant leaving the Fleet. She'd fully expected to live and die in a Fleet uniform, but with the exception of her childhood mentor, there was no one she respected more than Aurora, and no one she was closer to than Mya. She'd accepted the offer as soon as Aurora finished her prepared speech.

She reached for another sample, but paused when the door to Mya's office slid open and Aurora stepped into the med bay. They'd arrived about half an hour ago, and had been closed up in the office ever since. They could have worked at one of the lab tables in the main room, but she'd understood their desire for privacy. Aurora's dramatic collapse on the planet had clearly shaken her, and she suspected her friend needed time to lick her wounds.

Aurora crossed the room and slipped onto one of the stools beside Celia's workstation. "Got a minute?"

"Of course."

Aurora picked up one of the vials lying on the table and studied it, rolling the glass tube between her fingers. She opened her mouth. Closed it. Cleared her throat. Then she lifted her gaze, revealing the tension around her eyes. "Is there anything you'd like to ask me?"

Celia hadn't expected the subject to be broached so soon. "Do you have something you want to tell me?" she countered. Her job required her to pry into people's backgrounds and personal lives all the time, but only to protect those around her. She respected her friends' privacy, particularly regarding secrets they weren't ready to share.

The hint of a smile appeared on Aurora's lips. "Not going to make this easy for me, are you?" She placed the vial on the table and laced her fingers together. "I wanted to say thank you. I know I said it before, but in this case, it bears repeating."

When she paused, Celia waited. She'd been in this type of situation more times than she could count, and she'd learned silence was the best encouragement she could give.

"You know there's something different about me, don't you?"

It was more a statement than a question, but she nodded anyway.

"But you've never asked for an explanation. Why?"

"Why would I?"

Confusion clouded Aurora's gaze.

Celia rested a hand on her arm. "Whatever secrets you carry are yours alone. If you choose to share them, I'm always here. But sometimes there are things we need to keep to ourselves, at least until we're ready." She knew what she was talking about. She had an entire room full. "When the time comes, you'll know."

Aurora's expression relaxed, the tension fading away. "Thank you." She drew in a breath and gave herself a little shake. "So, any luck?" she asked, shifting back into her captain's role.

"No so far. I have another fifteen minutes before the meeting, but it's not looking good. What about you and Mya?"

Aurora grimaced. "Nothing. Mya's going to keep working, but she's not holding out much hope. Maybe Jonarel and Kire will have more success." She stood and pulled her tunic into place. "I need to check in with Star on the bridge, so I'll leave you to it. See you in the conference room."

After she left, Celia returned to her task, but she continued to mull over the scene on Gaia. She'd always had theories about her friend, some of which today's events seemed to have confirmed. And if she was right, there was a lot more to Aurora Hawke than most people imagined.

Eighteen

The crew had settled into six of the ten solid wood chairs surrounding the roughly circular table at the center of the conference room. Carved from the trunk of a native Drakar tree and polished until the surface shone like glass, the table was a stunning example of Kraed craftsmanship. But Aurora's focus wasn't on the table. She was too busy taking the emotional temperatures of the five people seated around it.

Kire and Jonarel had flanked her chair as soon as they'd arrived, putting her on red alert. Jonarel sat with his shoulders rounded forward and his arms pushed slightly away from his torso, giving him the appearance of a bouncer at a bar—the one you didn't mess with unless your judgment was seriously impaired by alcohol.

Kire's lean frame didn't lend itself to that kind of fierceness, but the intensity of his regard was no less intimidating for the lack of brawn. While he prided himself on his diplomatic skills, at the moment he looked more inclined to engage in a physical contest rather than a mental one. That told her more than anything else that they were dealing with more than dead plants on Gaia.

Celia was on Kire's right with Kelly next to her. Kelly's emotions were the same as always, since *placid as a lake* appeared to be her default setting. Celia, on the other hand, radiated a sharp focus that cut through the room like a laser. Clearly she still hadn't found the answers she wanted.

Mya had been the last to arrive, taking a seat next to Jonarel while she continued to scan the information on her data pad. Her emotions were a mixture of concern and frustration that matched the overall feel of the room. Hopefully this discussion would change that.

Aurora rested her arms on the tabletop. "Let's start with Celia's analysis of the samples. What did you and Mya learn?"

"I pulled vials from each of the collection kits and ran the plant remains and soil through several tests, checking for any sign of chemical agents, toxins and foreign matter. Nothing unusual showed up. The only materials contained in the vials were those that were also present in the base samples Mya examined earlier. If anything was introduced to cause the destruction, it was also extracted or evaporated afterwards without leaving any traces."

Mya picked up the thread. "I analyzed the samples for pathogens of a biological nature, such as a virus or bacteria, but had the same results. Even though all samples showed complete necrosis of the living tissue, the plants did not show any sign of infection or external trauma."

"So there was nothing unusual?" Kire asked.

"I wouldn't say that." Mya glanced at him. "The cellular breakdown was unlike anything I've ever seen. Most cells that are in a state of necrosis are the result of an internal virus or an external trauma that ruptures the cell wall, causing the nucleus to leak out. These cells looked like a physical trauma had occurred *inside* the cell, as though the nucleus was yanked through the cell wall, causing the rupture and the collapse of the cell."

Kire frowned. "So what could cause that type of destruction?"

"I don't know. I've worked with necrotic plant remains before, but I've never seen anything like this. However, it's unlikely it's a naturally occurring phenomenon."

"Meaning something, or someone, did this," Kire said.

Aurora turned to Jonarel. "Did the images we gathered yield anything?"

He nodded, his tension as palpable as Celia's. He touched the control panel and the video from their approach to the RC headquarters began playing. "The destruction to the vegetation is so complete that it is difficult to detect any patterns. This is particularly true in areas with predominantly low-lying plants."

He shifted the image, slowing it down. "However, in areas where the plants were taller, the borders and roadways revealed that the plants in a given area all died lying in the same direction, as if they were pushed down as they died, leaving a darker mark in the non-vegetated areas."

He switched the image to a close up from one of the fields and panned along several lines marked in red. "And there is something else."

A chill trickled down Aurora's spine. More footprints. Multiple sets, located at different points in one of the images. They appeared from nowhere, followed a broken path, and then disappeared just as abruptly, like a ghost that had temporarily gained substance.

"These prints look humanoid, but judging from the twisted shape, it is unlikely they are actually human. What species they might be, I cannot say." Jonarel's gaze locked with hers. "Most of the prints show up exactly like this, in the middle of the debris with no line going in or out. Star scanned all the images, and she located prints in nearly every one." His eyes flashed with anger, though his voice remained calm. "The destruction on Gaia is neither natural, nor random."

Celia tapped a staccato beat on the table with her fingers. "So this is a deliberate attack. But what's the motivation? This has been a peaceful colony for a hundred years, and no one seems to be profiting from this destruction."

"It could be Setarips," Kelly said. "They're certainly known for sudden violence against peaceful planetary systems."

"True," Celia agreed. "But Setarips are thieves and opportunists, not conquerors. Destruction follows them, but only because they want to obtain or protect something they value for their civil war. If they were involved, I would expect the crops to be taken, not destroyed, or somehow held for ransom. Since no one has contacted the Gaians and no demands have been made, it seems unlikely they're involved."

Kire nodded. "Prolonged secrecy isn't their strong suit, either. It's hard to imagine they would go to such lengths to cloak their actions without an obvious motivation for visible gain."

"Secrecy is only their pattern until the attack begins. Then they become pretty damn visible," Celia muttered.

Aurora glanced at Kelly. The discussion might have hit a little too close to home. However, Kelly didn't give off even a flicker of emotion. That was a little disconcerting.

"So we still don't have any idea who we're dealing with." Kire interlaced his fingers, rubbing the pads of his thumbs against each other as he gazed at Aurora. "Do you think we need to bring the Fleet in on this?" His voice indicated *yes*, but his eyes said *no*.

His internal conflict matched her own. It wasn't an easy question with a simple answer. "I've considered that. However, I don't think that's what we need right now." She gestured to the images. "These are guerrilla tactics we're dealing with, and if the Fleet moves in, the aggressors may just go to ground, then redouble their attacks when the coast is clear."

Kelly and Celia nodded.

"Right now, we're under the radar almost as much as they are, since we don't have to follow Fleet procedure and we don't have a set pattern they can predict. And, we've been designated as a science team. Very non-threatening. It's safe to assume they know we're here, but they shouldn't have any idea how we'll proceed."

Kire leaned forward. "So what's our next move?"

"First, we need to ferret out their hiding place. No ships have left the system since we arrived, so most likely they're still planetside. Our best bet is to monitor the area surrounding the most recent attack site and see if they show themselves. Then maybe we'll be able to figure out how they're destroying the plants."

"So you're thinking of an orbital surveillance?" Celia asked.

"For now. But we may not be able to get the answers we need that way." She felt a flare of concern from Jonarel, and glanced at him.

"And if we cannot?" His expression indicated he'd figured out where she was going with this, and he didn't like it.

"We'll arrange a surface surveillance."

Kire's voice held a note of disapproval. "And by *we*, I hope you mean us, not you."

She didn't agree with his conclusion. "I have no intention of staying on the ship." She held up her hand before anyone could raise an objection. "I spent most of the last hour down in the lab with Mya, and I handled every sample she tested. Nothing happened."

"So if you're not affected by the plants, why did you pass out?" Kire's face reflected the emotions that rolled off of him, his respect for her as his captain at war with his fear for her safety.

"I have a theory on that." She chose her words carefully, since each member of the crew had a different level of understanding of her unique skills. She glanced at Kelly. "I have a strong empathic ability that allows me to sense emotions in others." The comment elicited no emotional reaction from the younger woman. They were quite the pair—the empath and the blank page.

She sat back in her chair so that she could look at Kire and Jonarel as she spoke. "What I experienced was an intense emotional overload, triggered most likely by the strongly negative vibrations embedded into the affected area by the attacking force and the residents who suffered from the destruction."

Jonarel shook his head, his hair brushing his broad shoulders. "But you have been in places before that suffered destruction. The aftermath of Setarip attacks in particular, and you have never had a problem. Why now?"

Good question. And the only way to find out for certain would be to go back down to the planet's surface. "Maybe because I have a personal bond to Gaia as our sister planet, which heightened my emotional involvement. Or because my defenses were low as a result of our quick departure and a lack of rest." She laid her hands on the table, palms up. "I don't know. But that's not the point.

Whatever triggered it, the main problem was my lack of awareness. Now that I know what to expect, I can control it."

"Are you sure about that?" Kire asked.

She kept her gaze steady. "As sure as I can be. But it's a moot point at the moment. First, we have to locate our targets."

Nineteen

Kire set up a crew rotation while Kelly moved them into a geosynchronous orbit over the community that had been hit the previous night. He'd scheduled off-duty time for everyone during the long night, with the exception of Star, whose requirements for rest were minimal. Despite his objections, Roe had insisted on working the first shift while she ordered him off the bridge, but he'd relieved her a few hours later.

"Six hours to sunrise."

He glanced up at the sound of Star's melodious voice. A muscle in his neck twinged. Apparently he'd been focusing a bit too intently on the monitor in front of him. The captain's chair was comfortable, but his body still protested the prolonged lack of movement.

He rolled his shoulders and tipped his head from side to side, working the kinks out. Star had counted out each hour of the surveillance, and his optimism had faded in direct proportion to the passing time. Their prey still hadn't shown themselves. He really didn't want to end the long night empty-handed.

Leaning back, he gazed at the aerial image on the bridgescreen. Not that there was much to see. They were on the night side, and unlike Earth, Gaia didn't have an abundance of light sources marking the outlines of the populated areas.

They'd divided the target community into four quadrants. At the moment Cardiff, Jon and Kelly were on rotation with him, each watching a different section while Roe and Mya rested in their cabins. Star was overseeing the outlying areas as well as keeping watch for any incoming or outgoing vessels in the system.

So far, they'd located the decomposing hulk of a century-old transport, a group of teenagers breaking curfew on the outskirts of the community hub, and a herd of deer-like creatures headed for a large lake in an open valley surrounded by several large farms. But no sign of an attacking force of humanoids. He was beginning to feel like they were searching through the proverbial haystack, and possibly not even the correct one.

As he glanced down, a sudden flash of motion caught his attention. Snapping forward, he magnified the image as the screen rapidly populated with what looked like more than a hundred moving objects. However, unlike all the others he'd tracked during the night, these were concentrated together and their numbers appeared to be growing.

They expanded from a point near the base of the mountain range. It reminded him of a geyser, except instead of expelling water and steam, this geyser was gushing lifeforms. And they were fast. He estimated nearly two hundred had spread across a distance of more than a kilometer in less than a minute.

"Possible sighting in sector three." The silence of the bridge acted as an amplifier. "Twenty-nine point nine-six-six-seven degrees north, by ninety point zero-five-zero-zero degrees west. Visual onscreen." He sent the image to the bridgescreen.

The night vision filtering produced a green glow over the scene, but it also allowed for a definition that the lack of ambient light wouldn't normally provide in the visible spectrum. The targets were definitely using aerial transport as they skimmed over the landscape below, but he couldn't identify any specifics at this magnification.

Jon, Cardiff and Kelly all turned to face him, awaiting his orders. He started with Jon. "Get me infrared, and monitor any communication signals being transmitted to or from the targets."

Jon nodded and pivoted back to his console.

Kire glanced at Kelly. "Sweep the area for anything else that's moving, biological or mechanical. We don't want any surprises."

"Aye."

He continued around the semi-circle to Cardiff. "Get a close up on the visual and see if you can identify who or what we're looking at."

"Got it."

He finished with Star, whose three-dimensional image had appeared seated at the console to the left of the captain's chair. He knew her physical presence was a cheat to make it easier for the crew to interact with her, and that he could have whispered while staring at the floor or ceiling and she would have responded anyway. However, he appreciated being able to make eye contact. "Scan the area for any sign of a transport vessel large enough to carry at least two hundred humanoids."

"Yes, Commander."

"Infrared on screen," Jon said. "Picking up transmission signals among the various targets, but they are localized. No indication of external communications."

The main view split, with the night vision image on top and the infrared below. The figures continued their rapid movement across the valley, creating dotted rainbows from their heat signatures as they headed toward a section of rural farms to the southeast. They began to fan out, steadily forming a rough grid.

With the wide angle, the individual targets were difficult to see now that they were no longer clumped together, especially as they slowed and descended toward the ground, blending in with the surrounding landscape.

"Cardiff, give me a tag on each of those targets in the visual image."

Red markers appeared across the scene, defining the interior grid of the rough rectangle the targets had created. The scene remained fixed for roughly ten seconds. And then....

"What...the...hell." He could almost feel his pupils dilating as he strained to draw in as much light as possible. But that didn't help him process what he was seeing.

In the infrared, glowing hot spots bloomed around each figure, almost like a red and yellow corona of flame had been lit beneath their feet, setting them ablaze. But the visual image revealed something even more startling. Only moments before the area had been filled with the dark shadows of plant life. Now, like ripples from a pebble tossed into a still pond, the plants winked out of existence in expanding circles with the figures at the center. And yet, he couldn't see anything obvious that was causing the destruction.

His heart rate accelerated as he slapped his comband. "Captain?"

Several seconds passed before Roe replied, her voice thick with sleep. "Yes?"

His jaw clenched. He hated having to drag her out of bed when she obviously needed the rest. But this couldn't wait. "We have a positive ID on the targets."

This time, her response was brisk. "On my way."

Within moments she appeared on the bridge from the lift, securing her blond hair in a braid as she crossed to the captain's chair. He moved out of her way, but she didn't sit down, choosing instead to stand next to him as she faced the bridgescreen. A frown creased her forehead and tension lines around her eyes indicated she probably hadn't been resting easily even before he'd woken her.

"What's the status?"

He gave her a summary as she studied the images.

"Celia, any idea who or what we're dealing with?"

"I'm not sure of the *who*, but there are two different species down there." Cardiff tapped her console and a third image appeared on the screen to the left of the other two, showing a close up in night vision green of a hunched figure, the outlines of its head and the ends of each arm the only easily recognizable body parts. "This first one is canted at the hips rather than completely upright. It's possible they're used to walking on all fours, but from this angle it's hard to judge. We'd have a better idea from a ground perspective."

It looked a lot like the creature the child had drawn, although most of the torso was blocked from view by two large protrusions from its upper back.

"Are those wings?" Roe asked, taking a couple of steps toward the screen.

Cardiff nodded. "I tracked this figure on its approach, and the appendages were extended out during flight. They folded down when it landed. But they're mechanical, not biological. During flight, you can detect the energy pattern of the propulsion system."

"That would explain how they were able to move so quickly." Kire studied the close-up image. "And why the footprints in the debris appeared and disappeared." He glanced at Cardiff. "What about the second species?"

"They have the same wing apparatus, but their biology is very different." She added a second image that showed a significantly larger humanoid figure, this one fully upright and much closer in silhouette to a human. However, the figure's body was completely covered in some type of cloth mesh that obscured its features, making it impossible to identify. "And that looks like a rifle to me." She indicated the object the figure was holding.

So they *were* armed. However, judging from the heat signature, the weapon hadn't been discharged. And there was something else. While the plants around the hunched figure were rapidly disappearing, no changes were taking place to the plants around the armed target. The corona of heat didn't show, either. "This one doesn't appear to be part of the destruction," Kire murmured.

Roe nodded, her gaze thoughtful.

"How many of each?" he asked.

Cardiff had obviously anticipated the question. "Twenty of the second species, all around the perimeter, and nearly two hundred of the first within the grid."

Roe folded her arms. "So are the armed ones acting as guards? To protect the others?"

"That's the most likely explanation," Cardiff replied.

"The Gaians are lucky no one has stumbled upon them during an attack. It would probably have been a death sentence." Roe's focus remained on the bridgescreen. "Any sign of a transport?"

Kire glanced at Star. "Anything?"

She shook her head. "I have been unable to detect any sign of a transportation device in the area large enough to accommodate them. Since they appeared from the tree line at the base of the mountain range to the north, they may be using the rocks to block sensor readings. The area contains many gullies and valleys large enough to hide a vessel, and the mineral content in the area would make it difficult to distinguish a ship from the surrounding landscape."

Roe continued to stare at the images on the screen as though hypnotized. "When they head back, track them and see if you can pinpoint their final location." The muscles around her mouth and eyes pinched in a subtle wince.

Kire spoke in a low tone. "Are you okay?"

She glanced at him in surprise. It was the first time she'd looked away from the screen since she'd arrived on the bridge. "Why do you ask?"

"Because you just flinched."

She ran her fingers across her forehead as her gaze returned to the images. "I woke up with a headache."

"Are you sure that's all?" After what had happened on Gaia, he wasn't about to take any chances.

She nodded absently. "I'm fine."

He didn't believe her. Roe had a way of taking personal strength and self-reliance to extremes, and as her first officer, it was his job to protect her, especially if she wasn't watching out for herself. However, her explanation made sense, especially given her stress level and lack of sleep. He wouldn't push...for now.

"They're on the move again," Kelly said.

The wings on the two targets Celia had magnified shifted into place and lifted them into the air. Kire glanced at the infrared. The entire grid was in motion, although they didn't appear to be heading back to their starting point. Instead, they were on course to another large plot of unblemished land about two kilometers away. For the moment, the creatures stood out in stark contrast to the complete desolation they had left behind.

As the figures settled to the ground and the pattern started all over again, Roe moved to stand behind Cardiff's chair. "What can you tell me about their attack methods?"

Cardiff shook her head. "No idea. We're registering an intense increase in heat readings from the targets, but there's no sign of weaponry of any kind. The only explanation that's remotely plausible is that this is a biological attack."

"Even though you and Mya didn't find any traces in the samples?"

"We may have missed something. Or, we may be dealing with a new threat." Cardiff's expression revealed an understanding born of experience. "Never underestimate the humanoid ability to create methods of rampant destruction the universe never intended."

Kire grimaced. Sad but true.

"So we need more information." Roe crossed her arms and stared at the bridgescreen. "We'll monitor the rest of the attack and see if we can track the targets back to wherever they're hiding. But tomorrow night, we're going down to Gaia for a closer look."

Twenty

"She's going to do *what?*"

Cade stared at Reanne. He must have heard incorrectly.

Her expression remained neutral, but she looked pointedly at his hands.

He glanced down. He was gripping the edge of his desk so hard his knuckles had turned white. He pried his fingers open and sat back in his chair, his spine rigid. "How could the Admiral approve that? My team is much better suited to this than hers." He tried to keep the emotion out of his voice, but his strong overreaction had already indicated that his concern was not just a matter of professional pride.

Reanne's expression bordered on pity. "Her crew successfully identified those responsible for the destruction."

"So she gets to put herself in danger just because she has dibs?" He winced at his choice of words.

Reanne's voice took on a hard edge. "It's not your call. If the Admiral believes Aurora and her crew are the best people for the job, then you and I have to support that decision." Her tone gentled. "And remember that these are highly trained former Fleet officers. Aurora's intelligent and conscientious. She won't needlessly endanger herself or her crew."

Several swear words sprang to mind, but he kept them locked down. Reanne was right. But dammit, now that they knew their enemy was humanoid, he didn't want Aurora placing herself in harm's way, especially since this was exactly the kind of thing his team was trained for. Not that he had a say in the matter. The Admiral had already given her the go ahead.

Taking a breath, he focused on damage control. "But with Kelly on the ship, that leaves only five people for the surface team. You said that there are more than two hundred targets. They'll be greatly outnumbered if anything goes wrong."

Reanne shook her head. "This is a surveillance mission. They won't be engaging."

Cade ground his molars together. "A surveillance mission can turn into an active mission very quickly, particularly when the enemy is unknown."

"That's why you're here. The Admiral asked me to arrange for your team to establish a base of operations in a cabin located in the mountain region north of the valley. You can monitor the situation from there, and take any other defensive positions you deem necessary to protect Aurora and her crew."

That got his attention. "How close is the cabin to where they'll be?"

"A few kilometers. They'll land their shuttle on the far side of the ridge and use personal transports to reach their surveillance points. After they've taken up their positions, you should be able to move in closer. However, Kelly will be scanning the area, so you'll have to be careful. The Admiral provided the frequency they'll be using for communications, so you can monitor them that way."

She handed him a data pad with four locations marked in red.

"This is the cabin." She indicated a spot in the mountain range to the north. "Cardiff and Clarek will be here." She tapped a point to the east. "Emoto will be to the south, and Aurora and Mya to the west. You can set up surveillance, however, the Admiral emphasized that he doesn't want Aurora or her crew alerted to your presence unless they're in danger."

His chest tightened. He *already* thought she was in danger. Then something else occurred to him. "Why didn't the Admiral send the orders directly to me, instead of going through you?"

The sympathetic look she gave him grated on his nerves. "His message to you is on the pad. He knew you'd have...questions, and thought you might be more amenable after we'd discussed the matter."

He stared at her. The Admiral was right.

She stood. "Unless there's anything else, I'll leave you to it." She gave him a brief smile as she headed out of the office. "Good luck."

He gazed at the closed door for a full minute before picking up the tablet. He quickly reviewed the Admiral's message. It was short and to the point. Monitor the *Starhawke* crew, but do not interfere unless absolutely necessary. The Admiral's final words showed just how well he understood Cade's state of mind. *Stop worrying.*

Turning off the pad, he rested his elbows on the desk and stared at the worn wood surface. *Aurora, why are you doing this?* He knew the answer, of course—he just didn't like it. But he had his orders. Scrubbing his hands over his face, he stood and walked out the door.

Twenty-One

Aurora crouched at the edge of the shadowed orchard, listening to the sigh of the wind through the trees and the contented chirp of nighttime insects. The stars winked in and out as clouds drifted by, the subtle on and off switch of the moonlight the only marker of passing time. If she hadn't been on a surveillance mission against a hostile force, the scene would have been peaceful.

She'd been waiting for nearly four hours, and her muscles were starting to complain. Thankfully the headache that had plagued her since Kire had woken her the previous night had faded when they'd reached Gaia.

During the early evening, she and Mya had worked on placing sensors in the wooded areas within a seven-kilometer radius of their current location. Kire had done the same to the south, and Celia and Jonarel had tagged the tree line at the base of the mountain before heading up into the ravines in search of the enemy ship.

Regardless of the path the targets took from the mountains, they'd have to pass at least one of the sensors, giving Aurora and her crew a good look at exactly who they were dealing with.

Her earpiece hummed. "Jon and Cardiff are approaching the anticipated location of the transport," Kire said.

"Acknowledged."

After the previous night's attack, they'd successfully tracked the targets as they'd flown back to the woods, but as the creatures had entered the mountain range, the rocks and thick vegetation had wreaked havoc with sensor readings, making it impossible to pinpoint their final destination. With Star's help, Jonarel and Celia had plotted the most likely location for hiding a large transport. With luck, they'd find something soon.

Aurora gazed across the shadowed fields to where the mountain rose from the valley floor, the tall trees at its summit bathed in the soft glow of the waning moon. The targets had avoided the densely populated and wooded areas of the valley during the attack, which made sense given their aerial transportation and stealth movements. Besides, trees would likely be harder to destroy, and not worth the effort when they had so much open ground available. Last night, in the space of a few hours, they'd decimated roughly five square kilometers of land, mostly farms and grasslands. Only the structures had remained, standing out in stark relief in the resulting barrenness.

Tonight, she and Mya were stationed about a dozen kilometers southwest of the mountains, in a large orchard that climbed a series of hills to the west. Thick grasses covered the ground to the east, meeting up with the sprawling greenery and agricultural fields that filled most of the valley.

Kire had set up a command center in a wooded glen to the south that sat on a promontory and provided a nearly perfect view of the valley. Aurora had balked at the idea when he'd first proposed it. She didn't want him working alone. But he'd pointed out that three surveillance locations provided much better coverage than two.

They'd used Kraed gliders to reach their destinations. Designed for navigating the jungle-like forests of Drakar, the device resembled a narrow surfboard and required the same agility to maneuver, as it remained airborne when activated. Balance and speed were controlled by retractable handgrips that lifted out of the base, allowing the glider to carry up to three passengers.

Jonarel had grown up riding a glider, so he could navigate over any terrain, including the woods and ravines where he and Celia were currently searching.

Kire had taken to the glider immediately, having spent a fair amount of time surfing as a teenager. His comfort with the device had further calmed Aurora's fears about sending him out alone.

Aurora and Mya didn't have Jonarel's experience or Kire's skill in handling the device. They'd decided to stow theirs on the far side of the orchard near the main road after they'd realized the combination of hills and trees greatly increased the risk that they'd smack into something or go tumbling off. Aurora had made a mental note to ask Jonarel to give her a few lessons after they completed this mission.

The comm channel hummed again and Kire's voice came over the line. "Jon and Cardiff have located the transport and are continuing on foot."

Her heartbeat kicked up a notch. This was it.

From somewhere in the orchard, a night bird called, the elaborate series of trills and warbles reminiscent of a mockingbird. A breeze brushed through the trees, carrying the scent of blooming buds in the warm night air. A small rodent scuttled across the path, then disappeared into the underbrush.

Jonarel's deep voice rumbled over the comm. "The targets are leaving the transport and heading south toward the valley."

Aurora slid her surveillance visor into place and magnified the patch of sky in front of the mountain range where the creatures were most likely to appear. Time ticked by, but eventually a mass of dark shapes passed like a shadow over the paler clouds in the distance. Even at maximum magnification, the image resembled a swarm of bees. The sensors Celia and Jonarel had placed would be transmitting better visuals to Star and Kire, but Aurora hoped to get a closer look in person.

As if in response to her thought, the swarm arced toward the west, moving more or less in her direction.

"Looks like we're in luck," she said under her breath as she crouched next to Mya.

"Mm-hmm," Mya replied.

Aurora opened a channel to Kire. "Targets heading our way. Three kilometers and closing."

"Acknowledged."

She focused on the dark cloud as the images in her visual panel grew more distinct. She pressed against the rough bark of the tree and moved into the shadows. The sensor suits she and Mya were wearing should make them virtually invisible to visual and infrared scanners, but she wasn't taking any chances.

The targets continued their approach, their silhouettes slowly resolving into grotesque caricatures of winged angels. The pack broke up, the individual figures moving into the now familiar grid pattern. Like vultures descending on a carcass, they dropped out of the sky, their movements soundless, with nary a whisper on the wind.

As soon as their wings folded onto their backs, the hunched forms practically disappeared beneath the plants that surrounded them, making them seem smaller than they really were. They were definitely humanoid, with bodies as dark as the night sky above, but horribly misshapen, as if they had been molded from potter's clay crafted by a child.

The guards were a different story. The three closest to her looked completely humanoid. However, their backs were to her and the mesh cloth covering their bodies concealed their features.

A firm hand gripped her arm.

"What are you doing?" Mya asked in a harsh whisper.

Aurora glanced back in surprise. She'd taken several steps away from the tree toward the targets without even realizing it.

Mya tugged, trying to pull her back, but for some reason her feet didn't seem to want to go in that direction.

"Sahzade, *get down!*" Mya gave her arm a good yank that knocked them both off balance, tumbling them together like newborn pups. "Don't move." Mya righted herself and placed a hand on Aurora's shoulder, exerting pressure to keep her from standing up. "There's something very wrong with those creatures."

Aurora tried to peer around Mya. "What do you mean?"

Mya's full attention remained on the figures in the distance. "There's severe damage in their energy fields, almost like energetic scarring. I've never seen anything like it." She released Aurora's shoulder and crouched lower. "The targets are moving."

Aurora sat up, her heart thumping uncomfortably in her chest. The plants around the creatures swayed as an eerie silence descended.

A moment later, a wave of pain slammed into her, pulling at every cell in her body. Her chest heaved as she forced air through her constricted throat. She recognized the sensation as the empathic onslaught she'd anticipated, but that didn't make processing it much easier. However, this time her energy shield responded to her request with a roar, flaring to vibrant life and yanking her to her feet. The overload on her senses retreated proportionately.

A soft thump to her right made her glance over her shoulder. Mya lay flat on her back on the ground, her arms splayed on either side of her prone body. Her eyes were open, but she was blinking as though she couldn't focus.

What the hell?

Turning her back on the figures in the valley, Aurora dropped to her knees beside Mya. "What's wrong?"

Mya's gaze tracked to the left until it met hers, but the rest of her body remained perfectly still and languid. "I don't know." Her eyelids slid to half-mast. "I'm so tired." The words came out on a weary sigh.

Mya's energy field was engaged, the rich forest green pulsing around her body. But in contrast to the almost blinding vibrancy of Aurora's pearlescent field, Mya's was steadily fading out, like she was plugged into a dimmer switch and someone was turning off the power.

Reacting on instinct, Aurora grasped Mya's shoulders in both hands. The change was instantaneous. Mya's eyes snapped open and she drew in a deep breath, her energy field stabilizing.

A wave of anger at her own stupidity swept through Aurora as understanding dawned. What a fool she'd been. She'd agreed that partnering with Mya made sense because if anything went wrong, Mya would be able to help her. Unfortunately, it had never occurred to her that Mya might be affected, too.

Her earpiece hummed. Kire sounded tense. "Something's happened. The targets have stopped the attack and are breaking out of their grid formation."

She released her hold on Mya with one hand and tapped her earpiece. "Can you tell what they're doing?" She kept her gaze on the guards closest to them.

"No, but five of the creatures broke off from the group and are moving in your direction. The armed guard closest to them is following."

She and Mya exchanged a startled glance. This was definitely not part of the plan.

The creatures were tough to spot, although she could see the swaying of the greenery around them. They did appear to be coming closer.

She closed the comm connection and turned to Mya. "Time to go." Gripping Mya's wrists, Aurora pulled them both to their feet.

She had a decision to make, but their options were limited. They couldn't head east. North and south were a possibility, but that would keep them close to the valley. Their best bet to avoid the creatures was heading west into the orchard toward the glider. Unfortunately, even if they ran, it could take them ten minutes or more to cross the distance over the uneven, uphill terrain.

She released her hold on Mya's wrists. Mya swayed, her eyelids drooping. Snagging her arm around Mya's waist, Aurora made as much body contact as possible and immediately felt Mya right herself. Okay. Apparently they'd have to run together.

"I want you to lean on me. We're going to run as fast as we can into the orchard. Okay?"

Mya's entire being radiated misery. "I'm so sorry, Sahzade."

She gritted her teeth and shook her head. "No sorry. Just movement. We're going to make it out of here."

With that thought fixed firmly in her head, she pivoted on her heel and urged Mya forward with pressure on her back. However, her own feet felt a little sluggish, like she was running through calf-high water, even though the ground was fairly level in this section. Their motion as they stumbled along under the sheltering trees reminded her of a game they'd played as kids called the three-legged race. But this could well be a race for their lives.

"Roe! Can you hear me? Where are you?" Kire's voice held more than a touch of panic.

She tapped her earpiece. "I'm here. We're heading west into the orchard."

"The rest of the creatures and guards just lifted off. They're heading east toward the mountain. The other six are still following you."

She ducked under a low-hanging branch, grateful for the visor that provided a clear visual of the trees ahead. "Mya's in trouble, and I don't know if we'll be able to outrun the creatures. We need help."

He replied without hesitation. "I'm on my way."

She did a quick calculation. He was more than ten kilometers away. Even at full speed, the glider couldn't cover the distance in less than ten minutes. That might be longer than they had. But she wouldn't tell him that.

Maybe Star could buy them more time. "I need you to give me a direct link to Star."

"Done. And I'll be there soon, Roe. I promise."

The next voice she heard was Star's. "Captain?"

"Star, are you locked onto my comm signal?"

"Yes."

Mya stumbled as they hit a patch of slippery leaves. Aurora locked her arm more firmly around Mya's waist and pulled her upright. "Where are the six targets in relation to our position?"

"Three hundred seventy meters to the southeast, following your trajectory."

Maybe they could outmaneuver them. She changed course so that they were now heading due west. Leaves crunched under their feet and the rasp of their labored breathing filled her ears, but she forced her legs to pump faster, dragging Mya with her. After they'd crested a small hill, she spoke again, the air escaping her lungs in bursts.

"Now...where...are they?"

"Two hundred thirty meters. They adjusted their path to match yours."

Dammit! How could they possibly be tracking them? She kept moving, not because she believed they would outrun them, but because giving up just wasn't in her genetic code. She could reach into her tunic for her small pistol, but that would mean releasing her hold on Mya. Not a good idea since she seemed to be the only thing keeping her friend upright. The weapon would be a last resort.

She pushed forward, climbing another low rise, although her calf muscles were screaming and her lungs were on fire. That also didn't make sense. She was used to this kind of physical effort, had in fact run five miles during her morning workout. But for some reason, she felt like she was moving through glue, each step pulling at her, trying to stop the motion of her feet.

They were at least halfway through the orchard now, pale moonlight drifting down through the breaks in the trees above. She should ask Star how close the creatures were, but she honestly didn't want to know. The answer might sap what little strength she had left.

How much time had passed since she'd spoken to Kire? Four minutes? Five? She didn't know. And he was very far away.

As the thought tumbled through her exhausted mind, she heard a new sound off in the distance, coming from somewhere due west. She struggled to identify it over the pounding of her heart, but as it grew louder she nearly cried with joy.

It was the high-pitched whine of a jetbike.

Twenty-Two

The jetcycle screamed in protest as Cade pushed it to its upper limit.

Why hadn't he figured out a way to hide in the orchard? Instead, he'd set up three kilometers away in the closest wooded location. Stupid. He'd allowed his concern that Aurora would spot him override his instinct to stay close. What had seemed logical only a few hours ago felt ludicrous now that her life was in danger.

As soon as the six targets had moved in Aurora's direction, he'd put his team on alert. He'd barely controlled a flare of panic when Aurora told Emoto she needed help. He'd thrown his cycle into gear, determined to reach her before the creatures did.

He turned hard to the left as he crested the ridge west of the orchard and swept under the tree line. The moonlight flashed in alternating patterns of light and shadow as he raced through the grove. His visual display helped illuminate the trees, but they weren't planted in neat rows. He had to dodge around them while navigating the hills, which slowed him down.

The display lit up a moment later with a glowing red mark, indicating the location of Aurora's comm signal. She'd asked Emoto for a connection to Star, which didn't make sense. It could be a nickname she'd given Kelly, but Cade wasn't hearing an Irish accent. If they all got through this, he'd ask Aurora. Whoever Star was, she was providing updates on the locations of the creatures.

He glanced at the display. Aurora was further south than he'd anticipated and heading due west. He banked to the right, putting the bike on an intercept course. A moment later six heat signatures appeared at the top of the display, moving rapidly toward Aurora and Mya.

He was close enough now that she'd be able to hear his bike. Heart pounding, he scanned the area, trying to make out her form in the darkness. That's when he saw it—a pearlescent shimmer fifty meters ahead. Her energy shield was activated!

He adjusted his path so it would place him between her and the approaching figures. He kept his gaze fixed on the targets, who were now visible in the distance, as he swung in behind her, bringing the bike to a halt.

Aurora approached, her voice breathless and strained. "Thank you for stopping! We need hel–"

She cut off abruptly as he faced her. "Cade?"

"Get on the bike." He looked back over his shoulder. The figures were only a hundred meters away. He reached for the pistol strapped to his thigh.

"You need to help Mya, first."

That got his attention. Mya was leaning heavily on Aurora, her head drooping on her shoulder, even though he didn't see any sign of trauma.

"I'll take her." He wrapped his arm around Mya's shoulders and settled her onto the seat in front of him. She wobbled like an infant, and he tightened his grip. Whatever was wrong with her, it was serious.

Aurora hopped on behind him and slipped her arms around his torso. But rather than holding onto him, she placed her hands on Mya's upper arm and thigh. Cade felt a subtle tingle and then Aurora's energy shield enveloped them. His breath caught. He'd forgotten the incredible sensation of being surrounded by that energy.

A series of unintelligible shouts snapped his attention back to the creatures. They resembled rampaging beasts as they thundered toward him as quickly as their contorted bodies would allow, their arms flailing. The guard, however, had slowed, as though he was unsure how to deal with this new complication.

As Cade gunned the motor back to life, the outline of the hunched figures changed. Large wings unfolded from their backs, and they lifted off the ground, their voices and movements becoming wilder and more frenzied. A shot of adrenaline poured into his veins. Time to get the hell out of here.

Whipping the bike around, he took off in the opposite direction, the motor shrieking as it struggled to haul the weight of two additional passengers up the steady incline. Now that the creatures were airborne, it would be tough to outrun them, but they'd have just as much trouble navigating through the trees as he did. He could outmaneuver them, buying time for his reinforcements to arrive.

But when he checked the display, expecting to see the figures in pursuit, their heat signatures indicated they were moving to the east, back out of the orchard.

They'd caught a break. "It's okay," he called out to Aurora over the roar of the motor. "They're moving away."

She rested her head on his shoulder, her body sagging against him. Her energy shield flickered, too. She must be exhausted. She mumbled something he couldn't understand.

He slowed the bike so he could hear her. "What did you say?"

"I said, I know."

For some reason, her comment made the hair on his arms stand up.

They were almost to the edge of the orchard before she spoke again. "Stop."

He turned his head. "Stop? Why?"

"Kire. He still thinks we're out there."

Cade sighed. Now things would get complicated. She'd accepted his presence in the heat of the moment because she'd had to, but the questions would come fast and furious from here on out. And he was expecting a lot of furious.

Checking the display to confirm the figures hadn't changed course, he slowed to a stop. The sudden silence was oppressive.

She let go of Mya and tapped her earpiece. "Kire? Can you hear me?"

With her head so close to his, he caught Emoto's vocal response even over the distortion.

"Roe! I'm almost there. Where are you?"

"We're okay. Cade's here."

A pregnant pause followed her statement. Emoto had probably stopped his headlong rush so he could pay attention to the conversation. "Ellis is with you?"

"Yes. But Mya's not doing well. We need somewhere safe to go while we wait for Celia and Jonarel. Somewhere closer than the shuttle."

"Let me talk to Kelly. Hang on."

Cade turned his head so he could see her over his shoulder. "I have somewhere you can go." He'd already blown his cover. And now that he had her with him, he was determined not to let her out of his sight.

She was quiet for a moment. He would bet she was considering the wisdom of trusting him. Her voice didn't betray any emotion when she spoke to Emoto. "Cade has somewhere we can go."

"Where?"

"Where?" she asked him.

"It's a cabin about five kilometers up into the mountains."

She went very still. She was way too smart to think any of this was a coincidence.

And he was in serious trouble. Better to keep her agile mind working on the problems at hand. "I'll give you the coordinates and directions." He brought up the information on his comband and sent it to hers.

She took a moment to look it over before forwarding it to Emoto. "Kire, I've sent the information to you. Pass it on to Kelly, then contact Jonarel and Celia and apprise them of the situation. We'll discuss our next move when I see you."

He noticed she'd carefully avoided providing any identifying information as to where her crew was or what they were doing. She was at a disadvantage, something she would hate.

Emoto's tone indicated he wasn't pleased by the turn of events, either, but he kept his comments brief before signing off.

Cade restarted the motor and pointed the bike in the direction of the cabin.

Aurora brought her mouth next to his ear. "When we get there, you and I are going to have a long talk."

Her warm breath against the soft shell of his ear sent a tremor through his body, but her words produced a shiver of an entirely different kind. Odds were good he was heading into the lion's den.

Twenty-Three

They didn't speak as they drove up the winding mountain road to his team's temporary headquarters. Mya was unconscious, although her breathing was steady. Aurora's energy shield continued to surround them, but when they reached the clearing in front of the one story cabin, it abruptly disappeared.

He hadn't bothered alerting Drew, his second in command, to their impending arrival. She was in charge of monitoring all of the *Starhawke* crew's transmissions, so she would have already heard everything she needed to know.

He parked the bike next to the porch steps and shut off the motor. The front door opened and Drew stepped outside, her petite form temporarily backlit in the doorway.

She came down the steps, but halted a few feet away from the bike. "Emoto will be here shortly. Clarek and Cardiff are still in the ravine, but our team is in intercept range." The light from the front windows illuminated the wariness in her expression as she gazed at Aurora.

Aurora slipped off the bike and removed her visor. A similar wariness showed in her eyes. "How do you know my crew's locations?"

Drew glanced at him and he gave a slight nod. She turned back to Aurora. "I've been monitoring your communications."

The muscles around Aurora's mouth tightened. "I see." The two sharply clipped syllables spoke volumes.

Cade considered pointing out that without his interference, she and Mya might have been attacked or even killed by the creatures. But he liked his face the way it was, and Aurora looked far too eager to rearrange it for him. "What can we do for Mya?" he asked, swinging his leg over the back of the bike and lifting Mya into his arms.

The hostility dropped from Aurora's expression as she focused on her friend. "We need to get her inside. Do you have a bed or couch where we can lay her down?"

He nodded. "There are several rooms at the back. Come with me."

Drew held the front door open as he carried Mya through the doorway and down the hall. Aurora followed him into the small bedroom and turned on a light as he settled Mya onto the comforter. She was still unresponsive, and her skin had grayed out. He glanced at Aurora.

"Will she be okay?"

Aurora sat on the edge of the bed and clasped Mya's hands in hers. She took a deep breath and closed her eyes. Pearlescent energy bloomed to life, dancing around their joined hands and tripping lightly over their bodies.

The first time he'd seen that beautiful glow, they'd been in her dorm room at the Academy, absorbed in a passionate kiss. He'd felt the same tingling sensation he'd experienced tonight on the bike and when he'd pulled back to look at her, he'd seen that glow.

At the time, Aurora had been more shocked than he was. According to her, the energy was invisible to most people. For some insane reason, knowing that had made him feel special—that he could see a side of her that others couldn't. He'd cherished that knowledge, even after everything had fallen apart.

The glow faded and Aurora opened her eyes. "It's as though she's been drained of energy. I've done what I can, but the best thing for her right now is rest. I'll want to get her back to the ship as soon as the others arrive." She raised her hand to stifle a yawn as she stood. Her eyelids and shoulders were drooping, too.

He stepped closer. "What about you?" A lock of hair had pulled out of her braid and fallen over her forehead, adding to her road-weary appearance. "You look like you could use some rest."

She shook her head and pulled her shoulders back, though it seemed to take effort. "I'm fine." She placed her hands on her hips and fixed him with a steely gaze. "The only thing I need right now are explanations." Anger punctuated her words. "Like what the hell you're doing here and why you've been monitoring my crew."

Aurora was one of those people whose mere presence commanded attention, but when she was angry, she filled the space in a way that intimidated even the stout of heart. Of course, Cade knew better than most what she could do when provoked.

He rubbed a hand across the back of his neck to ease the growing tension there. "Those aren't easy answers to give." He gestured toward the hall. "Let's go to the main room so we don't disturb Mya."

She crossed her arms over her chest. "Okay."

The defensive posture told him just how wary she was. Either that, or she was tamping down the impulse to wring his neck. Either way, she had good reason for her anger. He was on very thin ice, with fissures in every direction. He'd have to tread carefully.

She followed him down the hall and into the small room that served as their command center. Cade motioned to Drew, who had resumed her seat at the monitoring station. "This is Bella Drew, my second in command. She's our tech specialist."

Aurora nodded at the other woman but faced him. "How many people are on this team of yours? And what exactly are you doing here?"

He was given a reprieve from responding by the sound of a male voice from outside and the banging of the front door. "Where are they?"

Emoto appeared in the entryway, his normally sunny expression eclipsed by a deep scowl. Justin Byrnes was right behind him. When Aurora caught sight of Byrnes, her mouth dropped open in shock.

He might as well start there. "You've already met my first officer, Justin Byrnes."

Justin smiled tentatively. "It's nice to see you again, Captain."

Aurora looked at a loss for words. She'd just learned the depth of the surveillance she'd been under. He didn't envy her that feeling.

She gave a tight nod of acknowledgment. "Mr. Byrnes."

Emoto crossed to Aurora, placing his hands on her shoulders. "Are you hurt?"

A ghost of a smile touched her lips. She shook her head. "No. I'm fine."

"Good." He glanced around the room. "Where's Mya?"

"In the back bedroom, sleeping."

"Is *she* okay?"

"She will be. I'll explain later. Have you spoken with Jonarel and Celia?"

"They're on their way."

She tilted her head in Cade's direction. "Apparently Mr. Ellis already has team members standing by to escort them."

The look Emoto gave him contained equal portions of dislike and distrust. "I had a feeling he might. Do they know where to locate them?"

"Their team has been monitoring us."

Emoto's expression darkened.

Aurora touched his arm. "I need you to tell Jonarel and Celia to rendezvous with Cade's team." She glanced at Cade. "Who will they be meeting?"

"Christoph Gonzalez, Tracy Reynolds, and Tam Williams." Or to be more specific, his weapons expert, security chief, and team doctor.

Aurora returned her attention to Emoto. "Contact Kelly and bring her up to speed, and find out the current status on the targets." She paused, her gaze swinging back to Cade. "Unless you already know the answer."

He didn't, but Drew spoke up.

"All of the targets have returned to the ravine. There's been no further sign of movement from them."

Aurora's head dipped as she bit her lip to keep from voicing her reaction to that statement. But she nodded in acknowledgment.

Emoto looked like he had some choice words to share as well, but after exchanging a glance with Aurora, he headed out the front door.

She rounded on Cade. "Is there somewhere we can talk? Privately?"

Time to face the music. He turned to Justin. "Contact the team and tell them to bring in Cardiff and Clarek. If anything changes, alert us immediately." He motioned to Aurora. "Follow me."

He led the way to the large family room. She settled on one end of the couch, so he sat in the overstuffed chair on her right, facing the doorway. She gazed at him steadily, saying nothing. He didn't have to be psychic to know she was reading his emotions. Most likely trying to ascertain where the deception ended and the truth began.

Emoto appeared in the doorway a moment later. "Everything's arranged." He joined Aurora on the couch. "Kelly will contact me if there are any problems."

"Thank you. Your timing is perfect. Mr. Ellis was just about to explain why he's been keeping us under surveillance."

"Good." Emoto looked like a general about to discipline a soldier who'd gone AWOL in the heat of battle. Not very reassuring.

Cade focused on Aurora. Admiral Schreiber might have his hide for what he was about to tell her, but the time for subterfuge was over. "Like your crew, mine is not an official part of the Galactic Fleet. We operate as independents on specific missions coordinated with the Galactic Council."

She cocked her head, digesting that bit of information. "So you report to the Council?"

"Not exactly. We're under the stewardship of one particular member."

"Which one?"

"Admiral Schreiber."

Frown lines appeared above the bridge of her nose. "He's the one who sent your team here?" She didn't sound as surprised as he'd expected.

"Yes."

Her eyes narrowed. "Did you receive your orders before or after my ship was commissioned for this investigation?"

"Before."

"So you would have been here regardless?"

He nodded. But she didn't look convinced.

She rested her head against the pillows that lined the back of the sofa. "What exactly *are* your orders?"

"Originally, it was my understanding that my team was being sent to Gaia for the same reason as yours—to investigate the cause of the destruction. If it turned out to be biological in nature, we would continue in our guise as Rescue Corps personnel to assist you in correcting the issue. If, however, it turned out to be a planned attack, we would handle the type of reconnaissance your team attempted tonight."

She frowned at his choice of words, but damn it, she had to understand how much better suited his team was for the job.

"Then why didn't Admiral Schreiber alert us to your presence after we determined the attacks were planned?"

Good question. "He believed your team could handle it on your own. He also didn't want us getting in your way."

"Hmm." Aurora's focus was starting to drift. Her head lolled against the couch cushions and her eyelids slid to half-mast.

Emoto spoke up. "I still don't understand why you've been keeping us under surveillance."

He chose his words carefully. "While the Admiral trusted your abilities, he was concerned for your safety. You didn't have the strength of a Fleet ship to back you up, and you're a small crew." He gazed at Aurora, who had finally lost the battle to keep her eyes open. "He wanted us close by so we could step in if needed to neutralize any threats."

Aurora's words came out on a sigh. "Which you did."

He nodded, although she couldn't see it. The stress of the evening had apparently caught up with her, her body claiming the rest it needed.

The silence stretched out. When she relaxed completely against the cushions and exhaled softly, Emoto sat forward, propping his elbows on his knees.

His tone was low but it cut deep. "That's fascinating background, Ellis, but what I really want to know is how you managed to be in exactly the right place at the right time to rescue Aurora and Mya tonight."

Cade was caught off guard. At the Academy, he'd only seen the fun-loving, easy-going side of Emoto. He'd never experienced Commander Kire Emoto, the Fleet officer. Even during their time together on the *Starhawke*, Emoto had chosen to ignore Cade rather than command him. But right now, despite his smaller stature and slim build, Emoto radiated authority, his every syllable indicating he expected his question to be answered to his satisfaction and without hesitation. Cade's respect for Aurora's choice in her first officer increased.

"We were monitoring your communications. When Aurora contacted you for help, per my orders from the Admiral, I provided assistance."

"And how did you manage to tap into our communications?"

"The Admiral provided the frequency."

Emoto swore. "So you didn't know that they would encounter a problem?"

"No."

"How did you pinpoint their location? They're wearing sensor suits."

"I used the comm signal."

Emoto glanced at Aurora. "But the creatures didn't have that information. How the hell did they know Aurora and Mya were even there?"

Cade was hesitant to give an opinion on that question. Something had occurred in the orchard that had driven Aurora to use her energy shield for protection. Whatever it was might also explain her reaction on the farm the previous day and Mya's strange collapse. However, he wasn't about to speculate. Emoto was her friend, someone she obviously trusted, but his line of questioning indicated Aurora hadn't revealed her secret to him. And Cade certainly wasn't going to be the one to tell him. "I can't say."

Emoto sighed, the fight going out of him. "Did your arrival scare them off at least?"

Cade snorted. "I don't think anything scares those things. They kept coming until their wings activated and they were hauled off their feet. The guard pulled them back against their will."

Justin appeared in the doorway. "The team has picked up Clarek and Cardiff. They'll be here shortly."

Wonderful. The temperature in the room was likely to go from cool to frigid once those two were in residence.

Justin's gaze flicked to Aurora, and his eyes clouded with concern.

Cade stood. "She's fine. Just resting." He turned to Emoto. "I think we should continue this outside."

Emoto followed him out to the front porch. The cool breeze felt good against Cade's skin, though it did little to soothe the growing tension in his body as he anticipated the impending arrival of Jonarel Clarek. He leaned against one of the railing posts, which gave him a clear view of the front door and the driveway while he remained in shadow. "Now I have a question for you. Who's Star?"

He'd surprised Emoto. To his credit, he recovered quickly. "Where did you hear that name?"

Cagey. He could respect that. "At one point Aurora asked you to provide her with a link to Star. I wasn't aware of anyone connected with the team who had that name. It sounded like she was on the ship. She definitely was helping with the surveillance."

Emoto gazed out into the darkness. "You'll have to ask Captain Hawke."

His use of Aurora's title was no accident. Whoever Star was, her presence on the ship appeared to be a carefully guarded secret, one Emoto was not about to share.

Movement in the driveway drew his gaze. Four shadows ghosted up toward the house, resolving into the forms of Reynolds, Gonzalez and Williams on their stealth pods, and Clarek and Cardiff on the Kraed glider.

"Take me to her."

Clarek's command wasn't directed at Cade, but it still grated up his spine, raising the hairs at the nape of his neck. It took every bit of willpower he possessed to keep his expression neutral as the oversized Kraed approached the house.

Cardiff was close behind, with Williams on her heels. The good doctor would want to assure himself no one from Aurora's crew needed medical attention. Reynolds and Gonzalez remained behind to secure the stealth pods.

As Clarek reached the porch, he caught sight of Cade. He paused with one foot on the bottom step, the light from the open doorway bathing his dark form in its glow. The hostility in the Kraed's eerie eyes would have intimidated most people, but this wasn't the first time he'd faced off against him. Last time, only Aurora's intervention had prevented a bloodbath. He held no illusions about how Clarek felt about him. The Kraed would gladly break him in half given the opportunity. Cade didn't plan to ever give him that opportunity.

"Where is she?" An accusation, not a question. Clarek's hands clenched at his sides as his lips pulled back from his teeth.

Cade gestured to the door. "Inside. She's resting on the couch."

Clarek exuded menace, but apparently his need to see Aurora overrode his desire to dismember Cade. With a low growl, he vaulted up the steps in a single stride and stalked into the house. Emoto and Cardiff followed.

The smart move was to stay put. However, contrarian that he was, Cade couldn't stop himself from heading inside, with Williams right behind him.

Clarek slipped silently into the family room. "Aurora?" He sat down beside her and cupped her face in his hands. "Can you hear me?"

Cade's stomach rolled. He'd suspected Aurora and Clarek were lovers, but he hadn't anticipated witnessing the depth of their emotional connection. He had the urge to punch something—hard. Clarek, if possible.

Aurora shifted, turning her cheek into Clarek's hand and whimpering softly, like she was in pain. Clarek pinned Cade with a hostile glare. "What happened?"

"She's fine." Cade hated the defensiveness in his voice. "She's just exhausted."

Surprisingly, Emoto came to his defense. "It's true. She was fine when I arrived. Tired, but fine."

Cardiff spoke up. "Where's Mya?"

Cade glanced at her. "She's sleeping in the back bedroom. Tonight's events took a lot out of both of them."

Clarek shifted his attention to Cardiff. "Is this what happened before?"

She shook her head. "This is different. If I didn't know better, I'd say she collapsed from extreme fatigue."

Clarek's thumb gently stroked Aurora's cheek. "Very well."

Cardiff glanced between Cade and Clarek, her gaze assessing. Trying to decide if a battle was about to ensue?

She turned to Emoto. "If everything's under control here, I'd like to go check on Mya." It sounded like she was asking for a second opinion.

Emoto's gaze flicked between Cade and Clarek as well. Clearly Aurora's entire crew knew there was no love lost between the two of them. Emoto nodded. "We're good here. Go ahead."

Williams moved to follow her. "If you don't mind, I'd like to join you." Doctors had trouble ignoring the unconscious.

Unlike Clarek, Cardiff didn't seem to be radiating hostility at Cade's team. "Of course." She led the way down the hall.

That left Cade, Clarek and Emoto with Aurora. Cade's anger at Clarek's proprietary behavior was a great antidote for his concerns about the creatures, his mission, and Aurora's safety. Clarek ignored him completely, his entire focus on Aurora, which only added to Cade's growing frustration. But what the Kraed did next nearly put him over the edge.

He began to sing.

The Kraed words were unintelligible to him, since he'd never studied the language, but the emotional content of the song was easy enough to follow. Judging by the expression on Clarek's face and tone of his voice, it was a song of love and devotion. And even worse, it seemed to be having the desired effect. A soft smile appeared on Aurora's lips and the color crept back into her pale cheeks.

Clarek shifted so that she was cradled against his chest with her head tucked under his chin, his arms around her in a loose hug.

Cade ground his teeth together. He must be a masochist, because despite his brain's continual urgings to leave the room, he couldn't get his feet to move. Not even when he realized Emoto was watching him, a speculative look on his face.

As the song ended, Aurora's mouth pinched in a subtle pout. Clarek murmured something to her, and her expression cleared as she relaxed against him.

Emoto walked over to Clarek. "We need to talk."

The Kraed finally looked up. His gaze flicked to Cade in warning, but he nodded. He tucked a pillow under Aurora's head as he slipped off the couch. He stroked the errant lock of hair off her forehead before he straightened.

Emoto's gaze fixed on Cade as they headed for the doorway. "You too, Ellis."

His temper flared at the command. But his curiosity got the better of him. With one last glance at Aurora, he followed them into the foyer.

Twenty-Four

Her body had rebelled. Aurora wasn't sure if she was dreaming or awake, but her limbs felt like iron weights attached to her torso. The slightest movement of her head created the uncomfortable sensation of being spun in a centrifuge, and her body ached as though she'd spent the day hiking uphill with a large sack of boulders strapped to her back.

She concentrated on breathing and reconnecting with her wayward muscles, testing one small group at a time. They responded, but with reluctance. Not a good sign.

Giving up on moving for a moment, she focused on her surroundings, trying to bring some order to her thoughts. How had she ended up in this condition?

Raised voices filtered in from somewhere nearby. The first one she recognized was Kire's. He seemed to be trying to diffuse a confrontation. The next voice surprised her. Jonarel. There was a forceful coldness to his words that sent a shiver of uneasiness through her. Then she identified the third voice. Cade. That clarified things.

Summoning what little strength she could muster, she forced her eyelids to lift against the pressure of gravity that very much wanted to keep them down. The sudden light blinded her. She blinked several times, bringing the room into focus. But nothing made sense. She was lying on a couch, not a bed, in a house that didn't look familiar.

The noise in the other room intensified. She turned her head, inhaling sharply as the room spun and dipped. Her gaze fell on the open doorway and the gates of her memory flew open. The creatures. Mya's collapse. Cade's rescue. The cabin.

Jonarel was here. And she had to get off the couch before the situation escalated.

Ignoring the protest from her aching body, she shoved to her feet, swaying on unsteady legs as she concentrated on keeping her balance. Her head pounded and her muscles shook, but she remained upright. Taking a cautious step forward, she tuned into the thread of the argument in the foyer.

When all the dots connected, her temper hit the red line in a heartbeat. Adrenaline poured into her veins, clearing the cobwebs and energizing her limbs as she stalked to the doorway.

Jonarel and Cade stood toe to toe. Cade's face had flushed red and he quivered in heated fury like a volcano about to erupt. Jonarel's golden eyes had darkened to black, his body poised like a cobra ready to strike. Kire's back was to her, but his arms were raised in a conciliatory gesture as he tried to get in a word between the increasingly rapid exchanges of condemnations.

"Enough!"

Silence swept the room as they all turned. Only Kire looked chagrined. Jonarel and Cade's postures continued to project the strong desire to commit bodily harm to each other. She understood the impulse. She felt the same way about both of them at the moment.

Some of that emotion must have telegraphed to her face, because they looked startled, though neither backed down from their aggressive stances. The anger in the room swirled around her, stalking her like a living beast, but she refused to give in. Taking a steadying breath, she held their gazes while she addressed her questions to Kire. "Where's Celia?"

He gestured to the hallway. "In the back bedroom with Mya."

Why hadn't the uproar brought Celia running? "Has Mya's condition changed?"

"Not that I know of."

Obviously he'd been too busy trying to prevent a brawl in the entryway. "Has there been any movement from the targets?"

Kire shook his head. "Kelly would have alerted me."

"How long since you checked in with her?"

"About half an hour ago, before you and I spoke with Ellis."

That was something at least. She hadn't been unconscious very long. She'd evaluate the *why* of her impromptu nap later.

"Check in with Kelly and let her know we'll be returning to the ship as soon as Mya's up to it."

"Yes, Captain." He stepped onto the porch, leaving her to face the two males responsible for the greatest challenges of her adult life.

Her anger simmered below the surface, but she held it in check. They'd both lost control. She would not.

Jonarel's hands were curled into loose fists, hiding the claws that protruded from the pads of his fingers. His posture was reminiscent of his Mr. Hyde impersonation in the *Starhawke*'s greenhouse. Time to get Dr. Jekyll back.

"Is there a problem, Mr. Clarek?"

His focus slid back and forth between her and Cade, a myriad of conflicting emotions spiraling around him. She kept her gaze on his face, willing him to let go of his anger. Slowly, his eyes lost their hard gleam. His body remained in a subtle battle ready pose, but he turned away from Cade and folded his hands behind his back. The movement emphasized the taut muscles of his chest and shoulders. "No, Captain."

"Glad to hear it." She had a lot more to say on the matter, but now was not the time. She still had to deal with Cade. "Go check on Mya and remain with her. I'll join you in a little while."

He didn't move. Instead, his attention shifted to Cade and his lip curled in a feral snarl. Clearly he did not want to leave her alone with his adversary.

In all the years they'd known each other, she'd never been in a position to discipline him for unprofessional behavior. This was the second time in as many days. She didn't like being in that role again, but his actions were forcing her hand.

She moved into his personal space and lowered her voice. "*Now.*"

His gaze met hers, revealing the battle raging inside. She'd seen that look once before. Ten years ago. In that instance, she'd had to take drastic measures to settle the internal debate for him. She would do it again if necessary, though she sincerely hoped he'd learned from that experience.

Apparently he had. Shooting a look at Cade that promised a slow, painful death if he stepped out of line, he gave Aurora the briefest nod of acknowledgment, then strode from the room without a word.

Not exactly the behavior she would have liked, but at least no one was bleeding.

That left Cade. He was watching her with justifiable wariness. She wanted to throttle him for causing trouble with her crew. And hug him for saving her life. Why did his actions always end up tearing her apart?

She glanced into the adjoining room where his team was intent on their tasks. Curiosity and discomfort pervaded the space. Mostly curiosity. She didn't want an audience for this discussion. She indicated for Cade to join her as she returned to the family room.

He followed, but chose to remain close to the doorway, his stance rigid.

Jonarel must have hit all his hot buttons. "What happened with Jonarel?"

Cade stared at the floor, the pictures on the walls, the ceiling—anywhere but at her. "Emoto wanted to talk about the situation with the creatures and Mya's collapse, to explain to Clarek why my team stepped in. But *your* boy wouldn't listen."

The emphasis on *your* caught her attention, as did the look in his eyes when he finally met her gaze. Up to this point his attitude had been guarded but friendly. Now, she was facing a stone wall.

She had no problem envisioning Jonarel as the instigator of the battle. His hatred ran deep. But what exactly had he said to Cade? Something awful, judging by the way Cade was reacting. He'd closed himself off behind a shield of rage.

She spread her hands in a conciliatory gesture. "I know you and Jonarel have never seen eye to eye, but he's a valuable member of my crew. And, given the parameters of your orders, the two of you will have to deal with each other on a regular basis for the foreseeable future." She took a step toward him and he flinched. She sighed. "Cade, I'm sorry I wasn't...available...to help smooth things over earlier. I knew any meeting between you two would be tense. This isn't how I would have chosen things to go."

The first chinks in his armor appeared, so she pressed on. "I never did thank you for rescuing Mya and me. I know you were doing your job, but I'm still grateful that you were there when we needed you."

She was making headway. Now he was studying her like she was a giant puzzle and he was missing several critical pieces. "You're welcome," he said at last, his voice husky. "How are you feeling?"

Awful. "Okay. A little out of sorts, but at least I'm back on my feet."

He frowned. "When you were sleeping, you reacted like you were in pain."

Oh, hell. She didn't want to think about Cade watching her while she was unconscious. She offered him a smile. "The encounter was an intense experience. I guess it wore me out. But I'll be fine."

His eyes narrowed. "Are you sure?"

She nodded, even though the motion made her head throb. "Absolutely. However, I do have one question that I need answered."

He tensed, but he held her gaze. "Okay."

"Can you work on the same team with Jonarel, or not?"

His eyes widened and his lips parted in surprise. Whatever question he'd been expecting, that wasn't it. "What do you mean?"

"Now that your team is no longer observing us covertly, the best way to accomplish our mutual goals is to combine forces."

"You want my team to work *with* you?" He stared at her in disbelief.

She stared back. "Yes. *If* you and Jonarel can learn to work together. I can't keep breaking up heated confrontations."

She could sense his internal conflict. His professional side would know she was right and might even be intrigued by the possibility. But his personal side probably loathed the idea of spending time with his mortal enemy. Which side would win?

Apparently his dedication to duty was stronger than his hatred. He nodded. "If there are any problems, it won't be because of me."

One huge leap accomplished. Hopefully Jonarel would have a similar attitude. "Thank you." She stepped toward the doorway. "I have a few things to discuss with Kire, but if your team will pack up whatever they need, they can join us on the shuttle to the ship as soon as we're finished here."

She'd surprised him again. His expression was truly comical. He managed to appear both horrified and delighted at the same time.

"You want us on the *Starhawke*?"

"It's where my crew will be." And it felt like karmic justice after his team had spent the past few days spying on her. Staying on her ship would shift the balance of power. It would also place Cade in close proximity to Jonarel, but she'd deal with that.

He cast out a weak argument. "I don't think the Admiral would approve."

"I disagree. He may not have wanted us to know about you initially, but now that we do, this plan makes sense. However, I understand if you want to discuss it with your team first. I'll give you a little time to talk it over." Without waiting for a reply, she headed out to the porch.

She found Kire standing near the railing, gazing up at the incandescent moon, as though he was trying to find some answers in its peaceful beauty.

He turned as she approached. Even in the dim light, worry lines showed on his face. "I'm so sorry, Roe." He shook his head. "I should have known better. I'd hoped Jon and Ellis could talk things out, that once I explained the situation, Jon would relax and focus on helping you. But those two are like flint and tinder. Jon struck the first spark and it all went to hell."

She leaned against the railing next to him. "It's not your fault. Jonarel and Cade in the same room would have been challenging in an ideal situation. Having them suddenly thrust together when I was incapacitated was a recipe for disaster."

"I heard what you said to Jon. How did you handle things with Ellis?"

She gave him a brief summary. "Hopefully I can extract a similar commitment from Jonarel."

"You will. His hatred of Ellis is strong, but his love for you is stronger."

Her heart squeezed. He was right, of course, but in many ways, that made the situation harder.

"What did Kelly have to say?"

"Not much. She and Star are going over the sensor data and will have a report ready when we return."

At least something had gone right. But she still had a plethora of questions. Maybe Kire could get some answers. "Would you be willing to hang out with Cade's team and see what you can learn while I go deal with Jonarel?"

The look he gave her said it all. "Of course."

Thank the universe for Kire. She honestly didn't know what she'd do without him.

Cade stood in the doorway to the temporary command center, talking with Mr. Byrnes, when Aurora and Kire stepped inside. Conversation ground to a halt as an undercurrent of tension pulsed around the room.

Time for diplomacy. "Kire and I would like to meet the rest of your team."

To Cade's credit, he didn't miss a beat. "Of course." He stepped into the small room and addressed his team. "I'd like you all to meet Captain Aurora Hawke and Commander Kire Emoto." He gestured to a trim blonde woman Aurora hadn't seen before. "This is Tracy Reynolds, our security specialist."

Reynolds gave a tight nod, her emotions indicating a reserve that contrasted sharply with the curiosity Aurora was picking up from everyone else. Then again, as a security specialist, her attitude made perfect sense.

Cade gestured to a stocky man with a shaved head and a serene expression. "Tam Williams, our team's doctor."

Ah, doctor. That fit with his calm demeanor.

Williams stood and extended his hand. "Captain." His tenor voice seemed at odds with his barrel chest and muscled physique.

She returned the handshake. He had a firm but gentle grip and kind eyes. "Dr. Williams."

Williams and Kire exchanged greetings as they shook hands.

The next member of Cade's team stepped forward. He was taller than Dr. Williams, with a tough, wiry build and a thin face full of laugh lines. "Christoph Gonzalez." He extended his hand before Cade could introduce him. "It's a pleasure to meet you."

The animated, positive energy he projected was infectious. She smiled. "And what's your specialty, Mr.

Gonzalez?" She was going to guess communications, or maybe reconnaissance.

"Weapons."

Her surprise must have shown on her face, because Gonzalez laughed. "Yes, I figure out how to blow things up for a living."

"Then I'll be sure to stay on your good side," she replied, earning her another chuckle as he shook hands with Kire.

Bella Drew, the petite brunette Aurora had met outside, introduced herself to Kire and Justin Byrnes stood to shake hands.

Aurora glanced at Cade. A flash of approval lit his green eyes. A small victory, but it was a start.

She left Kire to do what he did best as she headed for the back bedroom. The murmur of voices drifted out into the hallway.

Celia popped up from her chair when Aurora entered. "Aurora! How are you feeling?"

"Better." Which was mostly true. She wasn't unconscious anymore.

Celia's gaze swept over her. "I'm glad you're standing. When we got here, you looked like you were down for the count."

Aurora winced.

Celia's entire being radiated empathy. "Yeah, I know. I didn't want to leave Mya while she's still unconscious." Which explained why Celia hadn't tried to break up the confrontation in the foyer. "Care to fill me in on what's been going on?"

Aurora glanced at Jonarel. He was watching her intently.

"Jonarel and Cade had a disagreement."

Celia snorted. "So I gathered."

"I had a discussion with Cade, and we've made a preliminary plan for his team to work with ours." Jonarel growled, but she ignored him. "Can you go meet with them and set some ground rules? Find out what they can bring to the table to help us?"

"Absolutely."

Yet another friend she owed a drink.

Aurora walked over to the bed and sat down next to Mya. She brushed a lock of hair off Mya's forehead and clasped her hand. Her cheeks were still pale but her breathing was steady.

She glanced at Jonarel. "Things didn't go as we'd planned, did they?"

His expression was unreadable, his emotions carefully locked down. "No, they did not."

She sighed. How should she begin a discussion she'd never imagined having with him? Might as well be direct. "Are you ready to talk about the scene in the hallway?"

His voice was as devoid of emotion as his expression. "I am sorry you witnessed it."

Interesting word choice. "Sorry that I witnessed it? Or sorry that it happened in the first place?"

"I am sorry that we disturbed you."

Oh boy. His words fanned the embers of her anger, and she slowly counted to ten. She needed time to think. Jonarel didn't do anything without a solid reason. She just needed to extract that reason from his internal lockbox. "Talk to me."

She touched his arm and he flinched, but he didn't pull away. A muscle in his jaw twitched as his teeth clenched.

"Jonarel, tell me what happened." She dipped her head forward, trying to get him to look at her. "I need to know."

He remained silent, the seconds ticking by. He wasn't going to answer her.

But finally, ever so slowly, he bent his head to look into her eyes. The pain and sadness he revealed took her breath away.

"I am so sorry I failed you, Aurora."

She frowned. His words made no sense. "Failed me? How? By getting into an argument with Cade?"

The well of sadness deepened as he stared at her. He shook his head, his thick hair casting his face in shadow. "On the day we met, I made a vow to you. Whatever might happen to me, I would protect you, even at the cost of my own life."

How could she forget? She tightened her grip on his arm.

"You accepted me without question. You called me friend without hesitation. You stood by me without fear." His voice deepened with emotion. "I have honored that vow. I have watched over you, guarded you. But there was one thing I could not protect you from. One...person." The last word came out as a curse, and his eyes flashed fire.

"I wanted to avenge you at the Academy, but you stopped me." His muscles flexed beneath her hand. "Tonight, you encountered a threat I had not anticipated, one that might have cost you your life. That knowledge haunts me. But to discover that *he* had anticipated it. That *he* was there to protect you when I was not. I cannot..."

As his voice trailed off and he glanced away, she finally understood. Ten years ago, Cade had hurt her in a way that Jonarel had been unable to defend, to make right.

Apparently that failure had been a festering wound ever since, turning Cade into a living, breathing reminder of Jonarel's worst fear realized. And tonight, he'd succeeded where Jonarel had failed. He wasn't just angry at Cade. He was furious with himself.

She placed her palm on the side of his face, allowing the pads of her fingers to trace the delicate patterns on his skin. When he finally turned toward her, she leaned forward and brushed her lips against his before drawing back to hold his gaze. "I trust you with my life."

He reached a hand toward her.

"Sahzade?" Mya's voice was a faint puff of air, hardly even a whisper.

Aurora looked down. Her friend's eyes were open and focused on her. Their rich brown coloring looked dull, but at least she was awake.

She gave Mya's hand a reassuring squeeze. "Welcome back. How are you feeling?"

Mya licked her dry lips. "I've been better."

Jonarel removed his small hip flask and helped her sit up so she could take a few swallows of water.

She sank back down onto the pillows but her voice was a little stronger. "What about you? Everything's kind of a jumble." She glanced around the room in confusion. "Where are we?"

Not an easy question. Aurora wanted to keep the details to a minimum until Mya got her strength back. "A safe house. The rest of the team is here and we'll return to the ship as soon as you're up to it."

Mya looked between Aurora and Jonarel, picking up on the odd tension in the room. "I guess Kire rescued us."

Aurora shot a look at Jonarel, silently pleading with him not to contradict her. Mya was still weak. Aurora didn't want to add to the strain she was under by announcing the new complications that had resulted in their dramatic rescue.

Thankfully, he seemed inclined to follow her lead. "Everyone made it out safely," he said.

Mya sighed. "Thank goodness."

Celia appeared in the doorway. "Everything's set, Captain." She glanced at Mya and a warm smile lit her face. "Good morning, Sleeping Beauty."

Twenty-Five

Aurora had successfully outmaneuvered him. He shouldn't be surprised. She'd graduated at the top of her class for a reason. Still, Cade wasn't looking forward to finding out what the Admiral would have to say about the turn of events. He was also more than a little concerned about the promise he'd made regarding working with Clarek. He wasn't convinced it was one he could keep.

He'd avoided the Kraed during the move from the cabin, which had meant avoiding Aurora as well, since the male had refused to leave her side until they reached the shuttle. Byrnes had driven Emoto out to the orchard to pick up the other glider, and then they'd loaded the gliders, his bike, and the stealth pods in the transports. It had been tight, but they'd managed to fit everyone in.

When they'd reached the shuttle, Clarek had taken the controls and Aurora had settled into the co-pilot's chair. Cade was seated next to Byrnes and Drew in the first row of the main compartment, with Gonzalez, Williams and Reynolds behind them. Cardiff, Emoto and Mya had insisted on sitting in the back row. He suspected Emoto and Cardiff wanted to keep an eye on his team.

Mya still looked weak. She'd allowed Williams to do a bio scan before they'd left the cabin and he hadn't found anything physically wrong. She'd taken the news of the rescue well, and had actually seemed relieved to see Cade and his team.

Her reaction had surprised him. Mya was Aurora's oldest friend, so he'd assumed he'd be public enemy number one in her book. Apparently, his actions tonight had gone a long way toward altering that perception.

He still didn't have any idea why Mya and Aurora had needed rescuing in the first place. His brain kept supplying potential reasons, but he didn't have any facts to hang them on. Whatever the cause, he couldn't shake the feeling that the creatures tied in somehow.

Byrnes let out a low whistle as the shuttle approached the ship. "And I thought the shuttle was impressive."

Cade glanced out the window. He hated to admit it, but the *Starhawke*'s graceful design was breathtaking. He understood Justin's open appreciation.

Aurora glanced over her shoulder. "Kraed have a gift for blending function and aesthetics." She gestured toward the ship. "Jonarel designed her and oversaw her construction. Everything you see is a result of his efforts."

Cade tried not to be bothered by the admiration in her tone. He really did.

Her gaze shifted to him. "Kelly has arranged quarters for your team. She put you in the same cabin you had during the trip here."

"Thank you." Although he doubted he'd be spending much time in it. "And after we've stowed our equipment?"

"Report to the observation lounge. We'll meet you there to discuss our strategy."

Half an hour later, he joined the rest of his team in the lift, headed for the main deck. The doors slid open to reveal a curved walkway that followed the exterior wall and led toward the stern. At the end they encountered double doors with cutouts in curving shapes filled with colored glass or crystal. The design filtered light through from the room beyond, making the doors glow softly. They parted soundlessly as his team approached.

The observation lounge was aptly named. A two hundred degree curved panorama of the star field greeted them. A large table with a dozen chairs sat toward the back of the room, and smooth inclines led to smaller tables positioned closer to the windows. The tables looked like they had been carved from tree trunks, with the elaborate roots forming the base, surrounded by chairs of a similar design.

Byrnes pivoted in a circle. "The Kraed don't do anything halfway, do they?" He walked up one of the inclines and stopped in front of the tall windows, which offered a spectacular view of Gaia.

Drew and Gonzalez joined him. "You won't see this kind of set-up on a Fleet ship, that's for sure." Drew indicated a doorway at the back of the room. "What's through there?"

Cade followed her gaze. "The kitchen. Emoto said this room serves as a dining hall and off-duty space."

Justin ran his hand over the surface of the table to his right. "I can see why. If I were living on this ship, I'd certainly spend time here."

"Well you're in luck, Byrnsie." Drew punched him lightly on the arm. "For the next day, you *are* living on this ship."

Justin grinned at her.

Some inner sense prompted Cade to glance over his shoulder. Aurora stood at the back of the room, watching them with a bemused smile. He hadn't even heard her enter.

"What do you think of our observation lounge?"

He told her the truth. "Impressive."

Her smile widened. "If you're going to spend your life among the stars, you should have a great view."

She'd left him an opening, and he couldn't resist taking it. "Yes, you should." Her presence had definitely increased the appeal of the room.

An emotion flickered in her eyes as they stared at each other. Her smile disappeared, but she didn't look away. "Celia's put together some snacks to fortify us before the discussion."

"Cardiff cooks, too?" Justin murmured under his breath.

Cade had picked up on his first officer's infatuation with the *Starhawke*'s security chief.

Drew poked him in the ribs. "Just be sure to keep your tongue in your mouth, Byrnes. No woman likes a drooler."

Justin ignored her, focusing on Aurora instead. "This ship is amazing."

"Thank you. We're fond of her."

Behind her, a curved section of the wall pushed out in a gentle arc, the top opening like an oyster to reveal platters of fresh vegetables, fruits, and sandwiches. Another section opened onto a neat row of plates and glasses next to pitchers filled with assorted beverages.

Justin looked intrigued. "Is that tied to the kitchen on the other side of the wall?"

Aurora nodded. "It's much more efficient than hauling everything."

Drew seemed equally impressed. "What I'd like to know is how you acquired all this fresh food. It can't be from Gaia, since they're under quarantine. Did you bring it with you?"

"The food is from the greenhouse." They all turned as Clarek stepped through the main doorway and crossed the room, coming to stand beside Aurora.

The oversized Kraed had placed himself between Aurora and Cade. No way was that accidental.

"You have a greenhouse? On the ship?" Drew's eyes widened.

Clarek nodded. "The ship is designed to be self-sufficient for extended periods of time."

"But how do you accomplish that?" Drew had slipped into tech mode. "You don't always have a stable solar source."

"True. But the ship can store solar energy and reproduce it in the same conditions plants would experience on Earth. The greenhouse creates day, night, season and temperature changes, and even wind and rainfall. As far as the plants are concerned, they are growing on Earth, not on a starship."

"Incredible." Drew glanced at Aurora. "Could I see the greenhouse?"

Aurora smiled. "Of course. When we have time, I'd be happy to give you a tour."

A stab of irrational jealousy speared Cade. That was more than she'd offered him.

Drew lit up like a Christmas tree. "I'd love it. Thank you."

"Can I come, too?" Justin asked, his expression uncharacteristically subdued. He'd mentioned to Cade that he anticipated being persona non grata with Aurora's crew after playing a lead role in the covert surveillance.

But Cade knew Aurora better than Justin did, and she didn't disappoint him.

"Yes, Mr. Byrnes. You would be welcome, too."

Justin beamed. "Thanks."

And just like that, Aurora befriended two of his team members. From the looks on their faces, her natural charm was winning over Gonzalez and Williams, too. It wouldn't be long before they'd align themselves with her and follow her anywhere. Aurora had that effect on people, whether she meant to or not.

He should know. She'd done the same thing to him many years ago.

Only Reynolds seemed unmoved. But then again, that was her job.

Aurora gestured to the food. "Please, help yourselves. I'm sure you're all hungry. The rest of the crew should be here shortly."

His team filled their plates as the remaining *Starhawke* crewmembers arrived and everyone settled in at the table.

Cade selected the chair across from Aurora. Conversation was minimal as everyone focused on the meal, the platters of food rapidly emptying. But he could feel Aurora's gaze on him.

She took a sip from her glass and cleared her throat. As silence descended, she folded her forearms on the tabletop. "Before we discuss our plans going forward, I want to thank Mr. Ellis's team for agreeing to work with us on this mission."

The acknowledgment was unexpected. The flash of anger that appeared on Clarek's face was not.

"It's my hope that by combining forces, we can achieve a quicker and more effective resolution than either team could accomplish alone." She glanced around the table. "With that in mind, does anyone have a recommendation for how we might proceed?"

Cardiff wiped her fingers on her napkin. "We need to find a way to detain the—" She made a swirling motion with her hand. "Whatever we're going to call those creatures." She frowned. "They need a name."

"You're right," Aurora said. "Any suggestions?"

"How about Night Monsters?" Emoto said. "That's what the child at the RC headquarters called them."

Cade's head snapped up. Some child at the refugee camp had seen those things and no one had told him?

Cardiff shook her head. "Too wordy. We need something concise and descriptive."

"What about Leechers?" Justin suggested.

"Not bad." Cardiff replied. "Except these things kill. Leeches generally don't."

"True."

"Vile Vultures?" Drew volunteered. "It's what they look like."

"That's still long," Gonzalez said.

Silence fell. Everyone in the room seemed to give a collective shrug.

"Necri."

The word hung in the air like a dark cloud as the focus shifted to Aurora.

"Necri," Mya echoed softly. "Well, that definitely fits. They are death personified."

Having seen the creatures up close and personal, Cade had to agree. "Any objections?" No one offered a dissenting opinion. "Then Necri it is." He held Aurora's gaze. "And getting back to Cardiff's plan, she's right. We need to detain the Necri without putting the Gaians at risk. We also need to get onboard their ship. There's a good chance we'll find most of our answers there."

Williams leaned back in his chair, the weight of his upper body making the wood creak. "It's my understanding that Clarek and Cardiff got a good look at the transport vessel tonight. What are we dealing with?"

Clarek responded first. "The design is unusual. The hull is heavily shielded with smooth plates. The physical shields prevent sensors from penetrating the interior. They also extend to the ground, enclosing the landing gear and lower levels. We were unable to locate any access points."

"The Necri are using what appears to be a shuttle bay to exit," Cardiff said. "They left it open during tonight's attack. Our best bet is to slip in through the opening right after the Necri and guards leave." She tapped her fingers against the table. "But that bay is a good forty meters above the ground. Even if we found a way to get inside, a squad of guards could be waiting for us and we wouldn't know until it was too late."

"We could use the trees," Clarek said.

Aurora glanced at him. "What do you mean?"

Cardiff was already nodding. "You're right. We'd have visibility and access inside." She glanced around the table, her gaze settling on Reynolds, her counterpart on Cade's team. "The entire ship is surrounded by tall trees with wide branches. Climbing them would be easy, and it would put us on a level with the open bay door. We could see inside before we had to enter."

Reynolds looked intrigued by the plan. "And we could use zip lines to slip over after the Necri and guards have exited the ship."

"Sounds like we have the first two members of the assault team," Cade said. No surprises there. Cardiff and Reynolds had both been trained for this type of operation.

"Which brings us to the Necri and guards." He turned to Drew. "What do we know about them?"

Drew tucked her hair behind her ears. "Each of the winged units is controlled by a signal that's sent by one of the guards, approximately ten Necri per guard. The entire group follows a rudimentary flight path for their initial formation and return flight, but as the events from tonight prove, the guards can override those commands and take control of the individual Necri if necessary." She glanced at Aurora before continuing. "There's no indication of signals coming from the ship itself. Everything is handled by the guards."

"Which means if we control the ship, we still don't control the Necri and guards." Emoto laced his fingers together. "We need to be able to override those signals somehow."

Drew nodded. "There should be a way to hack in, but I need time to analyze the data from tonight's attack."

"How much time?" Cade asked.

"That depends." She looked at Clarek. "Are you available to help me?"

He nodded. "Of course."

Drew smiled. "Then we can be ready by tonight."

Cade glanced at Justin, who was gazing out the window at the planet. "Byrnes? Any thoughts?"

"Something doesn't fit." Justin's focus shifted to Aurora. "Captain, do you know how the Necri were able to track you and Dr. Forrest so easily?"

Aurora's expression shuttered. "No, I don't."

Justin sat forward. "But clearly they knew you were there. It just seems to me that the movement was focused, with obvious intent. What if they were trying to establish contact, to communicate somehow?"

Reynolds smirked. "No offense, Byrnes, but you always think everyone's trying to communicate. From what I heard, it was an aggressive move, not an attempt to chat."

Justin frowned. "Then why did the guards only send five of the Necri rather than the whole group? For that matter, why did the guard pull them back as soon as Cade arrived? One person shouldn't have made much of a difference considering their destructive capability. They also could have easily brought in reinforcements to finish the job if that was their intent. But they retreated instead."

It was an excellent point. Cade was embarrassed he hadn't considered it himself.

Aurora looked similarly stunned.

Reynolds scowled. "I don't know. But unless we get a look inside that transport or somehow capture the Necri, we'll just keep talking ourselves in circles."

"Which brings us to how we're going to handle the guards and Necri after we take control of their transport signals," Cade said. "It's unlikely they'll go quietly." He turned to Gonzalez. "Any ideas?"

Gonzo stroked the close-cropped beard on his chin as he considered the question. "I can establish a containment fence as a holding area, and disperse an inhalant so they'll be knocked unconscious. I just need someone with me to assist and monitor the targets after they're down."

"I can do that," Byrnes offered.

"I want Kire to join you as well," Aurora said. "We'll need both of you to keep the teams informed of the status so we can coordinate our efforts."

Cade leaned forward. "You said teams. Do you have a third team in mind?"

She nodded. "Since Mya and I don't know how the Necri were able to locate us, I think it would be wise if we avoided close contact. We can be in charge of transportation and act as the command center for the other two teams."

Good. That plan placed Aurora in the safest possible position, far from the Necri. "Can you fly the shuttle?" He honestly didn't know.

"Yes. But if Jonarel joined us, he could pilot the shuttle and then control the Necri and guards from our location." She glanced at Drew. "Are you okay with that?"

Drew nodded. "I'd much rather get a look at the ship."

Cade liked how this was shaking out. "Williams and I will fill out the assault team. I assume Kelly will be remaining here?" He glanced at the young pilot, who'd remained silent through the entire discussion. She nodded.

Aurora's gaze flicked briefly to his. "Then we have a plan. Let's get to work."

Twenty-Six

*Then why did the guards only send five of the
Necri rather than the whole group? For that matter, why did
the guard pull them back as soon as Cade arrived?*

Aurora sat at her desk, staring out the viewport.
Sorting through the mystery of the Necri felt a lot like
putting together a picture puzzle without knowing what the
final image looked like.

Why had the Necri tried to reach them? Byrnes's
comments made an attack seem unlikely, but what other
reason was there? What would have happened if Cade
hadn't arrived in time? And how the hell had they known she
and Mya were nearby in the first place? The Necri hadn't
taken note of anyone else, even though Jonarel and Celia
had been right under their flight path.

The physical response she'd experienced to the
Necri's nearness was not a coincidence. Of that she was
certain. The sequence of events indicated they'd sensed her
presence as well. It was the only answer that fit the facts.
But the implications staggered her. And it wasn't something
she wanted to share with the group, especially now that
Cade's team was onboard.

With a frustrated sigh, she shoved out of her chair
and headed toward the bridge, determined to do something
productive rather than running circles in her head.

The chime of the door stopped her. "Yes?"

When Cade's solid form filled the doorway she took
an involuntary step backward.

His gaze locked on her like a magnet. "I need to talk to you. If you have a moment," he added when she hesitated. But his expression made it clear she'd get an argument if she said no.

She really wasn't in the mood for a verbal sparring match.

He stepped directly in front of her. "Please." That was a word she'd rarely heard from Cade's lips.

She met his gaze. Worry lurked in his green eyes. Something was really bothering him. "All right." She gestured to the chairs by the viewport and perched on the one closest to her desk.

He dwarfed the second chair, making the room feel smaller, more intimate. He studied her closely. "I need to know what happened to you and Mya in the orchard."

So that's why he was here. She should have guessed. "Why?"

He made a noise in his throat. "Why wouldn't I? It's my job to protect you, and I can't do that if you're keeping key information from me." He rested his forearms on his knees. "I know something happened, and I suspect it's tied to your abilities."

She glanced out the window. What should she tell him? What *could* she tell him? After all, she had more questions than answers.

He must have taken her silence as a rejection, because he reached forward and clasped her hand in his. The contact sent a zip of energy up her arm. Her gaze flipped back to his. The intensity in his green eyes didn't help matters, or the warm timbre of his voice. "I won't share anything with my team that you don't want me to. I promise. But Aurora, I *have* to know."

He was right. Hiding the truth wasn't going to help their situation.

"I can't explain why, but Mya collapsed the moment the Necri began destroying the plants. It was almost like their actions were somehow draining the life out of her, too."

His eyebrows lifted, but he remained silent, obviously sensing there was more coming.

He wasn't going to like what she said next. "And my first instinct was to move toward the Necri, not away."

His hand snapped closed, caging her fingers in. His voice deepened to a growl. "If that's true, neither one of you has any business being down on that planet tonight."

She pulled her hand from his grasp. "I disagree. Mya was only affected when they began the attack, and activating my energy shield helped her. If everything goes to plan, there won't even *be* an attack tonight."

"And what does Mya think about this?"

"She agrees with me." In fact, they'd discussed this very point as soon as they'd returned to the ship. "Last time we were unprepared. That won't happen again."

"And what if you're wrong?"

"Then we'll be far, far away from the Necri where they can't affect us." He might not like it, but she couldn't ignore the persistent voice that was telling her she *needed* to be there.

He shoved his hands through his hair. "I don't know, Aurora." His gaze searched hers. "Why can't you wait until after we capture the Necri and the ship? Then you can get your answers without putting yourself in harm's way."

"Are you listening to yourself?" She shook her head. "I know you're worried about me." She stopped him when he started to protest. "Let's be honest, okay? And I appreciate your concern. But you have to understand that this is *my* command, *my* ship, and *my* choice. I'm not going to take unnecessary risks, but I have a job to do and I *will* be with the rest of the team tonight."

He swallowed hard, holding her gaze. "Why do I always feel like I'm in a no-win situation with you?"

She could feel his frustration, and a lingering sadness that pulled at her. But she couldn't help him.

He searched for signs of uncertainty in her gaze. When he didn't find any, he sat back. "I have one more question for you."

She waited.

"Who is Star?"

Her jaw dropped open. At least, that's how it felt. How the hell had he found out about Star? But the answer came to her in a flash. She'd been talking to Star shortly before Cade had arrived in the orchard. He'd said his team had been monitoring all their communications. He would have heard their conversation.

He was watching her, waiting for an answer.

And she realized she needed to give him one. After all, Star might end up being pivotal if anything went wrong. As the co-commander of the mission, he needed to have a working knowledge of the assets at his disposal. But that didn't mean she had to reveal the truth.

"Star is a member of the crew."

His eyes narrowed. "Meaning what? Was she a member of the Fleet? What's her role?"

"She has an extensive knowledge of the ship's systems and can manage just about every task the ship requires to function."

He frowned. "Why didn't the Admiral mention her?"

She stared him down. "Because he doesn't know she's onboard. And I would ask you to keep her presence a secret."

"A secret? Is she underage or something? Or a former felon?"

She almost laughed. Star was certainly not a minor or a criminal. "No. She's just very protective of her privacy. Our crew respects that. I'm asking you to do the same. If she can be of assistance, she'll contact you."

He wanted to push for more information—she could see it in his eyes. But he wasn't going to get anything more from her.

He let out a frustrated sigh. "Okay."

He stood. So did she. But he paused on his way to the door. "Promise me something."

What now?

"Stay close to Clarek tonight."

What? She must have heard him incorrectly. But the look in his eyes said otherwise.

He must be *really* worried about her. At least it was an easy promise to make. "I will."

After the door closed behind him, she drew in a deep breath, holding it to the count of ten before releasing it. What a fascinating and bizarre turn of events.

The door chimed a moment later. Was he back with more questions?

"Come in."

But instead of Cade, Jonarel stepped inside. Star appeared a moment later. An aura of tension followed them, but that might have been a result of passing Cade on the way. "What's up?"

"Tehar and I have been going over the information I gathered from the enemy ship. We have confirmed something I suspected when I saw it." His expression indicated whatever he had to tell her was leaving a bad taste in his mouth.

"And?" Aurora prompted.

"The hull construction is Kraed."

Aurora's mind blanked. *Kraed?* "You mean we're dealing with a Kraed ship?"

Jonarel's eyes flashed fire. "Definitely not. The design is nothing that a Kraed would create. But the shielding on the hull is the same compound used for all Kraed ships."

She worked hard to connect the dots. "But the Kraed have never shared that technology with anyone, have they?"

"No." His voice rumbled with anger. "That would go against our beliefs. The raw materials come from our home planet. Many are difficult to locate elsewhere. They are a part of our world, and we would never allow others to take them."

"But surely there are ways someone might have obtained the technology. What happens to ships that are severely damaged beyond repair?"

"They are brought back to Drakar so the Nirunoc can move into a new form before the materials are reused for another vessel."

"What if a ship can't be brought back?"

Star's voice filled the room. "That would mean abandoning the Nirunoc who inhabits it."

Which a Kraed would never do. "Have any ships ever been lost where no one survived, including the Nirunoc?"

Star's honey-colored eyes filled with sorrow. "One. Long ago, during our early interactions with the Setarips. We had not yet realized their true nature, and they took the ship and crew by surprise. During the battle the ship was caught in the gravitational pull of a nearby planet and crashed. All onboard were killed."

"Did the Kraed recover the ship?"

Jonarel's expression matched Star's, pain etched in his features even though the event must have occurred before his great-grandparents were born. "The planet generated lethal heat and radiation fields. Any salvage attempt would have resulted in the deaths of those sent to the surface."

Great. Now they had one more mystery to solve.

Twenty-Seven

Aurora sat cross-legged on the rock outcropping that served as the team's command post, her gaze to the west where the enemy ship lay hidden among the canyons and trees. The sun had long since slipped past the horizon, the lingering hues of red, orange and pink replaced with the black of night.

The running lights of the shuttle ten meters behind her illuminated Mya to her right, her short dark hair ruffling in the breeze. Inside the shuttle, Jonarel worked with Star in preparation for hacking into the Necri signals.

The remaining team members had left hours ago to take their posts. Kire, Byrnes and Gonzalez had headed into the forest area to the northwest, making their way toward a decimated field beyond the tree line. That part of the landscape had been subjected to a Necri attack prior to her crew's arrival at Gaia. It would be perfect for the containment fences they'd use to hold and incapacitate the guards and Necri.

Cade, Williams, Drew, Reynolds and Celia had made their way toward the ship itself. Their task was the most dangerous—safely accessing the ship through the open bay doors. Of course, that was only the first hurdle. They also had to face the small matter of taking over the bridge and disabling the ship's engines while incapacitating the crew.

That left Kelly and Star to intercept the enemy ship if it powered up and attempted to leave Gaia.

Aurora glanced at Mya. "I hope this works."

Mya looked at her in surprise. "What are you worried about?"

Apprehension tapped along her nerve endings, making her restless. "I don't know." She pictured the eight people out in the darkness, traveling into uncharted territory. "I just don't want to be wrong."

Mya's brows drew down. "You're really hard on yourself, you know that?" She shook her head. "Sahzade, I know you hate not having all the answers. I get it." She paused, her gaze assessing. "Are you worried because you're not on the front lines this time?"

Was that it? She'd never considered the possibility, but it rang true. In all her Fleet missions, she'd either been following someone else's orders, or she'd led the team, facing the same dangers as those under her command. In this situation, she'd given the orders but couldn't actively protect those around her. No wonder she was jittery.

She rubbed her forehead with the tips of her fingers, trying to ease the tension that had gathered there. "I'm not used to risking other people's lives without risking my own, too."

"I know. But you can't be responsible for everyone and everything all the time."

Leave it to Mya to tell it to her straight.

"I am curious about something, though."

Aurora glanced at her.

"Why haven't you told Kire your secret?"

Aurora blinked. The question seemed like a non-sequitur. "Why do you ask?"

"Because there've been a few instances during this mission when that information would have been valuable to him. But you haven't said a word. I'm just curious why you're holding back."

Why indeed? Mya was much better at handling the secret of her non-human ancestry without allowing it to define her life. "Kire's always been the tough one." Aurora traced the patterns in the rock with her fingertip, drawing strength from the solid feel of the stone. "Even though I've never said anything to him, I know over the years he's picked up on clues that there's something...different about me."

"But he's never pushed for explanations?"

"No." That wasn't his style.

"You trust him, don't you?"

"Of course I do. It's not that." This went deeper than trust. She sat up and brushed the dirt from her palms. "Honestly, I think I've always feared it would change our relationship. Jonarel was different. He found out the day we met, and he understood immediately. And Cade..." She let the sentence hang. No need to rehash that situation. Mya had been at ground zero. "But Kire is human, born and raised. And he's always assumed I am, too."

Understanding lit Mya's eyes. "You're afraid you'll lose the closeness you share."

"I know it may sound crazy, especially since his best friend is a Kraed. But if I lost his friendship, or even if it changed." She closed her eyes and swallowed around the lump in her throat. "I'm not sure I could handle having him look at me like I'm...*other*." Cade had taught her all too well how that felt.

"Are you so certain he would?"

"No. In fact he probably wouldn't." After all, Kire cared about her, loved her like a sister. He'd proven that time and again. "But what if I'm wrong? It's not something I can undo." And she needed him, now more than ever.

Mya's lips pursed. "True, but—"

Her reply was cut short as Cade's voice came over the comm line. "The bay door is opening."

Twenty-Eight

Celia surveyed the forest from her perch in the branches of one of the trees surrounding the enemy transport. Ellis, Williams and Drew were to her left, partially concealed by the massive trunk, their black sensor suits blending with the deep shadows of the foliage. Reynolds was propped against the branch to her right, her gaze fixed on the hull of the ship that rose thirty meters overhead, dwarfing the enormous trees in the steep ravine.

The trees provided the perfect spot to monitor the bay door ten meters below, where the Necri would exit and their team would enter. She and Reynolds were in charge of making the initial foray into the ship. Only after they'd secured the interior would the rest of the team join them. If all went well, they would be on their way to the bridge before the Necri and guards reached the base of the mountain.

She spotted movement a split second before Ellis's voice came over the comm channel. "The bay door is opening."

She lifted the small launching device that lay against her palm and sighted down the scope, then fired. A thin cable shot across the space between the tree and the ship, snapping tight as the anchor made contact with the ship's hull and locked on. She attached the device to the stabilizer wrapped around the tree's trunk, then grabbed the handgrips. Sliding down the cable, she landed silently against the ship's hull five meters above the doorway. Reynolds followed behind.

The Necri and guards exited the bay, the metal of their wings flashing in the moonlight as they flew through the trees.

Celia fed a second cable through the anchor and secured it to the harness around her waist. She crept to the edge of the bay, waiting for the command from Ellis.

"All clear."

She swung inside and dropped to the floor. The interior was shadowed, the only light coming from pale strips that ran along the floor, outlining the open space just inside the bay door. No sign of movement. That was a good start.

However, she was unprepared for the overwhelming stench of bodily excretions and other noxious odors that hit her olfactory system like a sledgehammer. Her gag reflex kicked into high gear, threatening to empty the contents of her stomach. The ammonia content of the air was so high her eyes began to burn. She slapped her left hand over her nose and mouth while she pulled out her weapon and panned it around the space

Reynolds's posture indicated she was having the same rough adjustment to their surroundings. The pithy swear word she muttered confirmed it, especially considering what they were smelling.

To the left and right of the entrance, doors swung wide on a row of vacant cells that formed a low wall five meters high. The cells themselves were tiny, no more than two meters square. Other than a long drain panel that ran along the back of each cell, they were empty—no bedding, seating or sanitization facilities. That explained the smell.

If this was where the Necri were kept in between attacks, they lived enclosed in spaces that were too small for them to even lie down and stretch out. From what she could see, the entire room was filled with cells just like these in rows that ran to the back walls on both sides.

She'd experienced this type of solitary confinement in the prison camps of her youth. She understood intimately the mental and physical anguish such conditions caused. At one time, such a sight would have triggered a violent emotional response. But she'd learned to deal with those memories so they couldn't hurt her anymore. However, the presence of the cells shed a very different light on the role the Necri played in the attacks.

Reynolds relayed the all clear to the rest of the team, her voice muffled by the hand she held over her face. "The bay is secure."

Within moments Williams, Drew and Ellis joined them. Drew was the first to speak, her voice incredulous. "They keep the Necri locked up in here?"

Anger carved grooves on Ellis's face as he approached one of the cells. "No creature should live like this." He shook his head in disgust and tapped his earpiece. "We've entered the bay. No sign of any guards, but the room is full of small cells. It looks like this is where the Necri are kept in between attacks."

"They're prisoners?" Aurora's voice indicated her shock.

"Apparently. And not well cared for, either. We're proceeding inside."

"Acknowledged." Aurora replied. "We'll keep the Necri and guards busy out here. Good luck."

Celia and the rest of the team followed Ellis as he moved toward the security panel beside the narrow door on the far wall.

Ellis glanced at Drew. "We need that open."

"Give me a minute." She placed a small device onto the panel and keyed in a command. Lights flickered, then the panel flashed green and the lock disengaged, the door sliding open to reveal a short corridor.

Ellis bypassed the open lift in favor of a metal stairway that disappeared into an opening in the floor. Dropping to the ground, he eased over the edge, weapon at the ready. Apparently satisfied, he indicated for Celia to lead the team down.

The smell on the lower level was considerably improved. Unfortunately, the corridor they were in led in one direction down the center of the ship, with no openings visible on either side. No cover or escape routes. It was minimally lit, much like the Necri holding area, but there would be no hiding in the shadows if they were discovered. They'd be targets in a shooting gallery. Not that they had any choice.

Keeping close to the walls, they crept forward. Celia raised her hand to halt their progress when the solid walls gave way to windowed partitions and doorways with open grills near the top. She strained to pick up any sounds coming from inside that might provide a clue to what they would encounter. Eventually she heard something, though it was so out of place that she didn't immediately identify it. It sounded like...crying.

Crouching below the line of the glass, she motioned for Ellis, Drew and Williams to stay put and provide cover. Reynolds moved to the opposite wall and followed her down the corridor until they were directly in front of the door where the sound was emanating. Celia pressed her body against the cool metal, sliding up until she could peer through the glass into the space beyond...and forgot to breathe.

Twenty-Nine

Kire glanced at the chronometer on his comband. Based on Ellis's last communication, the Necri would be in visual range any moment.

No sooner had the thought crossed his mind then the dark cloud emerged to the west, cresting the ridge and passing beyond the shelter of the woods.

Jon's voice came over the comm. "Overriding the signals now. Stand by to activate the perimeter fence and inhalant."

"Acknowledged."

Gonzalez stood to Kire's right, near the fence generators. He'd set up two separate containment zones, one for the guards and a much larger one for the Necri.

Byrnes was next to him, the signal pad for the inhalant emitters in his hand.

"On their way," Jon said.

In the distance, the swarm of dark shapes abruptly changed course, sweeping in a wide arc and heading for the edge of the forest where Kire's team waited.

As they drew closer, he could see the guards fighting with their wing harnesses. Some slammed them with their fists while others pulled out their weapons and took aim at the devices.

"Jon, we need those guards grounded ASAP."

Immediately the contingent of guards broke away from the Necri and moved in a rapid dive toward the ground. With a few meters to spare, the dark shapes abruptly swung upward in a tight three-hundred-sixty-degree loop. When the guards finally touched down they staggered, disoriented by the unexpected somersault.

That was Gonzalez's cue. The perimeter fence activated, trapping the guards inside. Byrnes triggered the inhalant and the figures began to fall like dominoes.

"The guards are down," Kire said.

"Bringing in the Necri," Jon replied.

Unlike the guards, the Necri seemed to accept the change in plan without any concern. Within moments they were assembled in a close pack on the ground inside the perimeter fence. The inhalant took longer to affect them, however, and the results were less obvious. Most of them simply dropped to their knees in a slumped position. Considering how close they were to the ground in their natural posture, it wasn't easy to tell the difference.

"Necri are out as well."

"Acknowledged," Jon said. "No changes from the enemy ship. They may be unaware that the attack force is not moving as planned, or they have not figured out how to respond yet."

Either way, that was good news for the assault team.

Thirty

Children.

In all Cade's theories about what they might encounter on this ship, he'd never imagined he'd be staring at a group of small children.

The room had the styling of a military barracks, with sleeping platforms in a row along the far wall and sanitization stations under the window, which served as a two-way mirror. Cade stood in front of it and surveyed the space without drawing any attention from the occupants.

Every bed held one or two huddled figures, illuminated by a faint bluish light cast by circular disks embedded in the floor. The crying child was a small boy who looked to be no more than six, being rocked in the arms of an older girl of eleven or twelve.

Were these children from Gaia? And yet that made no sense. No one had reported any kidnappings associated with the attacks. This room held twenty-three kids, but his team had discovered three other rooms along the corridor with the same set up, also containing groups of young children.

Unfortunately, this changed everything.

Reynolds slipped up next to him. "What's our plan?"

"I need to talk to Captain Hawke. Be right back." He moved to the alcove at the bottom of the stairway and opened a channel to Aurora. "We have a problem."

"Tell me."

"There are children onboard."

Several heartbeats passed before she responded. "*Necri children?*"

"No, human. But I can't imagine who they are or why they're here."

Another pause. "Could they belong to the guards?"

"No. They're locked up. Whoever they are, they're not here voluntarily."

"Hang on." He heard murmuring in the background as she discussed the situation with Mya and Clarek. When she returned, her voice held a steely note he knew well. "Can you get them out?"

"Most likely, yes. But that may alert whoever is in charge of this flying penal colony that we're here. We're nowhere near the bridge or engineering. We may not be able to free the kids and disable the ship at the same time."

He could almost hear her thinking, weighing the pros and cons, following all the potential what-ifs they might encounter. "As long as those children are onboard, we're in a no-win situation. If we focus on disabling the ship and ignore the kids, the guards could potentially use them as hostages to force our hands."

"I know."

She blew out a breath. "What do you want to do?"

"We have to get them out. Assuming we can get the kids to go with us, the best plan is to put Cardiff and Reynolds in charge. Children are likely to respond better to women than men, and if anyone can successfully sneak a large group of kids off this ship without anyone getting hurt, it's those two. Drew, Williams and I can continue with our plan to take over the bridge."

"Losing Reynolds and Celia is going to make your job a lot harder."

"I'm okay with that."

He could hear the smile of approval in her voice. "Then do it."

Thirty-One

The moments of déjà vu were coming faster now. As Celia stepped up to the door panel, she had a new appreciation for how her mentor must have felt as she'd approached Celia's cell all those years ago, intent on setting her free. But Celia wasn't a young teen trapped in a prison camp anymore. And whatever these kids had suffered, she had the power to end it. Now.

She pitched her voice low as she called out. "Hello?"

The children closest to the door jerked on their beds, their bodies contracting involuntarily as their heads whipped in her direction. Terror washed over every face.

"It's okay," she said in her most soothing voice. "I'm a friend. I'm here to help you."

Lots of blinking going on. And the exchange of worried glances.

"Can you understand me?"

No one responded, but the older girl who had been rocking the crying boy moved off the bed and crept toward the doorway. Tension showed in every muscle of her body, as if she was anticipating great pain.

Celia remembered that kind of fear. Raising her hands where the child could see them, she tapped her chest. "I'm a friend. Do you understand?"

The girl's puzzled expression indicated the language was unfamiliar to her.

Not kids from Gaia, then. No problem. She was an expert at non-verbal communication, another skill picked up during her long years of confinement.

Using her hands in conjunction with her words, she spoke slowly, placing heavy emphasis on the tone and emotional content of what she said. "I want to get you out of here." She gestured to the room and then out into the corridor. "Off the ship." She roughed out the shape of the ship with her hands and pantomimed the children moving away.

The girl's eyes widened, her mouth dropping open in surprise. She glanced at her companions, who had gathered into a clump at the center of the room. The girl stepped toward the door, but the instant she spotted Ellis and Williams, she recoiled.

Celia reached out one hand toward the girl and placed the other firmly on Williams's chest. "Friend." She gestured at herself, and then at Williams and Ellis. She drew her hands in together and cupped them close to her heart. "Safe." She swept her hand to indicate the rest of the children in the room. "All of you, safe."

The girl's gaze darted from Celia to the rest of the team standing in the hallway. Time ticked by, taunting, but Celia waited patiently. If they wanted these kids to trust them and work with them instead of against them, this first contact had to go well.

Finally the child spoke. The language was unfamiliar, but Celia got the gist.

"Yes. We want you to come with us off the ship. We want to get you free from here." She placed her hand on her chest. "Celia." Then she pointed at the other members of the team and said each of their names. She tapped her own chest again. "Celia." Then she gestured at the child.

The girl slowly lifted her hand and pointed at her own chest. "Maanee." The child's accent gave the word a lyrical quality, drawing out the vowel sounds. Then she pointed at Celia. "Ceeliiaa?"

Her name sounded better coming from the child. She nodded enthusiastically, then did her best to reproduce the child's name as she gestured back.

Maanee nodded and Celia smiled, earning her the barest hint of a smile from the child's lips in return.

Maanee glanced at the other children, most of whom were wide-eyed and trembling. She spoke softly, reassuring them. Then she gestured across the hallway and to the sides, something else Celia was able to interpret. She wanted to know about the kids in the other rooms.

"Yes, the others, too. Everyone." She gestured to encompass the entire space.

Maanee pointed up and spoke again.

Celia frowned and shook her head. "I don't understand."

The child pointed again, hard, sweeping her hands to encompass the entire ceiling.

An idea dawned, though it made no sense. "The Necri?" Hunching her shoulders, she did an imitation of the Necri form. "Is that who you mean?"

Maanee nodded rapidly, her hands sweeping the ceiling again, then around to include the children. She finished by mimicking Celia's gesture of leaving the ship and safe.

Celia stared at her in shock.

Reynolds spoke up. "Is she saying what I think she's saying?"

"Yes. She wants us to save the Necri, too."

"How would they even know about the Necri?" Ellis asked.

She glanced back at him. "I don't know, but obviously they do." She faced Maanee and gestured to the ceiling. She pantomimed doors opening and the Necri leaving the ship, followed by the hands to heart safe gesture. To her shock, tears appeared in Maanee's eyes. The child turned and motioned the other children forward.

Time to do this. "You're up," Celia said to Drew.

Drew took the device she'd used on the previous door from her utility belt and placed it on the security panel. She tapped in a command, and a few seconds later, the door slid open. She pulled the device off and fastened it to the panel on the opposite wall.

Maanee approached cautiously. Celia and the rest of the team members backed up to give the children plenty of room. When Maanee saw what Drew was doing, she stepped into the hallway and called out to the children on the other side of the door. A young female voice responded.

The security panel flashed green and the door slid open. This group was led by a girl who appeared to be slightly older than Maanee. The two spoke rapidly, glancing up at the ceiling as they talked.

Drew sprung the locks on the remaining two doors and the children pushed into the hallway like an incoming tide. They ranged in age from twelve to four or five, with the girls outnumbering the boys three to one.

Ellis and Williams moved down the corridor to minimize the fear factor their presence elicited. Drew joined them while Celia gestured for Maanee to lead the children to the stairway at the back of the ship.

Maanee shook her head and pointed down the corridor in the opposite direction.

"We can't go that way," Celia said. "This is the exit." She motioned to the stairway.

Maanee raised her hands with palms out and fingers splayed. She pulsed both hands once and then lowered one hand and held the other up with only four fingers showing. Then she pointed down the hallway towards Ellis. Celia shook her head and Maanee repeated the gesture, then placed her hand on her head and raised it as high as she could while keeping her palm level.

That's when Celia got it. "There are more kids down that way?" She repeated the ten and four gesture the girl had made. "Fourteen kids, taller than you?" She held her own palm over the girl's head to indicate the average height of a teenager.

Maanee nodded and pointed again.

"Okay." She turned to Reynolds. "Start leading them up to the bay and see if you can get them to take zip lines out to the trees. I'll join you as soon as I can." She faced Maanee again. "Will you tell them to go with her?" She gestured to the kids and Reynolds, and then up to the stairwell.

Maanee nodded, then spoke to the children. They began moving down the corridor as if they knew exactly where they were going.

Celia refused to think about why that path was familiar to them. "Come with me." She motioned to Maanee and strode to where Ellis's team waited. "There are fourteen more kids down this way, probably older teens."

Ellis glanced along the corridor, which stretched another fifty meters. He crouched down so he was on eye level with Maanee and gestured down the hallway. "Where?"

She darted down the corridor and they followed behind. She stopped in front of a smooth, unmarked door.

Drew stepped forward and began working on the security panel. She frowned when it didn't open. "Either there's more security on this door, or they know we're here." She continued tapping in commands, and after a few moments, the panel went green. "Got it. But our grace period is over."

The door slid open to reveal a hallway to the right. Along the opposite wall, individual cells stood in a row, their design somewhere between the barracks where the children stayed and the confinement cells where the Necri were kept. Maanee called out and was answered by a chorus of voices, both female and male, from behind the closed doors.

"Thank goodness for central controls." Drew moved to the panel on the near wall that showed a clear diagram of the row of cells and the locked status for each. Ellis and Williams waited at the open doorway with weapons drawn as Drew set to work disabling the system.

"Any chance we're going to have trouble with these kids once they're free?" Ellis asked.

Celia tapped Maanee on the shoulder, interrupting her conversation with a female on the other side of the third door. "Will they be okay coming with us?" She conveyed the concept as best she could. Thankfully, the child seemed to understand. She said one word and placed her hand on the door. Then she tapped her chest and touched the door and said the word again.

"Your sister?" The question was answered a moment later when the door to the cell slipped open. A pretty girl of about fifteen who had the same sandy blond hair and blue eyes as Maanee dropped to her knees and hugged her little sister close. When she lifted her gaze, tears spilled down her pale cheeks.

Teenage boys and girls emerged from the other cells, their attitudes indicating a mixture of hope, fear and anger. Understandable considering what they'd endured.

The teens began firing questions at Maanee. She gestured up toward the ceiling as she spoke, mentioning Celia's name several times as well. Some of the teens glared at Celia, their distrust in the adults who had freed them evident. But Maanee wasn't cowed, her expression fierce as she dared them to challenge her judgment. Her sister backed her up, and that turned the tide. The teens didn't look happy, but they grudgingly accepted the new paradigm.

"We need to get moving." Celia stepped toward the doorway and Maanee and her sister followed.

"They'll go with you?" Ellis asked as the teens joined them in the corridor.

Celia nodded. "Reynolds and I will get them off the ship, then we'll head down to engineering."

Ellis shook his head. "You can't leave them. We still don't know who they are or why they're here. We can't abandon them to wander through the forest. Get them out and then stay with them."

But that would cut his team down to three. Not good odds. She started to argue, but he held up his hand. "That's an order, Cardiff, from me *and* your captain."

Apparently while she'd been talking to the teens, he'd been talking to Aurora. Reluctantly, she nodded. "Good luck."

His smile was grim. "You, too."

Thirty-Two

Something was wrong.

Kire couldn't put his finger on what was bothering him, but for some reason, his subconscious kept nudging him to stay alert. He stared into the two enclosures as he contacted Roe. "Any word from the assault team?"

"Nothing from Ellis, but I just spoke with Celia. They're beginning the evacuation of the children."

"Good." He'd been shocked when Roe had told him about the kids and the Necri cages. It added an unpleasant twist to an already difficult situation. Apparently the guards were using the Necri to do their dirty work. But that didn't explain why the ship was also carrying a hundred captive children. "How long before they can get them out?"

"I'm hoping for ten minutes or less, but it will depend..."

Kire didn't hear the rest of the sentence. He'd spotted movement inside the containment fence. One of the guards was awake. He gestured to Byrnes to give them another dose of the inhalant, but his hand froze in mid-motion as dark shapes rose into the air.

He cut Aurora off. "Is Jon doing something with the guards?"

"No. Why?"

"Because they're airborne." And so was he. Leaping up, he raced toward the containment fence, weapon drawn, with Gonzalez and Byrnes on his heels. He managed a dozen steps before several blasts from the guards pocketed the ground in front of him. *They were awake!*

"The guards are not incapacitated!" he shouted as he reversed course and returned fire. More blasts rained down and he flattened his back against the nearest tree. Byrnes and Gonzalez took up positions nearby. "What the hell is going on?"

Byrnes answered without taking his attention off the approaching figures. "I don't know. I hit them with another dose but it didn't have any effect. They should have been out for hours."

Kire had trouble hearing Roe's reply over the sizzle of rifle fire. "Kire! Jonarel's lost...the wing harnesses. He's trying...back, but six guards...your way."

"Yeah, we know." More blasts touched down. He peered around the tree and did a double take.

The guards weren't the only ones moving. Like a swarm of locusts, the Necri rose from the enclosure and headed back in the direction of the ship, with several of the guards joining the tight formation.

Kire opened a channel to the entire team. "We've lost control of the wing harnesses. The Necri are returning to the ship, and they're bringing several of the guards with them." He paused to snap off a few shots as the guards landed. "It looks like everyone's wide awake."

A blast slammed into the tree near his head, obscuring any response. Hopefully the assault team had received the message, because they were about to be invaded.

Kire's next shot hit one of the guards squarely in the chest, but rather than felling him, he only staggered slightly and then kept coming. The scorch mark where the material of his tunic had burned away provided the explanation. Underneath he wore a suit of heavy body armor. No wonder they all looked like body builders.

"They're wearing armor," he called out to Byrnes and Gonzalez. And that was bad news. They were already outnumbered two to one, but this placed the odds even more heavily in favor of the enemy.

"Emoto. Get behind me!"

At the command from Gonzalez, Kire pushed away from the tree and darted through the intervening space. Two pops sounded and something whirled through the air. The guards dodged out of the way and kept coming.

A split second later the trees lit up in silhouette as dual explosions took down the two targets. The remaining attackers reconsidered their strategy and sought refuge behind the trees.

Gonzalez glanced at Kire with a wry grin. "Magnetic grenades. I knew those wings would come in handy."

Byrnes joined them. "I've figured out why the inhalant didn't work on the guards. They're wearing ventilators."

Kire frowned. "But they weren't last night when we conducted surveillance. We would have seen it on the sensor images."

Byrnes's expression was grim. "No, they weren't." His implication was clear. Somehow the guards had known what to expect this time and had planned accordingly.

Thirty-Three

All things considered, the evacuation was going smoothly. By Celia's calculations, about a quarter of the kids had already made it to safety.

The teenagers hadn't needed any urging to hustle up the stairway and into the bay. As some of the younger kids spied the new arrivals, they'd raced across the short distance and flung themselves into their siblings' arms.

Reynolds had set up a zip line and moved into the nearby tree. She'd brought a few of the older kids over first, stationing them at intervals below her to help the younger ones climb down. The girl from the second cell was helping Celia get the children set on the line.

Maanee and the teenagers stood off to the side, talking quietly as they gestured at the empty cells. It wasn't hard to figure out from their troubled expressions what they were discussing.

"Do you want to know where the Necri are?" she called out, pointing at the cages and doing her imitation of the creatures.

The teens moved closer, watching her intently.

Celia raised her hands, pantomiming the shape of a fence, then the Necri descending into the space. She then laid the side of her face on her palms and closed her eyes to indicate sleeping.

Maanee frowned, then made a series of gestures.

"You want to know how we got them to sleep?" Celia spread her hands in front of her face and swirled them to indicate a mist, then waved them toward her nose. She took a deep breath, letting her lips form a soft smile as she repeated the gesture for sleep so they'd know it was nothing harmful or traumatic.

Maanee frowned again and shook her head.

No? Did she not understand, or was she disagreeing? Celia's earpiece crackled to life before she could respond. She cupped her hand over her ear, barely catching Emoto's words over the background noise coming through the signal. "We've lost control of the wing harnesses. The Necri are returning to the ship, and they're bringing several of the guards with them." A brief pause was filled with the distinct sound of weapons firing. "It looks like everyone's wide awake."

The inhalant hadn't worked. Apparently Maanee knew something about the Necri they didn't.

The teenagers had also figured out something was wrong. Maanee's sister began a series of rapid questions Celia couldn't follow.

Reynolds's voice came over the comm. "Did you get that?"

"Yep. Working on a plan." Because they needed one. Now. "Give me a minute."

As she saw it, they had one option. And with two hundred Necri and ten or more guards due back in the bay within the next five minutes, she'd have to move quickly.

She motioned for the teens to huddle up so she could hide her movements from the younger children. She prayed she could get her point across and that the teens would go along with her plan.

She pantomimed the Necri and guards returning. The fear and anxiety that appeared on the teens' faces showed they got that point loud and clear. Next she mimicked the teens carrying the younger children down the zip line in groups, with the kids in their arms or holding onto their backs. It wasn't the safest method of transport, but they couldn't wait to go one at a time—not if they wanted to get all the younger kids into the trees before the guards arrived.

Most of the teens nodded, but a dark-haired girl and a brown-haired boy gestured to the Necri cells, their eyes clouded with concern and anger. They clearly didn't want to abandon the Necri to their fate.

Celia didn't believe in leaving others to suffer needlessly either, but in this instance the kids' safety took precedence. She worked to convey that idea, but several of the teens, including Maanee and her sister, indicated they wouldn't leave with the Necri still onboard.

That complicated things considerably.

Touching her earpiece, she opened a channel to the assault team. "Cardiff to Ellis." No response. She tried again. "Ellis, do you read me? Drew? Williams?" Nothing.

She glanced around the cavernous space, searching for inspiration. If the assault team had been ambushed or was otherwise incapacitated, anyone who remained on the ship would turn into a captive as soon as the bay door closed. Were the teens willing to accept that risk? Using gestures and pantomime to convey that idea she lifted her brows in question.

Most of the teens looked uncomfortable, but the dark-haired girl calmly held Celia's gaze. Seven others nodded, including the boy and both the sisters. Celia tried to talk Maanee into changing her mind, but the look of fierce determination on the child's face stopped her.

The dark-haired girl gave instructions to the rest of the teens and they immediately began gathering the kids into small groups.

Celia moved to the bay door so Reynolds could see her. "The older kids are going to help. They'll be coming down to you in large groups. Hopefully we can get all the younger ones into the trees before the guards are in visual range. But I have eight who refuse to leave without the Necri. I'll stay onboard and help them get the Necri out." How exactly she would accomplish that was still a big question mark.

The first group descended. Reynolds didn't respond until she'd helped them off the line. "Have you talked to Ellis?"

Celia shook her head. "They're not responding. That's another reason I have to stay. They may need backup." The next group headed down. The kids worked together amazingly well, with none of the friction or panic she'd expected. Their actions showed an efficiency worthy of a Fleet crew. To see it from a group of frightened kids was astounding.

"They may have encountered more resistance then we anticipated," Reynolds said as the group completed the trip down the line.

"You'll need to get the kids away from the ship as quickly as possible in case this thing powers up. After you're on the ground, see if you can reach Emoto or Byrnes for assistance. They may be able to help you communicate with the kids and keep them calm."

"Roger that."

Celia turned back to the teens. The Necri and guards would arrive shortly. They needed a plan.

Most likely the Necri would be placed in their cells for lockdown, which would resolve one issue temporarily. Then all she'd have to deal with was hiding eight teenagers from a squad of heavily armored guards in a tight space with no good exit. No problem. Right.

But that was better than two hundred Necri on the loose. Things could get ugly fast. The teens didn't seem to fear them, but Celia had witnessed their destructive power. She had a healthy respect for how deadly they could be if they chose to make her or the kids targets.

Thirty-Four

How could things have fallen apart so quickly?

As Aurora raced toward the shuttle, she focused on three important facts. The guards knew exactly where each team was located, the inhalant had not affected them or the Necri, and a large attack force was headed in their direction.

She flung herself through the open hatchway and into the co-pilot's chair next to Jonarel while Mya dropped into one of the seats behind them. Their harnesses snapped into place as the shuttle lifted off.

She'd briefly considered staying put to face the attack. But the sounds of weapons fire that had overlaid Kire's communications had nixed that idea. His team needed backup, and that meant bringing the shuttle down to the fight, even though their attackers would likely follow.

"Kelly and Star are en route." Jonarel banked hard to the left and brought them directly into the path of the oncoming figures. "ETA in eleven minutes."

Thank the universe. Whatever happened with the ground assault, they could still keep the enemy ship from leaving Gaia.

She brought up the weapons grid for the shuttle and targeted the eight guards and four Necri as they bore down on them. Now that she knew the Necri were prisoners, she wanted to avoid hurting them if at all possible. That would be tricky, since they were in the center of the oncoming pack.

She flipped on the forward lights, giving her a spotlighted view and temporarily blinding the guards. She let loose a barrage of blasts aimed at the outskirts of the approaching group, scoring a few hits that knocked the guards out of formation. The Necri, however, continued their collision course.

Jonarel took the shuttle into a dive that swept them under the Necri and down toward the ground. He leveled off their descent as they approached the open space where the containment fields had been set up.

The console indicated their attackers had changed course to follow them, but the shuttle's speed had earned them a precious minute of leeway before the guards and Necri would reach their location.

Flashes of light in the woods marked the unfolding confrontation with Kire's team, but she didn't try to contact him. He probably wouldn't hear her anyway, and she didn't want to distract him. His team should be holding its own in the fight. Gonzalez was a weapons specialist, after all, and Kire was no slouch with a pistol, either.

The shuttle touched down with a grace that belied the danger waiting outside. She unsnapped her harness and grabbed a rifle out of the weapons panel next to the open hatchway. Flipping her visor down, she surveyed the landscape. No sign of heat signatures near the trees that would indicate an ambush.

She turned to Mya, who had also snagged a rifle. "I'll lead in case we encounter any fire from the woods. Jonarel can watch our backs. Stay close." She slipped outside, summoning her energy shield as they raced across the open space. Halfway to the trees, she glanced over her shoulder and spotted the approaching guards and Necri, the heat from their bodies creating splotches of color against the night sky.

An explosion lit up the trees deep in the woods, indicating where they'd find Kire's team. She altered course and picked up the pace. They raced under the protection of the canopy, but a scattering of shots followed them as the guards descended. Jonarel's large form was cast in silhouette by the light from the blasts that streaked past him and slammed into the trees.

"This way." Aurora took off in the direction of a warm glow that appeared to be the beginnings of a fire caused by the explosion. The guards crashed through the underbrush behind them, but the trees provided decent cover.

At least until several forms dropped to the ground fifty meters ahead, the wings attached to their backs giving them an eerie outline.

"Down!" Aurora cried as she pulled Mya into her arms and spun her against the nearest tree. Blasts sizzled past. She kept Mya tucked firmly within the safety of her energy shield.

"Over there." Jonarel pointed to the right.

She spotted the tall forms of five guards moving their way, but she couldn't see the other three or any of the Necri. Dammit! The delay in reaching Kire was really starting to tick her off. "We need to get to Kire's team. Let's split up and circle to the sides. Either we'll slip around them unnoticed, or we'll go right through them."

Jonarel nodded. "Stay as low as you can. I will draw their attention."

If anyone else had said such a thing, she'd wonder if they were suicidal. Jonarel? He looked eager for the opportunity to rip the guards to pieces. She almost pitied them. She turned to Mya. "Ready?"

"Absolutely."

Jonarel took off to his left, firing several well-placed shots. A couple of the guards staggered while the others moved to intercept him.

"Let's go." She and Mya ran in the opposite direction, making an arc that would eventually bring them to their destination. They'd traveled about eighty meters when Aurora pulled to an abrupt halt.

The four Necri stood in a loose semi-circle directly in their path. Their dead eyes stared at her as they began stalking forward.

Mya's voice was breathless, and not because they'd been running. "They've been tracking us."

"I know." Just as they had in the orchard. Somehow the Necri were able to lock onto them with the precision of a laser beam. But she was getting a different feeling from these four than she had from the five the night before. They definitely didn't look like they wanted to communicate.

They were hunting.

Well, she wasn't willing to be prey. Raising her rifle, she fired a shot. It slammed into the upper thigh of the closest Necri and it stumbled.

Aurora barely noticed. She was too busy sucking in air as a flare of heat and pain scorched her own thigh, in the exact spot where she'd hit the Necri. *As if she'd fired on herself rather than the creature.*

Mya clamped a hand on her shoulder, her healing field pulsing like a beacon. The pain disappeared as the vibrant green melded with the pearlescent of Aurora's field.

"We can't fire on them." Mya's gaze snapped back and forth between the approaching Necri and Aurora. "We have to run. Now!"

Aurora didn't have to be told twice. "Back to Jonarel. This way." She pulled Mya in front of her and sprinted in the direction they'd come.

She didn't understand the whys of her connection to the Necri, but all signs pointed to *bad.* Empathic abilities were one thing. What had just happened? That was something totally different. If she couldn't fire on the Necri without hurting herself, how would they get out of this mess, let alone help the other teams?

At least this time she and Mya weren't having any trouble running for all they were worth. The Necri pursued, but they were slow by comparison. She spotted Jonarel up ahead. He'd taken out a couple of the guards, and several others were struggling to keep their feet. But two more were moving in from the left.

She lifted her rifle and fired at one of the approaching guards, scoring a direct hit on the arm that held his weapon. He dropped it to the ground and grabbed the wounded limb with his other hand. The second guard whirled in their direction. Mya dove for the ground as blasts streaked past. Aurora didn't bother to duck, allowing the energy shield to absorb the shots before returning a few of her own, forcing the guard to take cover.

Unfortunately, the brief pause had allowed the Necri to close the gap. She darted forward, but the remaining guards shifted their focus from Jonarel and sent a barrage of fire that lit up her energy shield so brightly it blinded her. Mya grabbed her hand, pulling her to the right, but they halted as two more guards appeared from behind the trees and opened fire. The guards who had attacked Kire's team must have joined the fight. That was bad news.

They spun and headed in the opposite direction, now moving parallel to Jonarel's position rather than toward him, but two of the Necri stepped into view up ahead.

Aurora changed course again, moving away from Jonarel as her energy shield flashed with blasts from multiple directions. She was forced to slow down to keep Mya within the shield.

"Aurora!" Jonarel roared. He was aware of their predicament, but it was a question of numbers. Too many guards and Necri attacking on too many fronts.

Two more Necri came toward them, their movements ape-like, their hands and feet pushing their ungainly bodies along the forest floor.

She and Mya pulled up, heading back once more toward Jonarel. He was wreaking havoc on every guard he could reach, but he was still overwhelmed. So was Aurora. The effort of deflecting the constant barrage of blasts to her shield was sapping her strength.

One of the Necri moved into view, cutting off their route. She slowed, halting in the middle of a small clearing. The guards ceased firing immediately, confirming what she'd suspected—they'd been driving Aurora and Mya into a net.

It was always going to come down to this. Whatever the connection was with the Necri, the time for running was over. Game. Set. Match. A sense of—if not calm, at least acceptance—settled over her.

The Necri's hunched forms crept out of the surrounding foliage in a rough circle with Aurora and Mya at the center. As they slowly raised their hands, she knew exactly how this would end.

Thirty-Five

The Necri and guards had arrived.

From her position on the floor near the far wall of the bay, Celia watched as the flock of shadows flooded the cavernous space and swept across the room.

Turning back to the four teens who crouched beside her, she waved the next one toward the opening in the wall that led into the air circulation system. The girl quickly disappeared into the dark hole.

It was far from a pleasant place to hide, but the intake air vent was sufficiently spacious to fit the nine members of her group. And it was relatively clean, unlike the Necri holding cells. She'd placed magnetic grips along the wall to allow the kids to climb to the upper ductwork. Unfortunately, only five of them had made it inside. Celia and the remaining three were still fully exposed.

At least they'd successfully transported all the kids down to the trees. Reynolds should be on the ground by now, moving them to safety.

Another teen slipped into the hole while Maanee and her sister mimicked Celia's posture, keeping their heads down and bodies still.

The Necri descended, deposited with quick efficiency into the cells. The doors swung shut behind them and the locking mechanisms clicked in place with a soft whirring sound. A sudden silence fell, broken only by the shallow breathing of the girls and the clanks and clatters of the guards removing their wing harnesses.

She'd hoped the guards would head for the exit, but their heavy footsteps approached across the floor and started down the rows. Apparently they were going to check the cells first.

Maanee scrambled into the opening, her sister right on her heels, adrenaline making their movements jerky.

Celia pushed off the floor, snagged the vent, and edged backward into the tight duct space, pulling the cover into place a split second before the guard reached the end of the row. She waited for the guard to pass by before climbing the rungs, keeping her movements as silent as a mouse. The space was pitch black, although she could hear the soft rustle of arms and legs pushing against the metal walls as the kids moved out of her way.

In a few minutes, she'd head down to the bay and verify that the guards had left. If they had, she'd try to reach Ellis on the comm. If his team still didn't respond, she'd have some decisions to make. She could leave the teens in the relative safety of the bay and go in search of the assault team, or she could follow through with the teens' plan to spring the Necri from their cells and turn them loose in the ship.

She wasn't crazy about either option. But for now, all she could do was wait.

Thirty-Six

Aurora pressed her back against Mya's and laced their fingers together. "Give me everything you've got," she murmured as she focused her attention on her own energy field.

Mya didn't reply, but her hands gripped Aurora's firmly, their fields blending in perfect harmony.

The blast struck. For a heartbeat, every detail froze. The beauty of the deep green and pearlescent swirls of energy. The wall of charcoal gray that leapt from the Necri and slammed forward, creating a hard line where the two fields met. The reflection of the blast in the cold eyes of the Necri. The roar of horror and fury from Jonarel as he rushed toward them. The intense pressure that squeezed every cell like a vise.

This is how we'll die.

But before the thought had even completed its path through her overloaded mind, the next beat pounded forward and everything changed.

The compression gave way to a release so powerful she and Mya were wrenched apart. The current of white and green exploded outward, driving the gray back at lightning speed and dispersing it as it went, taking Aurora forward with it. As she fell, the wave hit the Necri. Their bodies shot upright, their hunched forms altering as their spines were pushed ramrod straight, their arms hanging boneless at their sides.

She barely had time to get her hands in front of her before she smacked the ground. She grunted as the air was driven from her lungs. Her face pressed into the leaves as she stared at the tree trunks that now ran parallel to her line of vision.

She wasn't dead. But the battle hadn't ceased just because she and Mya were now lying on the ground.

Rolling over, she looked up at the Necri closest to her. The creature seemed different, and not just because of her weird angle. Upright, it appeared much more human than she would have imagined. Something in its face had also changed. The eyes were still creepy, but rather than the dead vacancy she'd seen before, now it appeared stunned—caught in suspended animation and awaiting the touch from a magic wand to bring it to life.

Mya was sprawled a meter away. She was breathing, which was a good sign. Then she turned her head, her gaze meeting Aurora's. The look in her eyes was such a confusing combination of "What the hell?" and "Damn straight!" that it prompted a snort of laughter.

"Aurora!"

The tortured bellow from Jonarel's lips, however, sobered Aurora in a heartbeat. She stumbled to her feet as the trees spun. Mya staggered, too, and they leaned on each other for support. Their energy fields sprang to life, a surge of power stabilizing their equilibrium.

One of the guards struck Jonarel from behind and he roared in pain. His knees buckled and he collapsed.

"No!" Fear and anger launched her forward. She grabbed the rifle from the ground, aimed at the guard who'd struck Jonarel, and fired. The blast hit him squarely in the chest and drove him back, but he didn't fall. The scorch mark revealed body armor underneath.

She fired shots at the guard's arms and shoulders as she raced past the catatonic Necri, with Mya close behind. She'd taken five steps when a sharp snap, like a rubber band contracting, halted her in her tracks and torqued her around. Her gaze met Mya's, who looked similarly shocked, her mouth sculpted in a perfect "O" as she crumpled like a rag doll in the arms of the Necri who had grabbed her as she'd passed.

The Necri held Mya gently, reverently, its arms cradling her limp form as her head lolled on its shoulder. But the creature's touch was causing Mya's energy to bleed out, flowing from her body into the Necri. The darkness that emanated from the creature like a toxic sludge swallowed the vibrant green in huge gulps. And Mya's distress was taking Aurora down with her, making her legs tremble and her vision waver.

The blast that hit her back burned like a thousand suns, startling a scream from her lips as she fell to her knees. A second blast hit her right arm, knocking the rifle from her hand. Pain radiated outward, contracting the muscles in her upper arm and numbing her fingers.

Strong arms gripped her upper body and lifted her. But she wasn't being helped to her feet—she was being hauled into the air by two of the guards. One of them ripped her visor and earpiece from her face and let them fall, while the other tore off her comband.

She didn't care. All her attention was focused on Mya, whose body was growing lax as her life force drained away.

No. She couldn't let Mya die like this. Somehow she had to stop it. Drawing what little strength she had left, she focused her mind and reached out to the Necri, sending a single thought. *Let her go. You're killing her.*

To her great shock, the creature did.

As it opened its arms Mya melted at its feet, her energy field as dim and gray as the Necri's. But the other three Necri were in motion. They'd joined the fight that still raged with Jonarel at its center, but instead of attacking him, they charged toward the guards.

The guard holding her legs reached up to his control panel and keyed in a command. The Necri's wings unfolded and began lifting them upward, pulling them out of range of the guards.

The trio howled with fury, but the fourth Necri reacted with savage ferocity, venting its rage on the harness. It tore at the undercarriage that held it captive even as it was lifted higher and higher into the air.

One of the guards on the ground headed toward Mya. Aurora cried out, her warning barely a whisper. But the guard didn't get very far.

From off to the right a series of blasts flashed, hitting the guard in the head and limbs. He fell under the sudden onslaught.

Three figures appeared out of the darkness. Kire! He raced toward Mya while Byrnes and Gonzalez joined Jonarel. Kire knelt by Mya's side, then glanced up.

His gaze fixed on Aurora. "Roe!" His cry carried in the cool night air.

She couldn't move. Couldn't respond in any way.

Three of the Necri flew in formation near her, their bodies now hanging in limp resignation. The fourth, however, continued to rage against the harness, tearing through the straps that held it captive. Its gaze locked on Aurora for a moment and she recoiled. In the shadowy moonlight, intelligence and serenity showed in its dark eyes. Then the creature let go.

The fall couldn't have lasted more than a couple of seconds, but for Aurora it stretched into infinity. When the creature's body slammed into the ground and broke apart, she opened her mouth and screamed.

Thirty-Seven

Kire wanted to believe his eyes were deceiving him. But as the two guards disappeared above the trees with Roe locked firmly in their arms, he couldn't escape into a fantasy where everything was still okay.

Turning his attention to Mya, he placed his hand on the side of her neck and checked her pulse. Weak. So very weak. And her breathing was a shallow, hitching gasp that seemed to take more effort than her body could sustain, even though he hadn't found a single mark or wound on her that explained her condition.

"Mya? Can you hear me?" No response. Her consciousness had apparently checked out along with her body. What the hell had the guards done to her?

Byrnes appeared, crouching on Mya's other side and taking her limp hand in his. He reared back in surprise. "She's ice cold."

"Let me see her," a guttural voice mumbled.

Jon and Gonzalez stumbled toward them. Jon leaning heavily on the slighter man, his steps hesitant but his eyes blazing with pain and fury. Byrnes immediately backed away while Gonzalez eased Jon down next to Mya's still form. Byrnes tapped his earpiece and began speaking in a low tone to the person on the other end of the connection.

Jon brushed the side of Mya's face with his fingers. "We need to get her to the ship."

Kire opened a channel. "Kelly, where are you?"

"ETA in two minutes," she replied. "We just dropped out of the upper atmosphere."

"What's happening with the enemy ship?"

"The engines powered up a moment ago and the last remaining guards have reached the bay."

Jon stared at him, his expression tortured. "They took Aurora."

"I know." He placed a hand on his friend's arm. "We'll get her back." He'd always wondered if Jon's feelings for Roe were more than just friendship. The devastation in his eyes made it clear that his emotions ran very, very deep.

"Kelly, we're heading for the shuttle. Mya's injured and we'll need to get her to the med bay as quickly as possible." Of course they didn't have anyone qualified to treat her. Williams was still onboard the other ship. But they'd deal with that later.

Byrnes sank down next to them. "I just spoke with Reynolds. Cardiff and eight of the kids are still onboard, and she hasn't heard from the rest of the team. Reynolds has moved the children out of range of the ship but they're terrified and she's having trouble keeping them calm. I'd like to help her."

Kire nodded. "Go."

Byrnes rested his hand on Kire's shoulder for a moment before sprinting off through the trees.

Kire returned his attention to Kelly. "See if you can block the enemy ship from leaving. We'll rendezvous with you in the shuttle. We've lost contact with the assault team. The kids are on the ground with Reynolds so do not fire. We don't want to accidentally hit our own people."

"Acknowledged."

He glanced at Jon. "Let's go."

"I have her." Jon slipped his arms under Mya's still form. However, as he stood, he staggered and went down on one knee.

That's when Kire spotted the trail of blood flowing steadily from a nasty gash in his back. "Whoa, big guy. You're leaking like a sieve."

"A scratch." Jon growled, but when he tried to rise again, his knees buckled.

Like hell. "Jon, you're in no condition to play hero. You know where the shuttle is. You lead and Gonzalez and I will carry her."

Jon growled again, but from frustration at his own weakness, not aggression. He allowed Kire to slide his arms under Mya's knees while Gonzalez supported her torso. Then they set off toward the shuttle.

Thirty-Eight

Aurora was in a fog, barely aware of the trees underneath her or the dark shapes of the guards above. A heartbreaking sadness held her in a melancholic lethargy.

She kept replaying two scenes in her head—Mya sliding to the ground as the Necri released her, and the look in the Necri's eyes just before it had dropped to its death. The Necri had known exactly what it was doing. It had chosen death. Why?

A pale light appeared in the darkness up ahead. An open bay door. They'd reached the enemy ship. The three remaining Necri grew restless, their harnesses creaking.

She could make out vague outlines of shapes in the ship's interior, including the cramped cells where the Necri were kept. The doors were all closed, indicating they were locked inside. An overwhelming sense of hopelessness filled the bay, settling over her like a blanket as the guards carried her inside. But something else came with it. As the guards' feet touched down, Aurora's energy field came back online with a vengeance.

A barrage of screeching and banging erupted from all directions when the three Necri dropped to the ground a few meters to her right. The guards glanced around in surprise and Aurora seized the opportunity.

Whipping her head to the side she sank her teeth into the arm of the guard holding her upper body while she jerked her legs toward her hips and kicked the second guard. The element of surprise worked in her favor. They released her and she flipped like a cat, landing on all fours.

Raw energy poured through the room like a raging river, flooding her with power and focusing her mind. Normally she wasn't an aggressive person, but after what had happened to Mya and the dead Necri, all bets were off.

She drew a knife from her belt as the first guard charged. She sidestepped the way Celia had taught her, following with an arc of her right arm that took the blade across the back of his neck, severing his spinal cord. He fell like a stone. One down, one to go.

She pivoted on the balls of her feet, getting in position to face the second guard. It was a wasted effort. The three Necri had already taken care of him. His mangled body and the remains of the Necri's wing harnesses lay in a litter of bits and pieces across the open floor.

She held her defensive posture, generating her energy shield as she waited for them to attack. They didn't. Their eyes were curiously vacant of thought or emotion, their bodies as relaxed as their crippled forms would allow. The sight was disconcerting.

Were they waiting for her to do something? If she moved, would they attack? Or stay where they were? She'd have to test it to find out. Keeping her gaze on them, she took a small step backward. All three Necri moved the exact same distance toward her. She halted. So did they.

Her heart hammered in her chest. What was going on here? These three had tried to kill her in the forest and they'd just ripped the guard to pieces. Why were they standing there like statues?

A strange thought took root and wouldn't go away. Shifting her weight, she took a tentative step forward. They immediately backed up a step. She was right! They were mirroring her movements. But why?

The Necri in the cells were also silent. That seemed strange considering the uproar they'd made when she'd first arrived. Keeping the three Necri in her peripheral vision, she peered into the cells to her right. The dark confines made it difficult to see anything, but the light from the floor reflected off two points at the small window of each cell. Every single Necri was staring at her.

The floor beneath her feet began vibrating, indicating the ship had powered up. A quick glance confirmed the bay door was now closed. Not good. Cade's team had failed. They might even be dead.

She shoved the unwanted thought away. If they were alive and onboard, she could help them. If they weren't, then she still needed to help herself. She was not going to end up in one of those cells.

She needed to get to the bridge. Turning back to the Necri, she reached for the weapon the guard had dropped. They didn't move to stop her. That was a good sign. She didn't trust them, but since they didn't seem inclined to hurt her right now, she'd lower her defenses a little and see what happened.

"I'm heading for the bridge, and could really use some backup." They couldn't understand a word she said but she felt better talking to them as though they could. "You three seem to be intent on following me, so I'm hoping we'll be able to work together on this. I don't know why you're acting the way you are, but if you can help me rather than trying to kill me, that would be great. If not, well, no hard feelings."

Giving them one last look, she turned her back and headed for the door.

Thirty-Nine

The cacophony that had erupted in the bay had echoed in the ducts like cannon fire. Celia had slapped her hands over her ears, but they were still ringing. Silence had fallen moments later, as abruptly as the roar had started.

She worked her way along the makeshift ladder, her gaze dropping to the pale light filtering through the vent onto the small patch of floor below. She couldn't see any shifting shadows that would indicate movement, but that didn't mean anything given how far she was from the central section of the bay. As the silence continued, she crept down, alert for any clues that might tell her what she'd find when she reached the bottom.

Settling onto her hands and knees, she closed her eyes and listened. A moment later, she caught the faint murmur of someone speaking in the distance, followed by multiple footsteps crossing the room, heading in the direction of the exit door.

"Ceeliia?" Maanee balanced on the grips, her blue eyes as big as saucers.

Celia lifted her finger to her lips, then slowly eased the vent out and pushed it forward. Judging by the pitch of the voice, the unknown speaker had been female. As every guard she'd seen had been male, she'd either encountered the first female, or Ellis's team had made their way back to the bay and she'd been listening to Drew. In either case, it was time to make a move.

Setting the grate on the floor, she slid through the opening and glanced toward the door. No one there. If Ellis's team had been in the bay, they'd left again. Leaning back into the duct she waved at Maanee to follow her, which she did with surprising speed, her older sister close on her heels. While the rest of the teens worked their way out, Celia opened a channel to Ellis.

"Ellis, do you read me?"

His voice was one of the sweetest sounds she'd ever heard. "Loud and clear. Where are you?"

"In the Necri bay."

"You didn't make it off the ship?"

"The kids and Reynolds did. But eight of the teens wouldn't leave without the Necri. Where are you?"

"Climbing down an access tunnel toward engineering."

She frowned. "Were you and Drew just in the bay?"

"No. Why?"

"Because a female was just in here. I thought it might have been Drew." She missed Ellis's reply as a low murmur caught her attention. The kids had all moved out into the bay, heading down the aisles of the Necri cells. She set off in pursuit, her gaze sweeping over the space to make sure no guards were lurking in the shadows. "I'm sorry, I didn't get that."

"Are you certain it was a female?"

"Pretty sure." She spotted Maanee and her sister in front of one of the cells, their fingers clinging to the edge of the small grilled opening in the door. They were whispering to the Necri inside.

The Necri's gravelly voice drifted out of the dark cell as it responded—in the same language.

Forty

Cade followed Drew down the rungs of the metal ladder. "Who else would be in the bay?" No response. "Cardiff? Are you there?"

Even over the comm, he heard her clear her throat. "No clue. But I think I just figured out why the children refused to leave the Necri behind."

"Why?"

"The Necri are their parents."

He almost missed the next rung. "*What?*"

"I'm looking at a Necri with blue eyes that exactly match Maanee and her sister's. And the Necri speaks their language. Fluently."

Their parents? How was that even possible? He couldn't believe that the Necri were the natural adult form of a humanoid species. Evolution would never produce something so unwieldy. Besides, the children looked completely human and the teenagers were only a few years from adulthood. "Are you sure about that?"

"Yes. If you could see the looks on their faces, you would be, too."

One more step down the rabbit hole.

Drew tapped on his foot and he realized he'd stopped moving. She gazed up at him, her eyebrows lifted.

He motioned to her to continue and got his own feet going, though his mind was already racing. "What's your next move?"

"Depends. Are you going to need backup when you reach engineering?"

"Don't know. We were boxed in by a squad of guards near the bridge that seemed to be waiting for us, but we held them off until Drew got us into the interior. It's likely they've anticipated this move, too, and will have engineering locked up."

"Then we'll see what we can do to draw their attention elsewhere."

Forty-One

From his position in the captain's chair, Kire stared at the image of the enemy ship on the bridgescreen. Each second felt like an eternity. Roe was on that ship, quite possibly as injured as Mya, who was lying comatose in the med bay with Jon keeping watch.

Not that Jon was in good shape, either. He'd been faltering badly by the time they'd reached the shuttle and lifted off. The gash on his back was deep and ugly, but all Kire and Gonzalez could do to help after he'd successfully docked the shuttle was slap an emergency bonding pad onto his skin to slow the bleeding and help prevent infection. Then they'd raced to the bridge.

Gonzalez sat in Cardiff's chair, with Kelly at the helm as the *Starhawke* raced the enemy ship past the Gaian moon. If they didn't stop the ship before it made an interstellar jump, it could take days to track its course. But they'd have to be careful in their attack. They didn't want to accidentally blow up the ship with Roe and the assault team still onboard.

Roe, what went wrong? The way she'd screamed when the Necri had hit the ground haunted him. The pain and anguish in that cry had torn his heart right out of his chest. And with Mya on the edge of death, he really didn't want to think about what would happen if he failed them now.

"In range of weapons in thirty seconds." Gonzalez didn't take his gaze off the control panel.

"Aim for the engines, but use the weakest settings you can. We don't want to breach the hull."

"Understood."

Kire believed him. After all, Gonzalez had three members of his own team onboard.

"Firing."

Before the word had left his mouth, blasts shot back at them from the other ship, slamming into the shields. Gonzalez returned fire and Kelly changed course as the enemy ship banked hard to the left. Another round of blasts continued the deadly dance, Kelly keeping them on the other ship's tail with calm precision.

"Our shields are down to seventy percent," Gonzalez said.

The other ship was hitting them with everything it had. Thankfully, Kelly was able to keep most of the blasts from finding their mark as she took full advantage of the *Starhawke*'s superior design and speed.

"Commander, the engine pattern on the other ship has changed," Star said.

Gonzalez's head snapped around in surprise, his eyes widening at the sight of Star seated at the console to the left of the captain's chair. Roe had never mentioned the ship's resident crewmember to Ellis's team. No time for explanations now.

"Is it the assault team?"

"Unclear, but very likely given the outcome. Power is building up in one of the cells that seems to be short-circuiting the main reactor. The ship will suffer engine failure any moment."

Kelly broke in. "The other ship is losing power."

"Engines are down," Star confirmed.

"What about life support?"

"Still functional."

Thank goodness for that. The loss of their engines, however, had triggered an increase in defensive blasts from the enemy ship. Kelly worked double-time to avoid the spray.

"Return fire but only enough to keep their attention," Kire said. "We don't want to back them into a corner." He activated the comm panel on the captain's chair. Time to see if they could talk to their team. "Emoto to Ellis." Static crackled over the connection. "Ellis, this is Emoto. Do you read?" Still nothing. "Star, can you do anything to clean up the channel?"

"One moment."

More static, and then Ellis's voice broke through. "You've been missing all the fun."

Kire released the breath he'd been holding. They were alive. And that meant he might be able to get Roe the help she needed.

Forty-Two

The engines had stopped. An occasional shudder passed through the deck as blasts from the *Starhawke* hit the ship's shields, but Aurora knew her crew wasn't trying to inflict damage. Just keeping the enemy busy now that Cade's team had succeeded.

The crew on this ship, however, would have no such reservations. They'd happily blow the *Starhawke* into a billion pieces. Odds were good they were doing everything in their power to achieve that goal now that they were immobile. She needed to get to the bridge.

She slipped along the corridor with the three Necri close behind. The corridor ended at a lift, but a quick inspection revealed a winding stairway down a short hallway on the right that would take her three levels up or four levels down. Every ship she'd ever visited had positioned the bridge on the upper decks. She started climbing.

So far she hadn't encountered anyone as her strange little band had made its way up from the bay. They'd passed a set of windowed rooms that had probably held the children Cade's team had found. From there they'd wound through several corridors and climbed a few shallow stairways as they pushed into the front of the ship. And yet, they hadn't encountered a single person during the trek.

She checked the landings of the first two floors they passed, but neither looked promising, so she continued to the top of the stairwell. The door to the third landing slid open as she approached. The Necri followed as she moved down the short corridor.

A klaxon blared, filling the narrow space with a deafening screech. She flattened her body against the wall and peered around the corner to her right. No one. She broke into a trot, the footsteps of the Necri keeping perfect time with her own. But before they reached the end of the passage, the thunder of running feet echoed down the hallway toward them. She leveled her weapon but kept going.

Three guards appeared at the far end, their steps faltering as they spotted her and the Necri. She squeezed off several shots, but rather than going for their weapons and returning fire, the guards split up and darted down corridors on either side.

Their footsteps faded as she reached the junction. The sight of three loose Necri might have triggered the panic she'd felt pouring off of them. She retraced their original path, which led directly to the bridge.

Empty. The *Starhawke* was visible on the bridgescreen, hovering off the starboard bow. She strode to the main consoles and studied the readings. Numbers flashed on the screen of the second console, currently at 8:24, but steadily counting down.

The guards had armed the autodestruct. That explained the panic she'd sensed from the fleeing bridge crew. They were heading for whatever shuttles or escape vessels the ship contained.

Cade's team probably wasn't aware of the danger. She needed to alert them.

The Necri stood like sentinels as she made her best guess for how to open an internal communication line. She avoided looking at the ominous numbers. The console pinged, the screen indicating she'd successfully opened a channel. "Can anyone hear me? Cade? I'm on the bridge. Please respond."

The voice she heard through the speakers was the last one she'd expected. "Roe? Is that you?"

"Kire!" Apparently she'd hailed the *Starhawke* instead. "Are you in contact with Cade or anyone else on this ship?"

"Yes. What do you need?"

"The guards started the ship's autodestruct sequence. I need Drew's help to disable it."

"Hang on. I'm patching you through to Ellis."

A few clicks and a brief silence followed, then Cade's voice boomed out of the speaker. "Aurora? Are you okay?"

"Yes. I'm on the bridge. We have about seven minutes before this ship is going to blow apart. Is Drew with you?"

"Yes."

"Can she access the ship's security system and shut down the autodestruct?"

"I'm not sure. Give us a moment."

She heard murmuring in the background, then Cade came back on the line. "Were you in the Necri bay earlier?"

How would he know that? "Yes. Why?"

"You need to head down there. Now. Cardiff needs your help."

"Celia's in the bay?" Why hadn't she seen her when she was there? "I thought she and Reynolds were on Gaia with the children."

"Eight of the kids wouldn't leave without the Necri so she stayed behind. She got the Necri out of their cells, and the kids have helped her keep them in the bay, but

Cardiff said the Necri are frantic to locate someone they saw earlier. I'm guessing that's you."

Apprehension settled over her. Her gaze fell on the three Necri standing between her and the door. They'd followed her here like living shadows, unwilling to let her out of their sight. What was it that tied these creatures to her?

"There's something else you should know. Cardiff is convinced the Necri are the children's parents."

A bone-deep certainty settled into place, clearing her mind and emotions. "Has Drew had any luck with the autodestruct?"

"She's working on it, but it doesn't look good."

"Can she isolate the location of the detonation device?"

"I think so. Why? Do you want her to try to disable it manually?"

"No. Just tell me where it is."

She waited, her gaze remaining fixed on the three Necri.

"It's on the upper level of engineering in the center of the ship."

"What's the quickest route from the bridge without using the lifts?"

Cade's voice held a warning. "What are you planning to do?"

She ignored the question. She didn't have time to explain and he wouldn't go along even if she did. "What's the quickest route?" she repeated.

His brief hesitation spoke volumes. "There's a small staircase down a corridor to the left after you leave the bridge. If you follow it to the bottom, you'll be on the deck you want. Go forward until you reach a T-junction, then left and through the doorway on the right. The device is embedded in a console in the center of the room."

"Got it. Kire are you still there?"

"Yes."

"Move the *Starhawke* to a safe distance."

"Wait a minute. We could bring a shuttle over and—"

"There isn't time. Cade, you're in charge of getting the rest of the team off the ship. And tell Celia to let the Necri out of the bay."

"To go where?"

"To find me."

Forty-Three

Kire stared at the image of the enemy ship on the bridgescreen. There had to be a way to help Roe and the rest of the team get off the ship before it blew. But how?

"Shuttle exiting port side," Gonzalez said.

"Disable that thing," he snapped. "They're not going anywhere."

"Firing." The spray of blasts slammed into the small craft, visibly rocking it. When it kept moving, Gonzalez hit it with a more forceful shot aimed at the engines. It shuddered, then stalled, starting a slow spin as the power cut out. "Two more shuttles leaving the bay." He fired on them as well, and within moments, they'd joined their companion in a slow drift.

Kire was tempted to leave them where they were. If the enemy ship did blow, it would take the shuttles with it, which would be the only satisfaction he'd get. But Roe wouldn't approve. Regardless of what happened to her, she'd want the occupants of those shuttles brought back to the Galactic Council to stand trial. And she'd be right.

He pressed his lips together. "Kelly, attach tow cables and haul them in, then move us out of range of the other ship."

"Yes, sir." But before Kelly could maneuver the ship into position to fire the first cable, an explosion lit up the bridgescreen.

Panic flooded through Kire as he gripped the arms of the captain's chair. They still had five minutes. Had the autodestruct triggered early? No. The enemy ship still hung in the background, untouched. But only two shuttles remained.

"Did you fire on the shuttle?" he barked at Gonzalez.

Gonzalez looked offended. "Of course not. The blast came from inside."

"Another autodestruct," Kelly murmured, just before two more explosions flashed and debris pelted their shields.

So much for taking anyone in for questioning.

Forty-Four

"If Captain Hawke thinks we're abandoning her, she's nuts." Drew pulled another device from her bag of tricks and continued working on the autodestruct sequence.

Cade wholeheartedly agreed. He opened a channel to Cardiff. "We just heard from Aurora. She was the woman in the bay."

"Aurora? She's on the ship?" There was a pause, as though Cardiff was mulling over the information. "Where is she now?"

"She's heading to the upper levels of engineering. She wants you to let the Necri out of the bay."

"And then what?"

"She ordered us to evacuate."

"Why?"

"The autodestruct sequence was triggered. We have less than five minutes before this ship blows up."

More silence. "Then why is she going to engineering?"

"That's where the device is located. I think she's going to try to disable it."

"And how are the Necri going to help with that?"

"I don't know. But she was very clear that she wanted you to let them find her."

"Okay. Hang on." Her voice faded for a moment as she spoke to someone in the background. Her next words were overlaid with the deep rumble of bodies in motion. "They're on their way, and I'm with them."

He smiled grimly. Cardiff wasn't about to abandon her captain, either. "I'll meet you there."

Closing the channel, he glanced at Williams and Drew. There wasn't a flicker of doubt in their eyes as they met his gaze.

He raced back to the ladder that would take him to the upper decks. As he climbed, the rungs vibrated, the result of the two hundred Necri Cardiff had unleashed. He hoped to hell Aurora knew what she was doing.

He jogged down a corridor and navigated several twists and turns he'd noted in the schematic he'd pulled up to direct Aurora. He almost didn't need it though. The foul odor of the Necri told him where to go. He rounded a corner and spotted Aurora.

She stood in the middle of the small room, but she wasn't alone. Eight of the teens, including Maanee and her sister, formed a circle around the console at the room's center, their hands joined with each other and Aurora. Three Necri stood just behind her like sentries, their gazes unfocused and their bodies unmoving. Several other Necri hunkered behind the kids, with more appearing from the opening across the way, their bodies rapidly filling every available space.

Cardiff slipped into the room, nodding in his direction before moving to stand as close to Aurora as the tightly packed Necri would allow. The Necri had surrounded him as well, jostling his elbows as they pressed forward, their attention on Aurora.

She hadn't made any sign that she knew he was in the room. Her gaze was laser-focused on the console as though she was memorizing its features. Her chest rose and fell as she took a deep breath, and then her pearlescent shield bloomed to life.

The gasp he heard could have been his. Or it could have been the sound generated by every being in the room. He certainly couldn't believe what he was seeing.

Aurora's energy field had always been beautiful, but the sight unfolding before him stole his breath. The pearlescent glow was nearly blinding, even though it didn't give off visible light. It filled the space around her body, then flowed down the chain of linked hands and surrounded each of the children. As it touched them, a softer aura of color blended with Aurora's energy, creating stunning ribbons that wove into the glittering field until it filled the circle of linked hands.

The energy continued to expand, encompassing the Necri who stood closest to the circle. And with each one, a burst of color flowed in, though the Necri's were grayed out compared to the rich and vivid hues being produced by Aurora and the children. The wave finally reached Cade, wrapping him in a blanket of interconnection and joy so intense tears sprang to his eyes.

This was her plan. When the explosion went off, she was going to try to contain the outpouring of energy within her shield. Her courage and bravery humbled him. A gruesome fate awaited her if she failed, but the emotion that surged through him wasn't fear. And it was as pure and beautiful as the energy swirling around her.

Forty-Five

Cade was in the room.

Aurora had sensed his presence long before the energy field had enveloped him, but that intimate contact had intensified a startling and unexpected emotion that was emanating from him. The shock had almost broken her concentration.

But rather than reacting, she'd allowed the sensations to sweep through her, adding to the strength of the web she and the children were creating.

She didn't question how she knew what to do, or why the kids had joined her without a word. Right now, all that mattered was the shield.

She'd isolated the reactive elements in the device from the surrounding casing, wrapping them in layer upon layer of webbing that grew stronger each second she maintained the connection with the children and Necri.

She didn't need to see the countdown. When the electrical signal triggered the detonation, a shift in the core announced the change a millisecond before the elements ignited.

All the energy of the room focused on that one point. And exploded.

The blast sent a concussion wave rocketing outward. It crashed through her while an intense flare of light like a miniature sun illuminated the room. Her eyes snapped shut and her muscles screamed in protest as the violent pulse of energy erupted, challenging the shield that surrounded it. She trembled, her hold on the hands of the children threatening to break.

Time and space lost all meaning. There was only energy. Unbelievable, unrelenting energy. And a battle for control that obliterated everything in its path. The pressure bore down on her, demanding her surrender.

She fought back, refusing to submit, even as the energy pressed forward, crushing her.

And then it shot through the shield. A cry of agony tore through her. She'd lost.

But instead of blasting her into nothingness, the energy shifted, dispersing as the tension eased and the bright light faded away.

Only one thing remained. Breathing. *She was breathing.*

Cautiously, she opened her eyes, afraid of what she might see.

A smoking mass of metal sat at the center of the room. The children were still standing, apparently unharmed. But the Necri behind them, most of whom lay crumpled on the ground, were twitching and writhing in pain.

The cry of agony hadn't come from her. It had come from the Necri. Somehow they'd pulled energy through the shield and into their bodies. Those standing closest had taken the hardest hits. Their sacrifice had released the pressure, allowing Aurora to dissipate what remained.

If not for their sheer numbers, it would have killed them. However, working as a collective, they'd minimized the damage. She sensed their pain, but not death. They would live. Especially if she helped them.

She took a step, breaking the connection with the circle, but her knees buckled. Gentle arms caught her around the shoulders and eased her to the floor as her head swam.

Something firm but yielding supported her upper body as her muscles relaxed into a puddle and her lids grew heavy.

But that didn't prevent her from spotting Cade's solid form standing among the Necri across the room. Or the look of awe on his face.

Forty-Six

She'd done it.

Cade stared at Aurora, uncomprehending. Somehow, she'd managed to contain an explosion that had the power to tear apart the entire ship and everyone in it.

The repercussions pounded into him, much like the wave that had blown out when the autodestruct ignited. He'd always known Aurora had power. But this? He couldn't even begin to grasp it.

It had clearly taken a lot out of her. Cardiff had settled Aurora into her lap, supporting her upper body so she was upright. But Aurora looked one step away from unconsciousness.

She held his gaze as he approached on unsteady legs. Maybe the explosion had succeeded in its deadly task and he was actually a ghost in an alternate reality. In some ways, that seemed more plausible.

He knelt, taking Aurora's hand in his. She watched him with an intensity that made his heart thump painfully in his chest. Emotion flickered in her beautiful green eyes, and an openness he hadn't seen in a long time, as though all of the walls she kept in place to protect herself had been wiped away.

Emoto's voice in his earpiece jarred him back to awareness of those around them.

"Ellis! Are you there?"

He tapped the device. "We're here."

"What happened? Did Drew halt the sequence?"

"No. The device detonated."

"It did?" Emoto's voice conveyed his confusion. Then it edged toward panic. "What about Roe? Is she okay?"

"Yes. She's right here."

Emoto exhaled audibly. "Thank the universe. What happened?"

"She can explain when she sees you." Cade gave Aurora's hand a squeeze, but she didn't return the gesture.

"Can you put her on? I need to talk to her about Mya."

"Hang on." He pulled off his earpiece and held it out to her.

She glanced at it but made no move to take it. Or more precisely, she acted like she couldn't.

Had she been paralyzed by the blast? Fear gripped him. He leaned toward her but two sets of hands held him back. Maanee and her sister appeared on either side of Aurora, blocking him from getting closer. The older sister shook her head and gently removed his hand from Aurora's.

He hated the loss of connection, but they seemed to have a plan. He stepped back as the girls held Aurora's hands while linking their free hands with each other, forming a small circle.

Aurora's gaze shifted to the two sisters. A blue glow formed around their joined hands, and she inhaled sharply. A moment later, her energy field flared to life and she bolted upright like she'd been plugged into an electrical conduit. And in a way, he guessed she had.

Forty-Seven

Aurora kept her focus on the two girls. The energy from their hands was cool and soothing, like being touched by love itself. And it was working.

After the blue light faded and they released her, her own field remained strong and vibrant. She rested a hand on each of their shoulders. "Thank you." She allowed her emotions to join the flow of energy she sent back to them in gratitude.

They gazed at her silently, a look that bordered on reverence on their faces. They nodded, rising to their feet and stepping away.

"Ellis? Roe? What's going on?" Kire's voice filtered out of the device Cade still held loosely in his fingers.

Aurora reached forward and captured it, then secured it to her ear. "I'm here, Kire."

"You have no idea how good it is to hear your voice."

The tremor in his was a good indicator. "It's good to hear your voice, too."

"I'm sending Kelly over with a shuttle. Can you get to the bay on the port side? It's three levels below the Necri bay and fifty meters to the stern. The guards left it open when they evacuated."

She frowned. "Why the urgency?"

"It's Mya. She's not doing well."

"Mya?" Her muscles contracted as a jolt of fear rocketed through her veins. With the cascade of problems she'd faced since the guards had brought her onboard, she'd temporarily forgotten the condition Mya had been in when she'd last seen her. She pushed to her feet. "I'm on my way."

"We need Williams, too. He's the only medic we have."

Her gaze locked onto the teens. "Williams can't help her. But I know who can." The teens stared back. "We'll be outside the bay when Kelly arrives."

She slipped the earpiece off and handed it to Cade without waiting for a reply.

Facing the teens, she allowed her instincts to guide her. She focused on an image of Mya with her deep green energy field glowing around her. She felt their surprise and knew she'd successfully projected the image into their minds. Then she shifted to the visual of the Necri holding Mya, and Mya's body slumping to the ground.

Shock and horror buffeted her as the image registered. A dark-haired girl of about seventeen looked ill and wavered on her feet. Aurora hated causing them distress, but they needed to know what they were up against. The final image she sent was a composite rather than a memory, with Mya at the center and the circle of teens standing around her holding hands with Aurora while they generated an energy field.

The teens began talking rapidly to each another, with some gesturing at the Necri while others glanced at her. She could sense their concern for the creatures, a concern she shared. Most of the Necri were unconscious on the floor, including her three bodyguards. They were also in pain—she could feel it—but their injuries were not life-threatening. She didn't have the same conviction regarding Mya.

Celia joined the conversation, the obvious rapport she'd developed with the teens allowing her to communicate despite the language barrier. After a few exchanges back and forth, the teens split up, with two boys and two girls moving to join Celia.

Celia's brown eyes filled with compassion and understanding as she held Aurora's gaze. Mya's safety meant a lot to both of them. "Take care of Mya. We're going to stay and help the Necri. The kids will keep everyone here calm so you can go."

Aurora gave Celia a quick hug. "Thank you."

The dark-haired girl, the two girls who had helped her, who looked like sisters, and a boy of about fifteen stepped toward Aurora. She motioned for them to follow her. "Come with me."

Cade joined her as she headed for the corridor. "Where are you going?"

"To help Mya." She continued down the hallway and turned left toward the stairway.

"Do you think you're in any condition to help her?"

"Yes." She was upright and she was mobile. Nothing was going to stop her from doing everything she could to save her friend. It wasn't open for debate. "I need you and Drew to stay here with Celia and keep the Necri calm, but I need Williams to meet us outside the bay. Mya may have physical injuries that will require treatment as well."

"As well?" He caught hold of her arm. "What happened to her?"

What could she tell him that wouldn't generate a hundred questions? She didn't have the time or strength for that discussion right now. "It's complicated."

He held her gaze. "With you it often is."

Funny, Mya had said the exact same thing.

Forty-Eight

Kire was waiting for her when she exited the shuttle. Without preamble, he hauled her into his arms and held on tight. "I thought we'd lost you." He pulled back and swept his gaze over her. "Are you okay?"

Such a difficult question. "I will be. Where's Mya?"

"In the med bay with Jon. Star's been watching over them."

Jonarel. She'd forgotten about him, too. "How serious is Jonarel's condition?"

"I think he'll be okay. He took some hard hits during the fighting, but nothing that can't be fixed. Unfortunately, he's a terrible patient. He's refused any treatment or pain killers until he sees you."

Then she needed to get moving. Motioning to the teens and Dr. Williams to join them, she and Kire led the way as they all filed into the lift. "Med bay."

The lift opened on the main deck, revealing the glass entrance to the med bay. Aurora's heart rate picked up. Mya lay on one of the platforms near the back of the room. She looked lifeless. Was she even breathing?

But far worse, Aurora couldn't *feel* her. She got no sense of her at all, as though the body on the bed was nothing but an empty shell.

"Aurora." The croak came from the med platform across the aisle from Mya's. Jonarel lay on his side, his face a mass of dried blood and grime that hid his beautiful skin. One eye was swollen shut. Pain radiated off of him, but his focus was entirely on her. He tried to push himself up, but she stopped him, resting her hand lightly on his arm and coaxing him back down on the bed.

"I'm here." She allowed a gentle flow of energy to slip down her fingers and into his skin. His expression relaxed as the pain eased a bit.

Williams whistled as he got a good look at the blood-soaked wrapping on Jonarel's back. "That's an impressive wound you've got there. Mind if I take a look?"

Jonarel shook his head, his gaze never leaving Aurora.

Williams glanced at her. "I've got this. Why don't you go help Dr. Forrest?"

She could have kissed him. "Thank you." She squeezed Jonarel's shoulder. "I'll be right over there." She gestured to Mya's bed. He nodded, though he continued to stare at her as if he was afraid to blink.

Kire cleared his throat. "I'll leave you to it, then."

"Wait." She didn't want him to go. He needed to witness this. It was time. "Stay. Please." She placed her hand on his arm. "It would really help if you're here."

Something shifted in his eyes, an awareness that hadn't been there before. He nodded slowly. "Okay."

She released him and moved to the foot of Mya's bed. The ache in her chest expanded as she gazed at Mya's still form. *Don't leave me. Please don't leave me.*

A gentle touch at her wrist startled her. The younger of the two sisters laced her fingers through Aurora's, a quiet calm that completely belied her years shining in her blue eyes. She joined hands with her sister, who clasped hands with the boy across the bed. The dark-haired girl completed the circle, taking hold of the boy's hand and Aurora's.

She wasn't alone. She'd brought help. Mya was going to be okay.

Aurora cleared her mind and focused on her connection with Mya's virtually non-existent energy field. The soft pearlescent glow of her own field flowed into the circle and was quickly joined by the blue of the two sisters and the red and yellow of the dark-haired girl and the boy. The colors danced and spun through the space, encircling Mya's body in a gentle web.

Come back to me, Mya. Please.

She repeated the last word over and over like a chant, willing some kind of response from Mya's body. She tuned into every breath, every beat of her heart, every touch of the hands clasped in hers. She sensed every life force in the room—Williams, Kire, Jonarel, and the four children. She even sensed Star's special presence.

But she felt nothing from Mya. Nothing. Not a whisper, not a flicker, not a—

The burst of green slammed into her so abruptly that it felt like she'd been punched in the gut. A hook latched onto her field, pulling her forward, drawing energy like a mosquito draws blood. She braced for the weakness she'd experienced on the ship following the explosion. But it never came.

Instead, Mya's energy field bloomed to glorious life, a cloud of emerald green that blended with the pearl of her own to create a stunning band. It spread outward, encompassing the four children. The feeling of power and healing that came with it shocked her, all the aches and pains she hadn't even been aware of now noticeable for their sudden absence.

She glanced down. Mya's eyes were open, though still unfocused. But her breathing had returned to normal and color was rapidly suffusing her skin.

The wave of energy pushed outward, washing over Kire, Jonarel and Williams. Kire inhaled sharply. He wouldn't be able to see the energy, but he would certainly feel it when it touched him.

This was the moment she'd avoided for years. But she couldn't hide from him any longer. She met his gaze, afraid of what she'd see in his eyes.

Only one emotion dominated his entire being. Joy. *Thank you* he mouthed silently as a small smile touched the edges of his lips.

Her heart warmed as her fears washed away. He *knew*. And he understood.

Movement in her peripheral vision drew her attention back to the bed. Mya's eyes had finally cleared. She was gazing in surprise at the four teens holding vigil around her. Her energy field had resumed its normal state, vibrating with health and vigor as it flowed around her body. The expanding wave from the circle slowly dissipated as Aurora released her own field.

The teens let go of their clasped hands and moved back. Aurora took Mya's hand in both of hers, grateful for the warmth and vitality that had replaced the emptiness. "How do you feel?"

Mya's voice rasped, unintelligible. She swallowed a couple times and tried again. "Strangely enough, I feel good." Then she grinned. "But you look like hell."

Aurora laughed. She was probably right.

Mya's gaze shifted to the teens. She pushed herself into a seated position while Aurora snagged a pillow off the nearby platform. She stuffed it behind Mya's back to prop her up.

"I think introductions are in order," Mya said.

Yes, they were. "They don't understand our language." Aurora indicated the teens. "But they rock at the non-verbal communication." She turned to the young girl beside her and indicated for her to start the introductions.

The girl gave a slight bow in Mya's direction. "Maanee." She touched her chest then gestured at her sister.

"Paaw," the older girl said.

Mya smiled and pointed at herself. "Mya."

Paaw smiled back shyly, and then executed a graceful hand movement that ended with one palm extended flat toward Mya and the other held palm-inward over her heart. She said a word in her language.

For some reason, Mya flinched.

Aurora frowned. "What's wrong?"

"Nothing." Mya avoided her gaze, turning to the teens on the other side of the bed.

The dark-haired girl spoke first. "Raaveen."

"Sparw," the boy said.

Then all four turned their gazes to Aurora and waited expectantly. "Oh!" She'd never told them her name. She placed her palm flat on her chest. "Aurora."

The children smiled and nodded, as though they approved. Then Paaw made the same elaborate hand gesture and indicated her. "Sahzade."

She froze, the small hairs on the back of her neck and arms lifting. She stared at the girl. "What did you say?"

Paaw frowned, glancing at Mya and her sister in confusion. She gestured at Aurora again. "Sahzade."

There was no mistaking it the second time. Aurora's voice leaked out in a harsh whisper. "*How do you know that name?*"

Forty-Nine

Kire's reality had shifted, but Roe looked poleaxed. All the color had drained out of her face.

How could the girl, Paaw, know Roe's childhood nickname?

The teen glanced at the others for support as Roe stared at her like horns had sprouted from her forehead.

Roe finally keyed into the girl's discomfort. "I'm sorry. I didn't mean to upset you." She spoke to the girl, but her gaze shifted to Mya. "I just don't understand how you could know that name."

Mya gave a subtle shake of her head.

Roe's spine straightened. She wasn't happy. But she was doing her best to hide it. She placed her hand on Paaw's arm. "It's fine." When she smiled, some of the tension eased from the girl's shoulders.

Motion to Kire's left caught his attention. Jon was sitting on the edge of the med platform with Williams behind him. The doctor was staring at the shredded remains of the tunic covering Jon's back. As Jon stood, Kire blinked. The deep green skin underneath that had been a mass of ugly now looked smooth and healthy.

And that wasn't all. Jon's movements as he rolled his shoulders and stretched were as relaxed as if he'd just woken from a nap. Even his eye looked perfectly normal. What exactly was going on here?

Roe glanced at Mya. "Are you up to working?"

Mya nodded without hesitation, swinging her legs over the side of the platform. "Of course."

"Good. We have a ship full of wounded Necri. Take fifteen minutes to gather whatever you need and meet me in the shuttle bay."

"What about the kids?"

"They can stay with you until you're ready to leave." She pivoted and stalked toward Kire, banked anger glowing in her eyes.

Roe was furious with Mya. Why, he couldn't imagine, but he didn't envy the good doctor the storm that would eventually hit. Roe had a long fuse, but when it blew, the pyrotechnics were spectacular.

She halted in front of him. "Send a message to the Admiral. Let him know we'll be bringing the enemy ship back to Gaia. Then contact Reanne and tell her we need accommodations set up in a remote location for three hundred refugees. An island near the equator would be ideal, but make sure it's somewhere the Gaians don't go."

"What about Reynolds and Byrnes? They have most of the children at the landing site."

"Right." She placed her hands on her hips and stared at the floor. "It would be best if we could move the children to the new location before we arrive with the Necri." She glanced up. "Can Byrnes arrange for one of the Corps transports to get them there without prompting a lot of questions about where the kids came from?"

"If anyone can schmooze his way through this without giving away any pertinent information, it's Byrnes. He'll make sure the kids are settled."

Aurora glanced at Mya and the teens. "I also want you to talk to Reynolds and see if she can locate the bodies of the guards and the Necri in the forest. We don't want one of the locals stumbling across them."

"What should she do when she finds them?"

"Is Gonzalez's containment field still down there?"

He nodded. "He deactivated it before we left, but it's there."

"Reynolds can use that. Have her move it to the forest and place it around the bodies. That should keep them relatively undisturbed for the time being." Her next words seemed to take effort to get out. "Ask her to cover the Necri as best she can."

"I'll take care of it."

"Thank you." Her voice dropped so low he almost didn't catch her next words. "Are we okay?"

The flash of concern that crossed her face made his heart ache. "We're more than okay."

She sighed, the soft exhale filled with relief. "Good." She turned to Jon as he approached. "Feeling better?"

"Yes."

The understatement almost made Kire laugh. He and Gonzalez had practically carried Jon into the med bay. Now only Jon's tattered clothes indicated he'd been in a battle. At some point Kire would have a heart to heart with Roe and find out exactly what had produced the dramatic change.

"I could use your help on the other ship." Roe said. "I don't know what Cade's team had to do to disable the engines, but I'm guessing you would be a great help in getting them back up and running."

"Of course. I will change clothes and join you in the shuttle bay."

Roe turned to Kire. "I'll snag a new comband so you can contact me. You'll be in charge of the *Starhawke* until we reach Gaia. I need to stay on the other ship to help with the Necri."

"Understood." He followed them out of the bay and into the lift. Jon and Roe exited on the crew decks while he continued to the bridge. He settled into the captain's chair and sent off the report to the Admiral before contacting Reanne. He'd expected to leave a message, since it was two in the morning at the RC headquarters, but she responded immediately.

"Aurora?"

Her voice sounded a little shrill. Maybe he'd woken her up. "No, it's Kire."

"What's wrong? Is Aurora okay?"

He gritted his teeth at her tone, which indicated she didn't want to be speaking to him any more than he wanted to be talking to her.

"She's fine. But she asked me to contact you. We need help setting up a refugee center on an isolated island on Gaia."

Several beats passed before she responded. "What happened? What is this for?"

"I can't provide details, but we need housing and provisions for a hundred children and two hundred adults." As he spoke, he heard her muffled voice in the background. She was talking to someone else while he was talking to her. Typical Reanne behavior. Might as well push through the rest of it. "We also need transportation for the children. Roe asked you to coordinate with Byrnes to arrange that."

When she replied to him, it was with cold efficiency. "Anything else?"

"No. Those were Roe's two requests."

"Then I'll make sure she gets what she needs."

Talking to Reanne always made his skin feel a little too tight. "Thank you. We'll be in touch when we're ready to bring in the adults." He terminated the connection before she could respond.

Fifty

Who am I?

Aurora slumped in the utilitarian deck chair, the hard edge biting into her neck as she gazed at the ceiling.

Two days had passed since her world had imploded, since the truth had sunk its teeth into her heart and torn a gaping hole that continued to bleed. In the blink of an eye, she'd lost her center. Reality no longer followed a logical path.

Through the anger, the frustration, the disbelief, and the anguish that had followed, she'd kept returning to the one conclusion she couldn't ignore, no matter how much she wanted to—her entire existence was a lie perpetuated by the people she loved most dearly.

She and Mya had worked side by side almost non-stop since they'd returned to help the Necri, but they'd only spoken when absolutely necessary. It was the only way Aurora could keep doing what needed to be done. If she looked too closely at the paradigm shift she'd tumbled into, she'd lose her mind. So she'd erected a wall, focusing all her attention on the Necri.

The results of their joint efforts had been startling. Her energy field gave Mya's healing abilities a booster effect, producing visible changes in the Necri's bodies. Mya had been able to repair much of the damaged cellular structure that had caused the physical abnormalities. They'd also learned that what they'd mistaken as a genetic trait for dark skin and hair among the Necri was often just an accumulation of filth and grime.

The wing harnesses had been another shock. The weight of the mechanical devices strapped to their bodies was largely responsible for the bent form assumed by the Necri. In many instances the harnesses had been in place so long that the surrounding skin had grown over the straps, embedding the tough bands into their flesh. Mya had been reluctant to risk infection from the filth that coated the Necri by making incisions to remove the straps, so they'd left them in place for the time being. But they'd cut the heavy wing carriages from the harnesses, relieving the pressure.

Physically, the Necri were healing. Unfortunately, the energetic connection to the Necri during the process produced a very unpleasant side effect for Aurora. It opened the pathways to their intense feelings of horror, shock, sadness and fear, which mainlined into Aurora, threatening to swamp her. Staying on an even keel took an insane amount of effort.

That was one reason she'd retreated to this small cabin. Sensing their physical pain had been hard enough. Processing their emotional pain as they slowly returned to a state of awareness was like swimming against an undertow.

The teens had appointed themselves as caretakers for the Necri. They'd moved them to a large shuttle bay on the lower level of the ship and grouped them based on their family connections and physical and emotional needs, making it easier for Aurora and Mya to treat them. The arrangement also allowed the teens and Necri to stay together, something they craved after their long period of isolated confinement.

Mya had admitted to a limited understanding of the language the Necri and teens spoke. She'd been able to glean a few details regarding what had happened to them on the ship. The teens were understandably reluctant to talk about it, and never brought it up when the adults were present.

Their halting descriptions painted a picture where the guards had used them as blackmail to keep their parents in line. When the Necri refused to do the destructive work that caused them so much pain and physical crippling, the guards had tortured the kids in full sight of the Necri. All resistance had ceased.

The kids had served another purpose as well. The destruction of the plants caused cellular breakdown in the Necri's bodies, weakening them. Each morning after the Necri had returned to the ship, the kids had been brought up to the cell bay to help mitigate the damage by sharing their energy fields. It was the only contact they had been allowed with their parents.

It was astounding that they weren't all clinically insane. Yes, they were struggling, but their deep sense of community seemed to be providing them with an inner strength that guided them during their recovery.

The teens were coping by working relentlessly. Dark circles had become permanent fixtures under their eyes. The three catatonic Necri who had been Aurora's personal bodyguards had turned out to be Raaveen and Sparw's parents. Raaveen hadn't asked about the fate of her mother, the Necri who had died on Gaia, but Aurora suspected the girl already knew the truth. The three adults remained unresponsive to their children, but any time Aurora or Mya stepped into the room, they would turn toward them, like flowers lifting their faces to the sun.

And then there was Maanee and Paaw. Aurora would never forget the look in their eyes as they'd introduced Mya and Aurora to their mother—hope and joy overlaid with a soft melancholy. Prior to the healing session, the creature they'd brought forward had been unidentifiable as a female. Her back had been buckled and misshapen, her head downcast and her body caked in dark muck. Only her blue eyes had indicated her connection to the two girls.

Maanee and Paaw's mother had been the first they'd taken to one of the ship's cabins for a shower, since her daughters could provide physical and emotional support during the potentially traumatic experience. Their mother had been terrified of leaving the bay and entering the enclosed space of the cabin, but Aurora had led the way and remained within arm's reach as the girls had gently removed the scraps of clothing that had glued themselves to their mother's body.

The girls had stepped into the shower enclosure with their mother and turned the spray so it hit the back wall rather than falling directly on her skin. The guards had routinely turned hoses on the Necri in their cells in an effort to cut down on the smell and accumulated waste. The trauma had made most of the Necri afraid of falling water.

The hunched woman who had stepped out nearly half an hour later had born little resemblance to the creature who had entered. Her skin had changed from charcoal gray to a healthier pinkish hue. The girls had managed to wash her hair as well, and while it was sparse and coarse, indicating prolonged periods of malnutrition, the water had revealed the true color, which was a darker version of Maanee and Paaw's blonde waves.

The woman's head had been down, her gaze at the level of Aurora's knees. She'd trembled as she'd clutched the front of the robe she wore, as if she feared the garment would be taken at any moment, but eventually she'd released her death grip on the fabric. She'd lifted her hands, her movements choppy, but Aurora had immediately recognized the gesture Paaw had made in the med bay, which was followed by the name she had come to dread.

"*Sahzade.*"

And so it had begun. Williams and Celia had worked on removing the wing carriages and treating open wounds while Aurora and Mya had focused on cellular healing and physical sanitation. Variations on the scene with Maanee and Paaw's mother had played out as they'd taken the Necri who were emotionally and physically stable enough to handle the shower process to the cabins, always with a couple of the teens there to assist. And after each transformation, the same gesture had been made, the same hateful name spoken as she and Mya were treated like royalty, adding fuel to the fire of her anger.

She'd sent Kelly to the *Starhawke* to collect clothing donations from the crew so that the Necri would have something to wear as they shed their filthy rags. Consequently, during her last visit to Necri Hall, as she'd come to think of the large shuttle bay where the Necri lived, she'd seen a growing assortment of males and females in outfits that looked very familiar.

What she hadn't counted on was that the Necri would be able to identify which garments had come from her and Mya. Those who had received her clothes went out of their way to show deference whenever Aurora approached. It made her want to scream.

That was another reason she'd escaped to this odd corner of the ship. Gratitude was one thing. Having people fall at her feet was something else entirely.

And finally, there was the information Celia had just shared with her. After they'd finished their work with the Necri, Celia and Williams had returned to the cell bay to retrieve the bodies of the two dead guards. They'd removed the armor and cloth mesh that had hidden the guards' faces and bodies and revealed the unmistakable scaly skin and heavy brow ridges of Etah Setarips.

The faction had been rumored as extinct following a particularly violent encounter with an opposing faction twenty-five years ago. Apparently some Etah had survived. And thrived. But how they'd managed to obtain the resources to build a ship, abduct the Necri, and launch a guerrilla attack on Gaia remained a mystery. And why?

Aurora sensed Mya's approach long before the door behind her slid open. She cranked her shoulders up to her ears and shifted her gaze from the ceiling to the opposite wall. So much for her moment of privacy.

Mya entered, but Aurora didn't turn around.

"Sahzade?"

She ground her molars together. That damn name was going to be the death of her.

"Aurora?"

Not as bad. But at this point anything from Mya's mouth was a spark to tinder. Her temper flared. If Mya refused to leave her in peace then she'd better be prepared for a confrontation. The question that had been haunting Aurora for two days shot out of her mouth like a laser. "Who am I?"

"What?"

She shoved her feet against the floor, spinning the chair to face the door. She gripped the metal arms so tightly her fingers cramped. Her face felt like she'd stuck it in a furnace. "*Who. Am. I?*"

Mya had the grace to look uncomfortable. Good. Aurora wasn't about to make this easy. She was sick of the lies and deceit. She wanted answers. Now.

"You are Aurora Hawke, daughter of Libra Hawke."

She stared. "And?"

Mya took a tentative step forward. "And...you are like a sister to me."

A harsh laugh scraped out of her throat. "Oh really? Well you have a funny way of showing it." Hysteria bubbled up, the result of physical exhaustion and emotional overload, but she couldn't stop now. "Hell, for all I know, I *am* your sister. In fact, I could be the frickin' queen of England and *I...wouldn't...know!*" The last three words came out on a roar. Betrayal by the one person she'd counted on as her rock had wounded her in ways that might never heal.

The corners of Mya's lips pinched as she held Aurora's gaze, anguish visible in the lines of her face. "I'm sorry," she whispered. "Aurora, I'm so sorry."

Mya was in pain, too. But Aurora couldn't take any satisfaction in that. She also couldn't bear the sight of her friend's tortured expression. She spun the chair back around and resumed her study of the wall.

"Please. Let me explain."

There was only one explanation she wanted at the moment. "What does it mean?"

Mya sounded confused. "What does *what* mean?"

"Sahzade. What does it mean?"

Mya didn't respond right away. Instead, she pulled up a chair and sat facing Aurora. "The closest literal translation would be *guardian* or *protector.* Your family has always been the guardians of the race, which has given you a place of distinction." She paused, and her next words came out slowly. "But the cultural meaning of Sahzade for our people is different. It's much closer to *Your Highness.*"

Aurora squeezed her eyes shut, as if that would block out the words. Nope. They continued to ring in her head. And she'd thought having secret abilities was a challenge. Ha.

Abruptly the fight drained out of her, leaving her empty and numb. "So I'm royalty. Is that what you're saying?"

"Yes."

The Necri had certainly been treating her that way. And Mya, too. "What about you? That name they call you—Nedale. What does that mean?"

"It means *healer*."

"And?"

To her credit, she didn't look away. "And something along the lines of *Your Grace.*"

"So you're royalty, too." Mya didn't deny it. "*Are* we related?"

Mya shook her head. "No, not by blood. But our families are connected. You are the daughter of the eldest female of the Guardian family, and I'm the daughter of the eldest female of the Healer family. Together, those two families form the basis of power for our race. Our unique abilities, which are passed genetically from mother to daughter, have provided for the safety and nurturing of our people for millennia."

"Our people," Aurora echoed. "I don't even know what that means." She resumed her study of the wall. "According to my mother, our homeworld was destroyed and *our people* decimated when she was a child."

"I know." Sadness weighted down those two words. "This is not my story to tell. Sahz...Aurora," she amended when Aurora glared. "And I don't know much more than you do."

Yeah. Right.

"You may not believe me, but it's true. My parents didn't agree with your mother's choice to keep your heritage from you, but they respected her decision. Since they knew I would hate keeping things from you, they decided it would be easier if I didn't know the details, either. But one thing I can tell you. Your mother's choices were designed to protect you."

"Protect me?" What a joke. She had an energy shield, a unique ability that had kept her safe her entire life. An ability that now defined her in a way she despised. She was the *last* person who needed protection. "From what?"

"From those who would seek to hurt or control you."

She snorted. "I'm not a weakling, and you know it."

"Neither is your mother. That's not the point." Mya swept her arm to encompass the ship. "Look around you. Look at what happened to the Necri and how it affected both of us. Can you honestly say you're invincible?"

"I don't know." And the uncertainty was driving her insane. This was exactly what she'd been avoiding. She didn't have answers. Only questions.

She had to get out of here. For the first time in her life, being around Mya was draining her. And she knew exactly where she wanted to go. Shoving to her feet, she headed for the door.

"Aurora."

She stopped, glancing over her shoulder at her lifelong friend. "I believe you, Mya. I do."

"Then let's—"

She held up her hand. "But I need *you* to understand that I can't deal with this right now. I just can't. And if you're the friend you say you are, please respect that."

Turning away, she stepped into the corridor as the door closed softly behind her.

Fifty-One

Cade sat alone on the utilitarian bridge, running through a final check of the navigation systems while he waited for the engineering team to give the all clear to take the ship back to Gaia.

He'd be bringing the ship in from behind the moon onto the night side of the planet, which would shield it from view by anyone on the planet's surface. Not that they were likely to see it anyway with the Kraed hull doing its job. He'd been stunned to learn that piece of information from Drew. He couldn't imagine how anyone had stolen the technology from the over-protective Kraed race, but the revelation had to be eating Clarek alive.

The back and forth communications with Admiral Schreiber over the past few days had been intense. He'd appointed Cade's team as the security detail for the Necri, at least for the time being. They were responsible for returning the Necri to the planet's surface and hiding the ship on the island while the *Starhawke* remained in orbit as sentry.

The official word given to the Gaian chancellor was that the guerrilla force responsible for the attacks had been killed when their ship self-destructed shortly after they'd left the planet. The *Argo* was due to arrive in a couple of days to take over the *Starhawke*'s position, which gave Aurora and her crew time to settle the Necri in their temporary housing and finish treating their injuries before any new personnel showed up.

Cade hadn't seen much of Aurora over the past few days. When he had, she'd looked strung out. He'd wanted to ask her what had happened when she'd returned to the *Starhawke* to help Mya, but the abrupt change in her attitude had held him in check. At least Mya seemed in good health, although tension lined her face, too. Then again, they all looked road-weary.

He'd spent most of his time on the bridge, figuring out the controls to the ship and getting everything back online. The auto-destruct system had completely disabled all the navigation controls. Whoever had built this ship had wanted to make sure no one else could take it over. If Aurora hadn't been onboard, they would have gotten their wish.

Not that the ship was much to write home about. The Kraed hull was the most remarkable thing about it, but unlike the *Starhawke's* elegance, this thing was a mish-mash of appropriated technology all grouped together in bizarre and often confusing ways. It was built like a battering ram, with heavy weapons systems and a hull and shielding design that could deflect damn near everything. But the controls left much to be desired. Drew had helped him sort some of it out, and she'd also spent time with Clarek in engineering, repairing the damage her device had caused to the engines.

When the *Argo* arrived, Cade would be responsible for training whoever would be piloting the ship back to Earth for storage and study. His data pad was already filled with detailed notes and images of the ship's quirks.

"Mind if I join you?"

He glanced over his shoulder. Aurora stood in the doorway, her slumped posture betraying her exhaustion. "Of course not."

He expected her to come over to his station or take a seat in the command chair. Instead, she bypassed both and settled at the console to his right. She clasped her hands in her lap and stared at the image of the *Starhawke* on the bridgescreen. But she looked a million miles away.

"Are you okay?"

She glanced at him briefly before returning her gaze to the screen. Her jaw clenched and her breath hitched in and out, as though each inhale cost her more energy than she had to spare. Her eyelids drifted down on a weak sigh. "No." Her voice sounded strangled. "No, I am most definitely not okay."

Oh, hell. Things must be much worse than he'd suspected. Pushing his console out of the way he faced her, resting his elbows on his knees. "Do you want to talk about it?"

She opened her eyes and met his gaze. "Not really."

Of course she wouldn't. It had been a long time since she'd viewed him as a confidant, and with good reason. That's why her next words threw him for a loop.

"I just needed to see a friendly face."

Him? The comment rocked him back in his chair and triggered all kinds of alarm bells. If she'd chosen to come to him rather than seeking out Mya, Cardiff or Clarek, who were all on the ship somewhere, something was *really* not right in her world.

He quickly reviewed the events of the last few days, looking for clues. She'd saved the Necri, they'd successfully taken control of the enemy ship, and no one on their team had been killed. He'd also heard from Williams that the Necri were doing amazingly well. So what was so wrong?

He gave her a small smile of encouragement. "I'm glad you think of me as a friend."

The corner of her mouth trembled slightly, a failed attempt to return the gesture. "Yeah. Well. I know we've had our issues, but I'll say this for you. You've never lied to me."

Wrong. The list of lies he'd told her could fill this bridge.

She paused, a small line appearing between her brows. "Well, that's not true. This mission involved quite a few lies. And I realize now you lied about the reason for your training at the Academy. But that's different." She flicked those major transgressions away with a flip of her fingers, then tapped the center of her chest. "You've never lied about what was in here."

Also not true. He distinctly remembered telling her before he left the Academy that he didn't love her anymore. Turns out he'd been lying to both of them. But now wasn't the time to bring it up. "Do you want to tell me what happened?"

She returned her gaze to the bridgescreen. "I could tell you, but..." She trailed off, her eyes going unfocused again.

"But then you'd have to kill me?" he finished, hoping to lighten the mood.

It didn't work. "No." She sighed. "Although the thought has occurred to me on occasion."

No doubt.

Her expression turned bleak. "I'm just not sure you'll believe me."

The hell he wouldn't. She was the most honest person he knew. It ran through her core like tempered steel. She could tell him she'd created the universe and he'd believe her. "Try me."

She studied him for a moment, her expression wary. But apparently the need to talk to someone overrode her concerns. She turned in her chair, mirroring his pose. "Okay, here goes." She took a deep breath. "I'm a queen."

What?

"Or at the very least a princess of some sort. Of the Necri."

The Necri? He hadn't seen that coming. "Did they confer some type of ceremonial honor on you for saving them?" Anything was possible.

She shook her head. "No, this has nothing to do with choice or gratitude. I wish it did." Bitterness overlaid her words. "Turns out my mother forgot to mention one teeny tiny detail when she told me about our family history. Her family...*my family*...is from the same homeworld as the Necri. The same species, actually. And in that society, my abilities proclaim me as the guardian of the race, and therefore, the ruler."

He blinked. Allowed the words to filter into his brain. Blinked again. "But..." He didn't have anything to add. His thought process had stalled. She was a queen? Of the Necri? He tried again. "But didn't you tell me that your homeworld was destroyed and your race exterminated?"

"Yep. My mother lied."

Oh this was not good, on so many levels.

"And that's not all. Mya has known all along and never told me."

Click. The pieces fell into place. Now he understood her mood.

She'd always been close to her mother, and Mya had been her best friend since birth. They represented her connection to her non-human half. If those two women had lied to her about something this major, the devastation to Aurora's faith in the world would have shaken her to her foundation, making her doubt everything and everyone who had been a part of that reality.

Anger flared, but he pushed it away. That wasn't what she needed from him right now. "I'm sorry." The words slipped out without conscious thought, followed by a soft oath. "I'm so sorry." He shoved a hand through his hair as he held her gaze. "Dammit, Aurora, you deserve better than that."

Her lips tilted up in a sad smile. "Thank you. Believe it or not, it helps to hear you say that."

And didn't that just make him feel all warm and fuzzy inside. "Then I'll say it again." He reached out and clasped her hand in his. "You deserve so much better than that."

She gave his hand a gentle squeeze. But as the moment stretched out and neither of them let go, his palm and forearm started tingling. The sensation had nothing to do with warm fuzzies and everything to do with the energy field that had appeared around Aurora and was moving up his arm from their joined hands.

The look in her eyes had shifted, too, but not in a way he would have liked. The woman he had always seen as a pillar of strength and confidence suddenly looked as fragile as an intricate blown-glass sculpture, one that was one small nudge away from smashing into a million pieces.

He needed to get closer. The distance between the two consoles was a little wide, but he was a tall man with a good reach, especially when motivated. And he was highly motivated to protect her from the impending maelstrom he saw brewing inside.

As he moved his center of gravity forward, he kept his focus on her eyes, those incredible green eyes that could shift from the bright color of forest leaves to the dark tones of a stormy ocean, but were always interwoven with flecks of hidden gold. At the moment, they resembled the flat gray of a dead calm sea right before a typhoon.

His knees hit the floor with a soft thud. He kept his hold on her arm with one hand, and moved the other up to her shoulder. Tension gathered around her eyes as she watched him. He didn't have her gift for feeling the emotions of others, but in this instance he didn't need it. She was torn between two conflicting desires—to let go and allow herself to be comforted, and to maintain the self-reliance for which she was so well known.

But as he wrapped his arm around her shoulders, she lost the battle, leaning toward him as her eyes began to close.

"Clarek to Ellis."

The Kraed's voice acted like a bomb, blasting them apart. A slew of obscenities swarmed through his head as Aurora jerked back, breaking the connection.

Cade slammed his hand on the comm switch. If he didn't know better, he'd think Clarek had them under surveillance. "What?" he barked.

"We're ready to power up the engines." Clarek's reply held an edge that indicated he didn't like Cade's tone.

Too damn bad. Cade was feeling hostile. The behemoth had interrupted a very private moment. Then the words registered. Engines? Oh, right. The ship. Heading back to Gaia. Work. Duty. All those things that had vanished like vapor as he'd gazed into Aurora's eyes.

No going back, either. She'd turned to face the screen and had crossed her arms over her chest, her body taut.

He came up with a few more choice names for the damn Kraed. "Fine. Ready when you are." He settled back into his chair.

The engine of this ship wasn't what anyone would call refined. In fact, as it powered up, all the objects in the room vibrated, creating a hum that cut through the silence.

Would Aurora use the departure as an excuse to leave? He watched her out of the corner of his eye. So far, she looked like she was staying put.

"Engines powered and ready. All systems functional," Clarek said.

"Acknowledged." He opened a channel to the *Starhawke*. "Ellis to Emoto. We're ready when you are."

"We'll follow you in."

"On our way." He engaged the system's navigation controls and eased the ship forward. It obeyed his commands, but man, flying this thing after being at the helm of the *Starhawke* was like going from his jetbike to a horse and buggy. However, nothing on the console indicated any sign of trouble. He glanced at his silent traveling companion.

She turned her head to meet his gaze. "So far, so good."

He nodded. "Seems to be."

Her expression was hard to read. She'd obviously slammed a few walls into place, but the sadness remained. "Cade, I..." She paused as if searching for the right words. "My head's kind of a mess right now."

"I can understand that."

"Just so you know, I'm not sorry."

"About what?" Almost losing control? Coming to him for comfort?

"About you. You and me. The past. Any of it."

302   *Audrey Sharpe*

Her admission stunned him. He'd always assumed she
had a slew of regrets when it came to him. Of course, she
was inclined to be charitable at the moment, considering her
friends and family had just blasted her into next week. It
didn't mean she'd feel the same way after the storm passed.

"And I meant what I said," she added. "I would like
to be friends."

Just friends? The question was on the tip of his
tongue, begging to be turned loose. But he'd never ask.
Besides, he already knew the answer. If what she'd told him
was true, and he had every reason to believe it was, she
was more unattainable now than she'd been at the Academy.
And they'd been doomed back then. "So would I."

The small smile that touched her lips was
heartbreaking. "I'm glad. That means a lot to me."

It meant a lot to him, too. More than she'd ever
know.

"I should probably get back to the Necri." She stood,
but a frown creased her brow.

"Something wrong?"

Her frown deepened. "It's that name. I really don't
want to keep calling them that, especially knowing..." She
shuddered.

"You could call them something else." Something that
fit their emerging identity. He pictured the beautiful energy
ribbons Aurora and the teens had generated. That was their
true nature, not the deformed beings the Necri had been
turned into. Despite appearances they, like her, were beings
of light, not darkness. And their name should reflect that.
"How about Lumians?"

"Lumians?" She mulled it over. "Lumians. Huh. I like
that." The bleakness ghosted over her face once more. "Much
better than being the queen of the dead, that's for sure."

His throat constricted. He didn't want her to carry this burden alone. "Aurora, I—"

She stopped him. "It's okay. Really. I'll be fine." She took a step toward the doorway. "Thanks for listening."

He nodded. "Anytime." And he meant it.

Fifty-Two

Aurora was losing her mind.

First the revelation about the Setarips, then the scene with Mya, followed by her encounter with Cade. What a day. Her behavior was completely out of character—proof positive that she was slipping into madness.

The Lumians, however, were remarkably calm. And why wouldn't they be? They clearly trusted her to protect them. How ironic. The more relaxed they became, the more tension she carried.

The trip down to Gaia was bumpy, the shaking continuing almost until they reached their destination. When they touched down, air hissed through the ducts as the room pressurized to match the exterior, then the bay doors opened. Outside, night held sway, the only lighting coming from small lamps that bordered the path to the camp.

Nodding at the teens, Aurora stepped onto the ramp. Like ducklings leaving a pond, the Lumians followed in her wake, with Williams and Celia on either side and Mya bringing up the rear. Aurora stopped briefly to slip off her boots, allowing the warm sand to caress her bare toes. She'd always been a sucker for the tactile experience of walking on a beach, but that was only part of the reason for the footwear change. The Lumians were all barefoot. If the path became rocky or uncomfortable, she wanted to know before their feet took a beating.

Leading the way, she followed the line of lights that Byrnes and Reynolds had set out to guide them to the camp on the other side of the island. What would happen when they arrived was anyone's guess. Some of the Lumians still had difficulty interacting with other adults, let alone their own kids. The shock of being together might be more than they were prepared to handle.

In her fantasy, the kids ran to their parents and everyone was instantly happy. But this was reality, and the adults and children had suffered deep, long-term trauma. It might be months or even years before they could experience openness and trust.

The soft shwoosh-shwoosh of the sand and the touch of a gentle breeze lent a feeling of serenity to the scene. Thank goodness their destination was a fairly long walk. It gave her time to breathe in the cleansing salt air and release the toxic emotions that had battered her for days.

As they drew closer to the camp, however, she felt a shift in the emotions coming from the Lumians. She also picked up on the emotional tenor of the children up ahead. A low-level fear and apprehension predominated for both, as well as resigned acceptance, but also flares of hope and even excitement.

The path broke through the trees a few moments later, revealing the large tents and open pathways of the rescue camp, as well as the anxious faces of the Lumian children. But none of them moved. Had Reynolds and Byrnes told the kids to stay put?

A quick look at the children's faces gave the answer. They were having trouble processing what they were seeing. In their recent experience, their parents were Necri—dark, crippled, filthy creatures living stunted lives of continual pain. The clean and mostly-upright men and women who were walking toward them would appear, by comparison, like strangers.

A shout rang out. A dark-haired woman pushed forward, stumbling in the sand as she called out what had to be a child's name. An answering cry broke from the line of kids. A little girl of about six raced across the open space and launched into her mother's arms, knocking them both to the ground.

It was the small stone that started an avalanche. More cries echoed from both sides as children and adults moved forward, some with the same zeal as the little girl and her mother, others with much more care and even shyness, as though they were meeting for the first time.

Aurora fell back to the edge of the clearing as tears filled her vision. The fierce blend of relief, sadness and joy that swept out from the Lumians overwhelmed her exhausted mind and body, the force of it so strong it triggered physical pain.

She staggered, her legs unsteady as she struggled to absorb the emotions of three hundred tortured souls. As her knees buckled, she reached out to catch herself. But a gentle hand caught her, instead.

Mya stood by her side, her right hand wrapped firmly around Aurora's outstretched arm as her left hand caught her about the shoulders, lowering her to her knees. Mya knelt beside her, her healing field slowly pushing back the incoming tide, allowing Aurora's thoughts and feelings to regain a foothold against the onslaught.

"I've got you." Mya maintained the physical connection as she gazed at the scene unfolding before them, her own eyes glistening.

Aurora couldn't think. Couldn't move. Couldn't do anything but stare at the familiar features of her childhood friend.

Mya turned her head. a sad smile tipping the corners of her mouth. "It's going to be okay. Sahzade."

She surrendered. With a sob wrenched from the depths of her soul. she turned into Mya's arms and let the world crumble around her.

Fifty-Three

Cade scanned his notes one more time, making sure he hadn't missed any important details. The temporary pilot the Council had sent would certainly be competent, but this ship had a lot more quirks than a typical Fleet vessel. If he could save someone unnecessary stress, he was all for it. And he had another motivation for delaying. The longer he fiddled with his notes, the longer he could put off heading to the Lumian camp on the other side of the island.

Reynolds and the security detail from the Rescue Corps had returned early that morning from their trip to the Gaian forest to recover the bodies of the Setarips and the dead Necri. Aurora had arranged for the Necri to be turned over to the Lumians for a proper funeral ceremony, which would take place the following evening.

Mya had already examined the bodies of the Setarips and confirmed they were from the Etah faction. The security team would be delivering them to the ship, where they would be placed in storage along with the other two from the Necri cell bay. Reynolds would stay with the RC team to guard the ship until the temporary crew arrived. With Reynolds on site, his presence was no longer required.

That left him with one place to go. He grimaced. He didn't have any illusions that the next few days would be a picnic, since he'd be in forced proximity with Aurora...and Jonarel Clarek. After what had occurred with Aurora on the bridge, Cade wasn't sure spending time with her was wise, especially with the overprotective Kraed watching them. Not that he had a choice.

His comband vibrated. "Yes?"

"The security team has arrived," Drew said. "Are you ready to head over to the camp?"

No. But he'd run out of excuses. "I'll be down in five."

"We'll wait for you."

Clarek had remained onboard so he and Drew could complete a survey of the ship's engine systems. He'd be waiting with her in the bay. As Cade walked down the corridor, he focused on keeping his expression neutral. A lot had happened since his last interaction with Clarek, and he didn't know what to expect from him. But he'd be damned if he'd give the Kraed a reason to pick a fight.

Voices drifted through the doorway as he entered. Drew, Clarek, Reynolds and five Rescue Corps personnel stood in a loose cluster inside the bay. Night still reigned outside, the row of lights that led to the camp casting a friendly glow on the sand.

"Commander." Reynolds walked toward him, a rare smile softening the planes of her face. "It's good to see you, sir."

He returned the smile. "You too. How are the kids doing?"

She shrugged. "As well as can be expected considering what they've gone through. But getting them back together with their parents was important. They needed that."

"I'll bet." He'd guessed it would be an emotional scene, and from the tone of Reynolds's voice, it had been. He was glad he'd missed it. He glanced at Clarek. "Everything set in engineering?"

The Kraed nodded, his expression neither hostile nor friendly. "We left notes for the incoming team. And Bella did a wonderful job on the patch. They should not encounter any problems."

Bella now, was it? Apparently a friendship had developed between the two.

Drew beamed. "It was a team effort. I couldn't have asked for a better partner." She smiled at Clarek with obvious affection.

Cade's jaw clenched. It was illogical to get angry because a member of his team liked the Kraed, especially since Clarek knew his job and was likely to earn their respect. The rest of his team didn't have Cade's personal reasons for disliking the male. But it still irked him.

"Good." He turned to Reynolds. "The ship is yours. Gonzo will notify you when the *Argo* arrives." Gonzalez had been more than willing to stay on the *Starhawke* as the interim security chief until the *Argo* arrived with the transport crew, at which point he'd catch a ride down to the surface. Cade motioned to Drew. "Ready?"

"You bet."

They walked down the ramp and onto the sand. Thankfully, Drew kept the journey from being filled with uncomfortable silence. She described all of the strange things she and Clarek had discovered while working on the engine repairs. Clearly the cobbled-together technology was not limited to the bridge.

He caught sight of their destination, a collection of tents in a clearing. Shadows moved inside, indicating they weren't the only ones up and about this early in the morning. Clarek and Drew headed toward the open tent flap, but he hung back, glancing at his comband. He had a couple hours until sunrise. Maybe he'd take a short walk down to the beach before settling in. It might clear his mind and help him sleep.

He followed a narrow trail that led through the trees, the sound of the surf calling him. When he left the cover of the foliage, an expanse of pristine sand greeted him. The low-lying moon had just begun to dip below the horizon, its reflected glow creating a ribbon of light on the water. A lone figure stood at the edge, her body cast in perfect silhouette. Aurora.

Should he leave? But something about her posture— the straightness of her back and the tilt of her head—made him stop. When he'd seen her on the bridge, she'd looked whipped. But as she stood with her feet planted on the wet sand and her face lifted to the breeze, she was the picture of confident strength...and beauty. Oh, who was he kidding? He couldn't leave if his life depended on it.

He slipped off his shoes and left them next to the path before closing the distance to where she stood. She didn't turn, but her voice drifted back to him.

"Hello, Cade."

As he stopped next to her, he realized her eyes were closed. She hadn't seen him coming. She'd sensed him. Was there ever going to be a day when that ability didn't fascinate him? "Hello."

The moonlight created a halo around her head as she turned and opened her eyes. Her hair fell in gentle waves around her shoulders. It was the first time she'd worn it down on this mission, and it made her seem more approachable. Her eyes sparkled with humor. "Fancy meeting you here."

His brain hiccupped. Was she actually *flirting* with him? He fought to keep his emotions under wraps as he tested the waters. "You shouldn't stand so close to the water, you know. Someone might mistake you for a mermaid."

This time, his attempt at humor had the intended effect. She laughed, the lilting sound warming him in all the right places. He grinned, delighted to see her vibrancy returning.

"Now that would be fun." She inclined her head toward the expanse of sand. "Care to take a stroll with me?"

As if he'd say no? He gestured for her to lead the way and then fell into step beside her as the waves snuck around their toes and raced back across the sand.

"Is everything set with the ship?" she asked.

He nodded. "We turned it over to Reynolds and the security team. I won't need to go back until the *Argo* arrives."

She smiled. "Whatever will you do with yourself until then."

What indeed? "Oh, I'm sure I'll think of something. This place has a lot to recommend it." Including his walking companion.

"I know. It reminds me of pictures I've seen of Hawaii. When I was a kid, I asked my mom if we could take a vacation there, but she wasn't interested. She said the tropics were too warm and humid for her." She lifted her face, encouraging the breeze to ruffle the thick strands of her hair. "But this feels like heaven to me."

His breath caught. For a moment she looked exactly as she had at eighteen, and his body responded accordingly. And that was a serious problem. The longer he stared at her, the harder it was to remember the long list of reasons why he needed to keep his distance from Aurora Hawke.

She turned, her expression puzzled. "I'm getting the strangest mix of emotions from you."

Whoops. He wasn't guarding his thoughts or emotions worth a damn. "What do you mean?" He hoped she didn't catch the telltale huskiness in his voice.

"A moment ago you were relaxed and happy, but that abruptly disappeared and now I'm getting an intensity that borders on anxiety. If I didn't know better, I'd think—"

He tried like hell to shut down his wayward emotions, but when she cut off abruptly and stared at him, he knew he'd failed miserably. She was putting it all together and coming to the inevitable conclusion.

"Cade?" She sounded a little breathless.

"Yes?" He held her gaze, determined to brave this out.

"What are you thinking?"

"The truth?"

She nodded without hesitation.

And why shouldn't he tell her? She already knew. "All right." He took a step closer, moving within a palm's width as he drank in the silver light that glistened on her skin. "Right now, I'm using every iota of willpower I possess to keep my voice steady and my hands at my sides, because what I want to do is haul you into my arms and explore every millimeter of your mouth with my tongue."

Bingo. He didn't have to look to know her energy field had enveloped him in its embrace, even though her body hadn't moved.

She moistened her lips. "And that would be a bad thing, right?" Her eyes had taken on a smoky quality, making her look even more like the lover he remembered, not the competent captain she'd become.

"Depends on how you look at it."

"How do *you* look at it?"

He felt a tug in the vicinity of his heart. How to answer that? He reached up and traced her bottom lip with his thumb. "You are the best and worst thing that has ever happened to me."

Her breathing changed, and she trembled as his fingers continued to explore her face. Her voice was strong, though. "Believe it or not, I understand. That pretty much describes how I think of you, too."

"That doesn't surprise me." He allowed his index finger to slide up her jaw, his palm capturing the side of her face as his thumb continued to stroke her cheek. "Complications seem to follow wherever we go."

Sadness flickered in her eyes. "I know."

That brought him up short. He stepped back. "So we should—" He halted as she grabbed hold of his wrist, keeping his hand right where it was.

The look in her eyes intensified, as did the feeling of warmth from her energy field. "But here's the deal. We have unfinished business, you and I. And when this mission is over, we may not get another chance to resolve it."

He wasn't sure where she was going with this, but he wasn't an idiot. He'd stay right where he was and find out.

"When you left the Academy, our last moments were filled with anger and bitterness. And I thought I had come to terms with that." She shifted closer, bringing them a hair's breadth from contact. "But I realize now that I haven't. All this time, I've been wanting a better ending, one that has joy and pleasure, not pain."

His heart thumped erratically in his chest. Was she saying what he thought she was?

"Now we're here together, on a beautiful beach in the moonlight, just the two of us. I couldn't ask for a better setting. So I have a request to make." And then she got him right where he lived as her gaze drifted to his mouth.

Thoughts he had no business thinking played leapfrog in his head. He had to clear his throat before he could get a word out. "Okay."

"Will you please give me a proper goodbye kiss?"

No! He closed his eyes as her words registered. He *was* an idiot. A complete and utter moron to be exact. She wasn't asking about the future. Hell, she wasn't even asking about the present. No. What she wanted was a better ending to the past.

Her request would shred him. It might bring closure for her, but it would drop him into a Hell from which he might never find relief. But after what he'd done to her ten years ago, he owed her this. And he'd do it right.

He opened his eyes. She was gazing at him with worry lines forming between her brows. Those had to go. "Yes," he whispered. "It would be my pleasure."

Relief flashed in her eyes as the tension drained away.

She'd honestly expected him to say no. And that stung almost as much as his impending loss. He'd caused her so much pain, done so much to destroy her faith in him. But he would grab this opportunity to finally make amends. Even if it killed him.

Lifting his hand, he cradled her jaw and gazed into her eyes, watching the play of light over her features, memorizing every line. He could feel the rapid pulse in her throat, the subtle tension of anticipation beneath his fingers.

Leaning down, he allowed his breath to brush lightly over her skin, his lips hovering just out of reach as he traced up her cheek and over her forehead. He placed his first kiss in the space between her brows, allowing his lips to warm her skin and release any remaining tension there. But he didn't linger. Instead, he continued his slow exploration, touching down again and again, seeking points of exquisite sensitivity until a soft sigh escaped her.

Then, only then, did his focus move to his final destination. The velvet sweetness of her lips brushed like butterfly wings across his mouth once, twice, before he settled in with a sigh of his own. The contact sent a charge of electricity through his entire body, upping his temperature by several degrees in a heartbeat. The intensity of the emotions that assailed him threatened to break him, but he held them back, determined to enjoy every sensation he was creating for her.

He captured the back of her head in his palm, exerting just enough pressure to bring their mouths into the perfect angle to...*yes.* How had he gone ten years without this?

Her energy field enveloped him, tricking his brain into believing nothing existed but the two of them in the warmth of the cocoon. And that was something else he'd forgotten. The energy wasn't held back by little details like clothing. Oh no. It penetrated the fabric, stroking every millimeter of his skin while her lips settled onto his with assurance and familiarity, sending shockwaves of sensation through every cell in his body.

How far would she allow this to go? He changed the angle and swept his tongue against her bottom lip, his breath stuttering as she opened for him. Heaven. He was in heaven, and he never wanted to leave. Never.

Fifty-Four

She'd stepped out of hell into paradise.

The physical, mental and emotional trials of the past week blew away like dandelions as she sank into the wonder and joy of Cade's embrace. His lips and tongue caressed hers, at once achingly familiar and yet subtly different. He'd been a gifted lover before, and the intervening years had only enhanced his skills. She'd asked for a better ending, and he was giving her more than she'd ever dreamed.

Which was precisely why this needed to end. Her body wanted more, and more she could not have—for so many reasons. She'd felt his initial reluctance, but he'd agreed to her request anyway, probably out of a sense of obligation. She'd been willing to accept that, but as the touch of his fingers and the stroke of his tongue sent rivers of heat through her, everything began to tip from deliciously wonderful to potentially painful. She wanted a positive memory to soothe the wounds of the past, not a negative one that served as a reminder of what she'd lost.

Cade had made it clear at the Academy that her abilities and non-human ancestry were not something he wanted to deal with. Now that he knew about her connection to the Lumians? He might still crave her body, but he'd have to suffer a lobotomy before he'd consider becoming a part of her life again. In his eyes, she'd be even more of a freak now than she'd been ten years ago.

But oh, how she'd miss this.

Releasing her grip on his shoulders, she slid her hands down to his chest, putting pressure on the firm muscles beneath her fingertips. She met with resistance. His lips followed hers as she shifted away from him, the back of her neck pressing into his hands as he held her in place. She pushed a little harder, breaking contact with his mouth.

"Aurora?"

Hearing her name in that husky tone was sexy as hell. She almost gave in and made contact again. Almost. But self-preservation kicked in.

Keeping a tight grip on her emotions, she opened her eyes and took a step backward. He moved his hands to her shoulders, but his heated gaze told her he was waiting to see if she'd change her mind. The darkness made his green eyes appear nearly black—or maybe that was the aftermath of the heady kiss. Either way, the look was intense.

Emotions she didn't want to feel tried to worm their way through, but she didn't let them. This was a goodbye kiss, nothing more. He didn't want her. They both knew it. Oh, maybe after revving his engines he was reconsidering whether he wanted her body, but he didn't want *her.* Not really. He'd never given her any reason to doubt that—not at the Academy and certainly not on this mission. So why did it suddenly feel like *she* was rejecting *him?*

"Thank you," she whispered as she took another step back and released her energy field.

This time he let go, his arms dropping to his sides as the intensity faded from his expression, leaving him as dark as the night sky.

Something was wrong. She could feel it. But before she could pinpoint the problem, his emotions shifted.

A cocky smile spread across his handsome face, wiping away the darkness like a sunbeam. "You're welcome."

He winked at her. "That was fun." He glanced in the direction of the camp. "But we should probably head back before someone sends out a search party."

What was going on? She struggled to get a fix on his emotions, but all she encountered was static. Maybe she was projecting her own feelings, wanting to see something that wasn't there. After all, she was the one who'd propositioned him. And she'd been courting disaster with that kiss. Time to switch gears.

She joined him as they walked along the water's edge. "I'm surprised Jonarel hasn't come looking for me." A blast of emotional heat scalded her and she winced. "Sorry."

"Don't be. He's probably eager to see you, too."

He'd given her an opening, and she took it. "I've been meaning to thank you."

He glanced at her. "For what?"

"For keeping your promise to work with Jonarel. I know it wasn't easy for you." He didn't contradict her. She gestured to the camp tents that were now visible through the breaks in the trees. "None of this would have been possible otherwise. I want you to know how much I appreciate your willingness to set aside your personal feelings for a while. It means a lot to me."

He placed a hand on her forearm, pulling her to a halt. "There's something I want to tell you, too."

"Okay." Although from the tone of his voice, she wasn't one hundred percent sure she'd want to hear what he had to say.

"You told me you don't have any regrets about us, and I'm glad if that's true. Unfortunately, I can't say the same thing." He stared at the waves breaking on the sand. "I regret how I treated you, and the pain it caused. It was wrong, and I have no excuse, other than the idiotic behavior of a bull-headed male." He looked back at her, his gaze intense. "But know this. If there's ever anything I can do to help you...*anything*...all you have to do is ask. I won't let you down again."

Shock kept her nailed to the ground as he placed a gentle kiss on her forehead before turning and walking away.

Fifty-Five

The arrival of the transport crew gave Cade a much-needed break from the forced goodwill he'd been projecting ever since his encounter with Aurora on the beach.

Throwing himself into work had always been his go-to distraction whenever he couldn't stop obsessing about something. But in this case, his work—protecting the Lumians and getting them settled in the camp—brought him in close quarters with the object of his obsession.

Aurora did not seem similarly distracted. Instead, she looked weighted down by the responsibilities she now carried. Her first task had been leading the ceremony for the dead Necri. She'd handled it with grace, standing as a pillar of strength and compassion for the Lumians as she bid farewell to a Necri she'd never known. But the look in her eyes had revealed her suffering.

Her words had been foreign to the Lumians, but they'd hung on every one. The Necri's daughter, an older dark-haired girl named Raaveen, had also spoken during the short ceremony. The lyrical Lumian language had been beautiful to listen to, despite the obvious heartache that had threaded through each syllable.

Cade had questioned Byrnes about the events leading up to the death of the Necri, but Justin hadn't been able to provide many details. By the time his team had arrived on the scene, Mya was already unconscious and Aurora was in the hands of the Setarip guards. The one moment Justin had witnessed was Aurora's reaction when the Necri had torn herself free of the wing harness and hit the ground. He said Aurora had screamed as though she was dying.

Considering her connection to the Lumians, and her empathic abilities, Cade could easily imagine how traumatic that moment had been for her. What had caused the Necri to take such a rash action? And how had the Setarips managed to get a hold of Aurora in the first place? Unfortunately, the only person with answers to those questions was Aurora. Cade wasn't inclined to bring up a subject that was guaranteed to cause her pain. Or that would necessitate a private discussion where he'd be tempted to haul her back into his arms. Better to keep his distance.

The transport crew had arrived three days later. The Admiral had sent Hugh Winters to pilot the ship, a man Cade had admired ever since he'd given a symposium at the Academy during Cade's final year. The seasoned navigator was nearing retirement, although Cade couldn't imagine him ever slowing down. They'd talked almost non-stop from the moment he'd taken the transport team over to the ship, trading stories of the vessels they'd piloted and the adventures they'd experienced.

The small crew was rounded out by an engineer, a communications officer, and the *Argo's* first officer, who was the acting captain for the journey. She was an older woman who had transferred from the *Cromwell,* taking over the position Aurora had vacated the previous month. However, she lacked the warmth and sincerity that made Aurora such a fine captain. Cade doubted Knox Schreiber was as enamored of his new first officer as he'd been of his previous one. To hear the Admiral talk, Knox thought Aurora hung the moon.

Cade gave Winters the data pad with all of his notes, and walked the crew through the layout of the navigation and communication consoles. After saying his goodbyes, he left the crew to their preparations and exited the ship for the last time. He stepped off the ramp and felt the sand sink beneath his boots. Finally. He wouldn't miss dealing with that bucket of bolts.

The soft lights led him along the path through the darkness. Reynolds and the RC security team had already returned to the camp, along with Drew and Clarek, who had finished their tutorial with the engineer.

The ship would be powering up shortly. After it reached orbit, it would join the *Argo* for the trip to Earth. The Admiral hadn't set a permanent plan for the Lumians yet, but Cade suspected his team would remain with them on the island, at least for now. Whether the *Starhawke* crew would stay was unclear.

The ground under his feet trembled as he reached the camp, followed by the distant roar of thrusters. The ship was taking off.

His comband vibrated. "This is Ellis."

"We're on our way," Winters said. "Thanks again for all your notes. I suspect I'm gonna need 'em. I can already tell this thing flies about as well as a locomotive."

Cade laughed. "You're right about that."

"You sure you don't want to take over this job? I might let you talk me into making a switch if things keep shimmying like the ship's trying to molt."

Cade's smile widened. "Yeah, but then I'd be up there working and you'd be sitting down here with nothing to do." The ship's running lights appeared in the distance as it rose above the island and began a steady ascent over the dark water.

"Oh, I'd find things to do. Don't you worry about that." The ship blended seamlessly with the starry sky. "A little sun, sand, and surf sounds about per–"

His voice cut off abruptly as a flash lit the sky like midday and static screamed through the communication line. Cade slapped his hands over his ears. A split second later he registered where the light had come from. *The ship!*

"No!" He shouted into his comband, even as his subconscious whispered that it was futile. "Winters, come in! Winters! Respond damn it!" Dead silence.

He blinked repeatedly to clear the image the explosion had left on his retinas. In the sky, yellow and orange balls of flame bloomed in an ever-expanding cloud, like a grotesque, misshapen firework. And still his mind rebelled. It couldn't be. It just...couldn't.

"Cade!"

His neck creaked as he turned toward the voice. Aurora sprinted across the sand in his direction, followed closely by the rest of his team. Her eyes widened as she caught sight of the dying embers of the blast that had turned the ship into a million falling meteors.

"What happened?" She clasped his upper arm like he needed support. Maybe he did. His feet weren't as steady as he'd like.

"I don't know. They were lifting off and then..." He gestured to the dark patch of sky where the ship had been only moments before. But his numbness didn't last long. Years of training kicked in and he opened a new channel. "Ellis to Schreiber."

The background chatter of intense activity overlaid Knox Schreiber's clipped voice. "What the hell happened, Commander?"

"I was hoping you could tell me."

"We don't know. There's no sign of an attack, but we're scanning the area for ships. I'll have that information forwarded to your team." Schreiber gave a muffled order to his crew, then came back online. "Was the ship over the island?"

"No. It was already over the water. We need shuttles to begin a search for survivors."

"My security officer is assembling a team now. We'll have several shuttles down to you within the next fifteen minutes."

"Thank you."

Aurora was talking in low tones with Emoto on the *Starhawke*. Cade turned to Reynolds, who was already reviewing the data coming in from the *Argo*'s sensors. "Anything?"

She shook her head. "Doesn't look like it. No energy traces other than those produced by the ship, and no indication of a projectile of any kind. The data indicates the blast came from inside the ship."

Another auto-destruct? The same question showed in Reynolds's eyes. But how could that be, when they'd successfully powered up the ship and landed it here without incident?

Aurora joined them. "Kire was running sensor sweeps when the ship took off. He confirmed that the explosions emanated from inside. He's analyzing the data and will let us know what he finds. In the meantime, my crew is at your disposal."

It was the beginning of a very long day. Aurora, Mya and Cardiff remained on the island to guard the Lumians, while Cade and the rest of the team focused on the search and rescue mission. Unfortunately, it didn't take long to confirm that all four crewmembers had been killed in the explosion. The crushing pressure of the ocean depths had consumed the remnants of the ship. The few bits of debris they were able to salvage were no larger than a grapefruit.

Aurora met him at the head of the pathway when he returned, looking as tense as he felt. "I need to talk to you." When he gestured to the tents, she shook her head. "Alone."

She moved across the clearing and down the path to the beach. Had it only been four days ago that he'd walked this stretch of sand with her? If felt like an eternity. And the mood was oh so very different this time.

"I just spoke with Kire," she said without preamble as soon as they were out of earshot of the camp. "Star's finished analyzing the data on the explosion, and she's identified four distinct blast points from within the ship."

"*Four?*"

"Yes. One in the corridor outside the containment rooms where the children were kept, one in the crew quarters, one from engineering, and one from the bridge."

He swallowed. At least the location of the blasts meant the crew was killed instantly. Brutal, but painless. And far better than being conscious as they dropped out of the sky. "So this was deliberate."

"Yes. Star was able to pinpoint the exact location of each device to within millimeters. I showed the specs to Jonarel, and the device that went off in engineering was in a section where he and Drew were working to repair the engine damage. There's no way the device could have been there prior to the return to Gaia without their seeing it."

A chill raced down his spine despite the warmth of the setting sun. "So it was placed on the ship while it was on the island?"

She nodded. "That's right."

"But we've had the ship guarded at all times. I was onboard until the security team took over, and they remained with the ship until the transport crew arrived. Are you saying someone sneaked onto the ship undetected?"

"No. It turns out Star had a little free time on her hands, so in addition to the surveillance I asked her to perform, she also keep a visual scan of the ship running at all times. No unauthorized personnel have entered or exited the ship. It was an inside job."

His stomach contracted like he'd been sucker punched. Anger set in a split second later. "You're not suggesting that my team—"

She held up a hand. "No, I'm not. I trust you and the members of your team implicitly. Even if you had some bizarre secret order from the Admiral to destroy the ship, you would have found a way to do it without killing four innocent people."

The tightness in his shoulders eased. But the hard light hadn't left her eyes. "You have a theory."

"If we eliminate you, Jonarel, Drew and Reynolds, that leaves the five Rescue Corps members who were with Reynolds, and the transport crew. Jonarel said the engineer was with him the entire time that he and Drew were on the ship, and that the bridge crew was with you. Is that true? Did anyone leave at any point for any reason?"

He shook his head. "No, they didn't. Winters and the communications officer were working with me, and the captain remained on the bridge with us."

"And you left as they started their flight preparations, correct?"

"That's right."

"Captain Schreiber confirmed that the crew were checking in from their stations at regular intervals from the time you left until the blasts went off. No one had the opportunity to place devices in the containment corridor and crew cabin. Even if they'd had a motivation, these were experienced Fleet officers on a mission to bring the ship back to Earth. Blowing it up and killing themselves in the process serves no logical purpose."

He held her gaze. "Which leaves the Rescue Corp members."

She nodded. "How well do you know them?"

"Not at all," he admitted. "Byrnes might be able to give you a little insight, since he talks to everyone, but they were selected and sent by Reanne. I can't vouch for them, or their actions."

She started to pace. "I don't want to draw conclusions without facts, but if someone at the Rescue Corps is involved it would explain so much."

She was right. He'd provided Reanne with the details of their mission since day one. How well had she guarded that information? If someone had infiltrated the Rescue Corps and had Reanne's ear or access to her office, they may have been privy to everything that was being planned and done. And they could have gotten themselves posted to the security team when they realized the ship hadn't been destroyed. Placing the devices during the intervening days while guarding the ship would have been child's play.

Something else occurred to him. "What about the Lumians? If what you're saying is true, wouldn't whoever's responsible try to eliminate them as well?"

Aurora's face changed from flushed to ashen in a heartbeat. Without a word, she turned and sprinted in the direction of the camp.

Fifty-Six

Aurora's heart pumped in time with her feet as she raced toward the camp. How could she have been so blind? She'd been focused on solving the mystery of the explosion and hadn't even considered the possibility that someone might be planning an attack on the Lumians.

The dry sand of the path pulled at her boots, slowing her down. She fought the panic that gripped her by the throat. A few seconds might not matter, but logic had taken a backseat.

She burst through the flap into the main tent, the heavy canvas giving a loud *whomp* that mimicked the hammering in her chest. She stumbled to a halt in front of Mya.

Mya's eyes widened. "Sahzade? What's wrong?"

"Are the Lumians okay?"

"What?"

"The Lumians. Are they okay?"

Mya frowned in confusion. "Yes. They're fine. What's going on?"

Aurora took a deep breath to calm her racing pulse. "They may be in danger."

"Danger? What kind of danger?"

"Someone in the Rescue Corps may be responsible for blowing up the ship. And may have been feeding information to the Setarips ever since we arrived."

Mya's lips parted in surprise. Her gaze shifted to the sleeping chambers where the Lumians were resting until nightfall. "And you think they may go after the Lumians?"

"It makes sense. Someone doesn't want us to have evidence of anything we've seen. That means the three hundred eye witnesses on this island are a liability they'd want to eliminate. I need to talk to Byrnes."

"Looks like Ellis found him." Mya pointed over Aurora's shoulder.

Cade and Byrnes were walking toward them from the back entrance.

"Cade told me what you've learned." Byrnes said as the two men joined them. "I'm afraid I can't give you much information about the five Corps members. And they're gone."

"Gone? What do you mean gone?"

"After the search was called off, one of the *Argo* shuttles took them back to RC headquarters. We didn't have anything more for them to do here."

She closed her eyes and cursed softly. Well, at least they were off site. But that didn't mean the Lumians were safe.

She turned to Cade. "I'll contact Reanne and have the Corps members placed under surveillance. In the meantime, debrief Reynolds on exactly what occurred while the RC team was on watch with her. We're looking for any kind of tangible evidence that will tell us what happened on that ship."

The intensity in Cade's eyes gave her hope. "Understood."

"How can I help?" Mya asked.

"Find Gonzalez, Drew and Jonarel, and have them do a sweep of the entire camp for incendiary devices. If they find anything, alert me immediately. I'll see what information I can get from Reanne."

Slipping out of the tent, she walked down to the beach, turning her back to the water so she could see anyone who approached. She didn't want this conversation interrupted.

"Reanne, it's Aurora."

"Aurora! I've been so worried ever since I received the report about the ship explosion. What happened?"

"That's what we're trying to determine. I could use your help."

"Of course. Anything."

"The five RC members who worked the security detail here returned to headquarters earlier today. Have you seen them?"

"Yes. They checked in about an hour ago. Why?"

"Are they staying there?"

"For now. I haven't reassigned them yet. What's this all about?"

"I need you to keep them at HQ."

"Why?"

"There's a chance one of them was involved in placing explosives on the ship."

Reanne inhaled audibly. "*What?*"

Aurora gave her a concise rundown of what they'd learned, ending with her request that Reanne keep the RC team under surveillance.

Reanne sounded horrified. "I can't imagine anyone from the RC doing such a thing, let alone one of our security officers. It goes against our core tenets to help those in need. There must be another explanation."

Unlikely, but Aurora dialed back her response, not wanting to push Reanne into a defensive posture. "It's just a working theory. We want to cover all the potential explanations so that nothing's overlooked. But since all five

of them had unrestricted access to the ship for several days.
we need to monitor them as a precautionary measure.
Hopefully we'll know more soon."

"I suppose that's reasonable." Reanne didn't seem
happy. "I can place them on rotation at the check-in stations
here at HQ. That will keep them close by and visible."

"That's perfect. Thanks, Reanne."

"You're welcome. But just so we're clear, I really
don't think they're involved."

"I understand." And she did. She wouldn't react well
to someone accusing a member of her crew, either. Reanne's
loyalty was admirable. "I promise to contact you as soon as I
have any news to share."

She ended the conversation as quickly as possible,
then opened a channel to Kire.

"How can we help?" he asked. "I spoke with Jon, and
Star's already started a sweep of the camp."

She so owed him a drink. "Can you do a bio-scan of
the island and check for any unauthorized personnel? There
should be two hundred and ninety-seven Lumians and the ten
members of our team. If you locate anyone else, I need to
know who and where."

"I'm on it."

Three hours later the sweeps were completed and
the team was gathered around a table in the main tent. No
devices and no unauthorized personnel had been found. For
now, the Lumians were relatively safe.

Reynolds had given her report, though there wasn't
much to be gleaned from it. She and the RC security
personnel had worked paired rotations on both the bridge
and in the shuttle bay, but during off duty hours they'd been
free to roam the ship and make use of the cabin facilities.

Anyone could have accessed the four target areas without drawing undue attention.

"We need to send a contingent to RC headquarters to question the security team." Aurora glanced around the table. "Volunteers?"

"Me." Reynolds's eyes were frosty and her tone matched, although her ire was directed within. She'd taken the destruction of the ship personally, especially now that it looked like someone under her command was responsible.

Cade rested his forearms on the table. "I'll go, too. And I'd like Justin to come with us."

Byrnes nodded. "Absolutely."

"Do you want to join us?" Cade asked Aurora.

Did she? While her empathic abilities might come in handy to spot a liar, her emotional readings were not admissible as evidence. They needed facts, not impressions, and Cade's team was much better qualified to extract them.

"I'll stay here, at least for now." And if she was just the tiniest bit nervous about leaving the Lumians, well, that was only logical.

Fifty-Seven

Since they didn't know which members of the RC they could trust, Cade asked Captain Schreiber to send one of the *Argo*'s shuttles to take them to RC headquarters. Reanne hadn't been exactly thrilled with his request for a meeting with the security team, but she'd agreed to set it up.

The *Argo* pilot settled the shuttle on the landing platform outside HQ and extended the exit ramp. "Do you want me to wait here, sir?"

Cade shook his head. "It might be a while. Why don't you come inside with us? There's a staff lounge near the director's office that would be a lot more comfortable."

She smiled in gratitude. "Thank you, sir."

Two sirs in a row. He'd been working with seasoned officers for so long he'd forgotten that particular habit of new Fleet cadets. It always took them a while to stop adding that moniker to every sentence they spoke to a superior. He'd be willing to bet this was her first post out of the Academy.

The guards at the checkpoint waved them through after they showed their IDs. But as they walked down the long corridor toward the second checkpoint, shots rang out, followed by shouts from somewhere inside the building.

Cade palmed his weapon and sprinted down the hallway, Byrnes and Reynolds beside him. The second checkpoint was empty, and it wasn't hard to figure out why.

In the open space that led to the Corps offices, a male security officer lay on the floor, unmoving, with a large scorch mark in the center of his chest. A female officer pressed a weapon to the temple of a hostage she held in a chokehold. Two additional officers stood opposite her with weapons drawn, though they looked unwilling to shoot and risk hitting the hostage.

Cade had a clear line on the target, but even a perfect shot could cause the woman's finger to squeeze the trigger, which would not end well for the hostage. He needed to reach her before she became aware of his presence.

"You can't get out that way," the hostage said. "Ellis's team is due to arrive any minute and they'll stop you."

And what do you know, the female officer turned her head in his direction. So much for the element of surprise. She adjusted her stance, giving him a good look at the hostage. *Thank you very much, Reanne.*

"Stay back!" the security guard snarled at him. She pushed the pistol tighter to Reanne's head. "I'll kill her, I swear I will."

Amazingly, Reanne's voice remained completely calm, although her words indicated she might have lost her mind. "No, you won't. You're not going to hurt me and you're not going to escape. It's time to end this."

She was dead. No doubt about it. You didn't tell a lunatic with a gun that she had no way out.

And yet, the strangest thing happened. The look on the woman's face changed from wild anger to serene acceptance between one breath and the next. Then she did the unexpected. Lifting the weapon from Reanne's temple, she raised it to her own and fired.

As the security officer toppled over, she dragged Reanne with her. The woman was dead before she hit the ground.

Reanne, however, was staring up at Cade in shock, her mouth hanging open and her eyes blinking rapidly. He clasped her hand to help her up, and she took it like a sleepwalker. She glanced behind her as she rose to her feet. "No," she whispered, her hands coming up to cover her mouth as she stared at the dead woman. "Oh, no."

She repeated the denial several times as she shook her head, tears streaming down her face. She listed sideways and Byrnes wrapped an arm around her shoulders to keep her upright.

Time to take charge of the situation.

Cade contacted Captain Schreiber while Justin secured the area, placing additional guards at the checkpoints to prevent anyone from entering or exiting the building. Reynolds handled the removal of the two bodies and directed all personnel who had witnessed the scene to report for debriefing.

Many hours later, Cade's office was cleared of everyone except Byrnes, Reynolds and Reanne. Reanne sat in one of the chairs in front of his desk, a mug of coffee gripped tightly in both hands and a blanket wrapped around her shoulders. Despite the summer heat that permeated the building, she'd been shaking off and on for hours. Shock could do that to you.

"I just can't believe it." Her voice was hoarse, her nose and eyes both red and watery. "They used the Rescue Corps as a front to steal confidential Council information. Who does such a thing?"

Cade kept his tone gentle. "Someone who knew it was the perfect cover. Someone who excelled at giving the appearance of goodness to hide their real purpose."

And boy, had they. While he and Byrnes had conducted the debriefings, Reynolds had investigated the quarters of the two guards. She'd found exactly what they'd suspected—all the information Reanne had been privy to, including files stolen from her office that contained her notes and communication records. In short, everything the Setarips needed to keep one step ahead of them and plan a counterattack.

"It's all my fault." She stared into her mug. "I'm the one who trusted them. I'm the one who assigned them to their posts. I'm the one who didn't think twice about whether anyone was listening to my communications or going through my private data." She shook her head. "I almost cost all of you your lives."

Byrnes knelt beside her chair. "It's not your fault. These were security officers who had been vetted before they were ever assigned to the Rescue Corps. You didn't have any reason to question their motives."

She took a sip of her drink, the cup rattling slightly as she set it on the desk. "Thanks. But I still feel..." She shuddered, pulling the edges of the blanket tighter over her shoulders. "What do we do now?" She glanced at Cade.

"I'll contact the Admiral. All the evidence indicates only those two officers were involved. The Admiral will probably want a full inquiry, but for now, we can focus on protecting the Lumians."

"Lumians?" She frowned. "Who are the Lumians?"

"That's what Aurora has been calling the refugees."

"I thought you were calling them Necri."

"We were. But Lumians is a better fit now that they're healing."

"I see." Reanne's frown deepened. "Are they in danger?"

"Possibly."

"So you'll be staying on the island with them?"

He nodded.

"What about Aurora?"

He shrugged. "I don't know. Her crew may be needed elsewhere."

Reanne nodded, her gaze drifting to the door as she slid the blanket off her shoulders. "Well, you've spent enough time babysitting me. I'll get out of the way." She stood and draped the blanket over the chair. "Unless you need me for anything else?"

He shook his head. "Not until I've spoken with the Admiral."

After she left, he leaned back in his chair and exhaled on a sigh. "Not quite the day we'd anticipated."

Reynolds perched on the edge of the desk. "It would have been much better if we'd been able to take them into custody. We have the evidence to prove their involvement, but we didn't find anything that would tell us how they were keeping in contact with the Setarips or what the endgame was. We're at another wall." And Reynolds hated walls as much as he did.

For now, they'd have to focus on the tasks at hand. "Give me a few minutes to send a message to the Admiral, and then we'll plan our next move." He glanced at Byrnes. "How's our shuttle pilot holding up?"

"She's pretty shaken. Poor kid's never been in this type of situation before, and she's struggling. I left her in the staff lounge with one of the RC counselors. We may want to suggest to Captain Schreiber that she get some time off."

"Why don't you go ahead and contact the Captain and bring him up to speed. He may want to send some personnel down here anyway before we head back to the island." Cade turned to Reynolds. "What about the physical evidence? Is it secured?"

She nodded. "They're not set up for this kind of thing, but I've installed new security protocols on all the data sources in the HQ system, and moved the physical evidence to the *Argo* shuttle for now. Only the three of us and our pilot can access it."

"Good." He could always count on his team. "I'll meet you in the staff lounge as soon as I've contacted the Admiral."

Fifty-Eight

Aurora had always enjoyed change. It was one reason she'd wanted to join the Fleet. She never knew what each day would bring, and no two were ever the same.

However, right now she was yearning for a little mundane routine just so she could catch her breath.

First Cade had informed her about the hostage situation and the deaths of the two security officers responsible for passing information to the Setarips. Then Kire had contacted her and told her the Admiral had ordered all *Starhawke* crewmembers to return to the ship as soon as Cade's team reached the island. Oh, and she was supposed to bring Cade with her.

Which was why she was in the process of packing her minimal belongings in preparation for departure. Celia and Mya had already finished packing and were in the main tent saying their goodbyes. Aurora had no idea when she'd be back, or why her crew was suddenly being rushed off the island. Her one consolation was that Cade's team was staying behind to protect the Lumians. But the situation made her very uneasy.

Jonarel entered as she was tying her bedroll. His was already looped over his shoulder. He stopped beside her. "How are you feeling?"

Might as well give him the truth. "Upset. Worried. And more than a little confused."

He brushed a strand of hair out of her face with his thumb, letting his fingers trail over her cheek. "I like that answer much better than *fine*."

Yeah. And he knew as well as she did that *fine* was her default setting. "Good, because I'm not in the mood to gloss over things. I'm hoping once we reach the ship we'll get some answers about what exactly is going on here."

"I suspect we will."

"Then let's get going."

"Are you going to say goodbye to the Lumians?" he asked as they walked down the alley past the main tent.

Was she? She hesitated for a moment, then kept walking. "No. Celia and Mya have already talked to them, so they know we're leaving. I don't know what more I could say." And to be honest, she was a little afraid of how they might react. If they panicked, she'd be in a no-win situation. Far better to slip away quietly.

The Lumians, however, had other plans. They were waiting for her when she reached the clearing in front of the main tent, despite the glare of the late afternoon sun that had to be hurting their eyes. Mya and Celia stood with them.

Aurora caught Mya's gaze, but her friend shook her head to indicate the gathering hadn't been her idea.

Aurora stopped a few feet in front of the large group, her gaze sweeping over the increasingly familiar faces. She was going to miss them. Like it or not, she was already in a no-win situation.

Raaveen stepped forward, her head held high. Words in the Lumian language flowed with lilting grace from her lips. Aurora didn't understand the meaning, but she got the subtext just fine when, as one, the Lumians went through the familiar gesture that ended with the term of respect they all accorded her. "Sahzade."

How could she deny them? She inclined her head in acknowledgement.

But Raaveen wasn't finished. She glanced at Mya, who nodded in encouragement. When Raaveen spoke this time, she used words Aurora understood completely. "Weee...graatiiituuude...yooou."

Now her throat was closing up. She had to swallow several times before she could respond. She projected her voice so that everyone in the clearing would hear her. "I am grateful for you, too." She swept her hands out to emphasize her point.

And then the most amazing thing happened. The Lumians surged forward, surrounding her in their version of a group hug. Their energy fields lit up, and she responded, sending energy out in a flowing wave, interweaving with theirs as a sense of peace and joy wrapped around her.

And she'd been trying to avoid this?

She had no idea how long the moment lasted, but as if by unspoken command, a collective sigh went through the group and the Lumians retreated, leaving a pathway to the shuttle.

Aurora stepped forward and clasped Mya's hands. Damp tracks marked her friend's cheeks. Mya could probably see the same thing on hers.

She held Mya's gaze. "We'll see them again."

It was a promise—to Mya, to the Lumians, but most of all, to herself.

Fifty-Nine

Aurora's boot connected with the solid floor of her ship for the first time in weeks. But it felt like years. She wasn't even the same person. This ship, this reality, belonged to someone else.

And Cade was back onboard. That seemed to be a recurring theme ever since they'd started this mission. She hitched her pack onto her shoulder as she glanced at him. "I need to stop by my cabin. Go on up to my office. We can contact the Admiral from there."

"Okay. See you in a few."

When she arrived on the bridge, Kire moved to intercept her. "You have a visitor in your office."

"Cade. I know. I sent him up here."

He shook his head. "He's in there too, but I was referring to someone from the *Argo*."

"What? You let someone onboard the ship without asking me?"

He didn't flinch. "When you see who it is, you'll understand."

She was so tired of secrets and mysteries. Giving him a long look, she walked to the door of her private sanctuary. But when it opened, her feet stopped moving. "*Admiral?*"

The older man was seated in one of the plush chairs by the viewport, with Cade in the other.

The Admiral stood. "It's good to see you, Captain." He clasped her hand in both of his. "Please forgive the intrusion. I'm not in the habit of boarding ships uninvited, but under the circumstances, I felt it was necessary."

The Admiral was not at Council headquarters. He was standing on her ship. And apparently had been on the *Argo*. But for how long? Since it arrived?

"We need to discuss matters of grave importance." He gestured to the two chairs in front of her desk. "Shall we?"

She glanced at Cade, but he shook his head and shrugged. He was as lost as she was.

Aurora settled in behind the desk, her focus on the Admiral.

He laced his fingers together, resting them lightly across his stomach. "How are the Lumians?"

"Good, but I suspect they're still in danger. Your presence here seems to support that assumption." He didn't deny it, so she pressed on. "Do you have some idea of who's been orchestrating all this? I can't believe the Etah are acting alone."

"I'd like an answer on that as well, Admiral," Cade said. "A Setarip force might have viewed Gaia as a potential target to exploit. But the attempted abduction of Captain Hawke, the deaths of the Setarips and the RC security personnel, and the destruction of the ship doesn't fit with that scenario." He frowned. "Although you don't seem all that surprised by the course of events."

The Admiral's eyebrows lifted. "Surprised, Commander? Oh, I am surprised. Or I should say I'm sorry my concerns for the Captain's safety were justified." He paused, tapping his thumbs together as his attention shifted to Aurora. "You need to know that the decision to send you to Gaia was not mine. Several members of the Council specifically requested that you lead the investigative team, and it was a majority vote that resulted in approval."

"So it wasn't your order?" She'd assumed he'd been the one behind her crew's presence. Apparently not.

He shook his head. "With the wisdom of hindsight, I can now see that if you had still been assigned to the *Argo* when the call had come in from Gaia, those same Council members would have made a case to send the *Argo* instead. As it turned out, that became unnecessary because you had your own ship and a crew that was able to carry out the mission." His gaze held hers. "But your presence on Gaia was the key."

A sliver of ice trickled down her spine.

Anger flashed in Cade's eyes. "Are you saying she was the ultimate target of this entire attack?"

"Quite possibly, yes."

"Me?" Aurora stared at the Admiral.

He nodded.

"But that doesn't make sense." And she couldn't accept it. "You're talking about a plan that stretched out over weeks, involved hundreds of people and a massive ship. That's a lot of effort just to lure me to Gaia so they could capture or kill me. Why would someone do that?"

The Admiral didn't respond, simply waited for her to provide her own answer.

Cade wasn't nearly as serene. His lips pressed into a thin line. "I think you know why, Aurora, and it's connected to the Lumians. Their presence here is the reason the Council sent you."

She shot him a warning look to shut down that line of reasoning. The cover on her secret was thin enough already.

The Admiral's gaze grew speculative. "I agree. Someone clearly wanted you here. Whatever the end goal was for this attack, it involved you *and* the Lumians."

She sighed. "But they already had the Lumians. If someone wanted me that badly, why not kidnap me before we left Earth? It would have been easier."

"Would it?" Cade didn't seem to agree with that assumption.

And he was right. She'd been virtually untouchable until she'd come in contact with the Lumians and discovered they were her strength *and* her weakness. Because of them, she was vulnerable in a way she'd never been before. And capable of more than she'd ever dreamed.

The Admiral cleared his throat. "What's important now is how we'll proceed. Given the involvement of members of the Council and the Rescue Corps, I'm going to ask you to do something that goes against all your years of Fleet training. I'm going to ask you to lie."

She hadn't seen that coming. "Uhh...okay. About what?"

"First, there will be no mention of Commander Ellis's team or the Lumians in any of the records for this incident. The official story will state that the attack was carried out by the Etah Setarip faction in cooperation with a couple of rogue RC officers. They used the destruction of the vegetation as a diversion while they stole food and supplies."

Interesting way to spin it, and tough to disprove.

"Your crew uncovered their plan and launched a counterattack. During the resulting conflict, the Setarip ship self-destructed, killing everyone onboard."

Okay, not so bad. It would definitely cut down on the panic factor that would be generated by the truth.

"I will return to the *Argo*, and Commander Ellis will rejoin his team on the island while the *Argo*'s crew conducts a full investigation at the RC headquarters."

The Admiral turned to Cade. "Your team is responsible for the safety of the Lumians until Captain Hawke completes her next mission. I have arranged for a small but fast transport to be delivered secretly to the island at oh-two-hundred hours tomorrow. As soon as it arrives, you will move the Lumians to an island three hundred kilometers to the southeast. I'll have the coordinates for you. How you choose to handle the safety of the Lumians after that will be up to you. You have full authority to move them to any location of your choosing, on or off planet."

The Admiral glanced at Aurora. "I will also inform the RC Director and the Council that the refugees are being taken off planet. We'll be sending a decoy ship the following day that will be operated remotely from the *Argo* by Knox and myself. We will see if there's any reaction to its arrival or, more importantly, to its departure."

The Admiral had left out a key piece of information that pertained to her. "What *is* my next mission?"

A small smile touched his lips. "You're in charge of finding the Lumians a new home."

"A new home?"

"That's right. And you are not to share any of your findings with me or anyone else on the Council. I've reported to the Council that your ship suffered damage during this encounter that will require repairs on Drakar. To make the story plausible, you will need to act quickly to locate a suitable planet for the new Lumian colony."

Her head was spinning. "Why don't you want me to report to you?"

"Because I don't know who we can trust."

"Then what do I do when I find a suitable location?"

"You will contact Siginal Clarek."

"*Jonarel's father*?" That was a surprise. She wasn't even aware the two men knew each other.

The Admiral nodded. "He's expecting you. The Clarek clan will provide you with the resources and labor you need for construction. When the settlement is ready, you will contact Commander Ellis and arrange transport of the Lumians to their new home. The two of you can work out the best way to keep in touch during the interim."

She didn't want to look at Cade. She really didn't. But she had to.

A wry grin spread across his face. "Guess you're not getting rid of me after all."

She wished like hell that realization hadn't made her heart stutter.

Sixty

Less than an hour later, Aurora was back on the bridge. The Admiral and Cade were on their way to the *Argo*, and her crew sat at their stations, preparing for departure. That left her with one important task.

She walked over to the communications console and knelt beside Kire's chair. "Do you have a minute?"

He glanced at her in surprise. "Of course."

She kept her voice low. "We haven't had a chance to talk since the incident in the med bay."

"No, we haven't."

This was long overdue. "I just wanted to say I'm sorry."

"Sorry?" He frowned. "For what?"

"For letting you believe all these years that I was completely human." She held his gaze. "For not telling you about my abilities or my background."

He studied her. "Can I ask you something?"

"Anything."

"Why *didn't* you tell me?"

She weighed her words carefully. "Fear, mostly. I was afraid that it might ruin our friendship."

"That's flattering."

"What do you mean?"

"I can understand having a secret you were reluctant to share. We all do. What bothers me is that you thought so little of me that you believed telling me would make any difference in how I feel about you."

Her throat started closing up. She'd hurt him. "I'm sorry." She shook her head and sighed. "Kire, I'm so sorry. Honestly, I don't think it had anything to do with my faith in you. I was projecting my own fears. And I hurt you instead." His friendship was one of the greatest gifts of her life, and she'd damaged it. "Can you forgive me?"

His smile was warm but tinged with sadness. "Of course I can. That's the point. Nothing you do or say will ever change our friendship. Ever."

Tears pressed at the back of her eyes. "Thank you." She stood, resting her hand on his shoulder as she allowed her energy field to envelope them both so that he could truly feel how important he was to her.

His body jerked in surprise, but then he grinned. "*That is so cool.*"

Happiness bubbled out in a laugh of pure joy. "I think so, too."

She settled into the captain's chair. Star's ghostly image appeared beside her. "Do you have our first destination selected?" Aurora had placed Star in charge of cross-referencing and compiling all known systems to identify potential planets suitable for a Lumian settlement.

The family-focused Nirunoc had seemed positively giddy with the task. "Yes, Captain. I have already sent the coordinates to Ensign Kelly. It is a super Earth-sized planet around a G class star."

"Very good." She contacted Jonarel. "What's the status on the engines?"

"Ready to go at your command." He sounded happy to be back in engineering.

"Kelly, is the course set?"

"Yes, Captain."

She relaxed into her chair. She had a laundry list of unanswered questions regarding the Lumians, her past, and her future, but in this moment, none of that mattered. Her crew and ship were with her, and the glitter of space beckoned. "Then take us out. We have a homeworld to find."

Continue the adventure in

THE CHAINS OF FREEDOM

Starhawke Rising Book Two

Her past made her a guardian. Her choice made
her a leader. Now, the hunt is on.

"Kire, run!"

Captain Aurora Hawke grabbed Kire Emoto's upper arm and yanked him forward as her boots dug into the loose sand of the wide beach.

The thunder of a lake's worth of water hitting the ground fifty meters behind them kept her first officer from offering any resistance. Together, they sprinted toward the grove of trees that swayed gently in the balmy tropical breeze.

Aurora smacked her comband, praying her navigator hadn't taken the rest of the team too far into the island's interior. "Kelly, get back here. Now!"

"On our way." Bronwyn Kelly's complete lack of emotional inflection didn't indicate a sense of urgency, but Aurora had no doubt she'd have the shuttle at their location in record time.

Aurora snuck a quick glance over her shoulder as the sand trembled beneath her feet. What she and everyone else onboard the *Starhawke* had mistaken for giant lava rocks at the edge of the coast had just been revealed as something altogether different. The creature that was making its way up the beach with enormous strides resembled a moving rock formation, but with limbs the width of redwoods and a hinged mouth rimmed with saw blades.

Captain's Log

The Spark

It's a standard question. "How did you get the idea for your series?"

In this case, the answer is fairly simple. The spark came in 2013. Over a two-month period, I saw *Star Trek: Into Darkness* in the theatres five times. What can I say—I was addicted.

But I had one issue with it, an issue that shows up in *Star Wars* as well. The cast is almost all male.

Now don't get me wrong. I love guys. I grew up with brothers, not sisters, so I'm a big fan of guys. My older brother is one of the most incredible people I know. And guys are fun to write about. I could write about Cade all day long.

But when I thought about what type of story I wanted to tell, I knew I wanted more parity of the sexes. And, I wanted to tell it from the perspective of a female captain. Aurora Hawke was born.

My friends have asked if I based Aurora on myself, and the answer is, "Yes, and no." I understand Aurora. She has a lot of my strengths, and definitely my weaknesses. I never have to ask, "What would Aurora do?" because I know what Aurora would do, even if what she's about to do isn't in her best interests. But every character I've written, even those inspired by real people, evolve over time, becoming uniquely and wonderfully different from how they started. And that's one of the joys of writing—watching your characters grow and change.

Mya, Celia and Kelly showed up early in the process. They're the kinds of friends I wish every woman had. Their presence tipped the scale of Aurora's crew to predominantly female, but Jonarel and Kire were happy to fill out the remaining spots.

But then Cade's team showed up on Gaia. Predominantly male.

Add Aurora's crew and Cade's team together and you get six women and six men. That's no accident.

"But what about Star?" I hear you cry. Yes, Star does give a slight edge to the women on the *Starhawke*. But there's a new character you'll meet in book four who will restore the balance in ways Aurora can't possibly imagine. It'll be fun to see how that turns out!

Children

This is a case of what I call Magical Moments.

When Celia peered into the room on the Setarip ship, she had no idea what she'd find. What you might not realize is, neither did I.

I'd never planned to include children in this story. I had an image of the Necri from day one, but children? Uh-uh. Not even a blip on the radar. But when Celia started down that long corridor, she told me she heard something. And we both paused to listen.

That moment changed the entire course of the story, and in fact, the entire series. What I'd planned as a dramatic gunslinger-style battle on the ship between Cade's team and the Setarips became a rescue mission instead, one that allowed the characters, Celia in particular, to really shine. Who doesn't enjoy seeing brave soldiers saving innocent children?

I learned so much about Celia from her interactions with Maanee, Raaveen, Paaw and Sparw. The trust and cooperation that rapidly developed among them as they stood bravely in the face of fear, Celia's acceptance of their abilities and in turn, Aurora's abilities.

Without the children, so much of this story wouldn't have evolved. The containment of the auto-destruct explosion, the healing of Mya, and the revelations about Aurora's connection to the Lumians. The teens needed to be there to make those happen.

Magical Moments are special. I'm delighted the children joined the story. And all because Celia and I paused to listen.

Enjoy the journey!
Audrey

P.S. – I always write to music, so if you'd like to experience this story the way that I did, listen to the film score for *Thor* while you read.

Audrey Sharpe grew up believing in the Force and dreaming of becoming captain of the Enterprise. She's still working out the logistics of moving objects with her mind, but writing science fiction provides a pretty good alternative. When she's not off exploring the galaxy with Aurora and her crew, she lives in the Sonoran Desert, where she has an excellent view of the stars.

For more information about Audrey and the Starhawke universe, visit her website and join the crew!

AudreySharpe.com

CPSIA information can be obtained
at www.ICGtesting.com
Printed in the USA
BVOW03s1729221217
503317BV00035B/635/P